BETTIE ENGLISH STARTER COLLECTION

CONNOR WHITELEY

DEDICATION
Thank you to all my readers without you I couldn't do what I love.

INTRODUCTION

I flat out love private investigator stories.

I'm not exactly sure why but I seriously love these stories, because they're often fun, interesting and light-hearted. Also, they just tackle crime in a slightly different way than police or detective fiction, because police detective fiction is limited or has to follow police rules and regulations. That is brilliant for some stories and I do enjoy police fiction.

However, police fiction can only take place when a crime has been reported or occurred, and that (to some extent) is a dividing line between police and private investigator fiction.

Since there are only two "real" rules in private investigator fiction, the private eye has to solve the case and be interested in protecting their business. Besides from those two rules, you really can do whatever you want in private investigator fiction to a large extent.

For example, a private eye can be hired to investigate a crime that *might* have happened and the story is about finding out whether the crime occurred or not. Equally, a private eye could be hired to investigate a crime whether that's alongside or in conflict with the police depending on the character and author. Or a private eye could investigate something small or big because they're better equipped to investigate it.

In reality, private eyes mainly just do background checks and no one likes stakeouts because they are just as dull as dishwater. But considering I grew up on TV programmes like Private Eyes, Frankie

Drake Mysteries, Shakespeare and Hathaway Private Investigators and so on. I seriously love this subgenre of mystery.

As a result, this volume focuses on a gut-punching, tense and unputdownable series that I flat out love. It is my *Bettie English Private Eye Mysteries*, which I cannot get enough of because it's a powerful, stellar, gripping mystery series that might be my favourite series of all time.

Therefore, in this volume, you get to enjoy twenty unputdownable short stories allowing you to explore the wide range of cases, crimes and criminals that Bettie English and her team comes across. Some of the stories are light and sweet and family-centred whereas others are darker and more shocking.

Whilst you might not be able to guess the tone without reading the first few paragraphs, I can promise you all the stories are positive, fun and Bettie English is a brilliant character.

Also, what I really like about this Starter Collection is that you'll notice how Bettie changes over the course of the series so far. The first five short stories are before I started writing the novellas and then as the short stories go on, you can see how she changes and grows stronger, more powerful and more determined to help people in more ways than one.

In addition, as a rule of thumb, I don't actually talk about the inspiration for any of my series very often, because I don't like to. Yet this series was inspired by my love for the genre and my love for strong female characters. Since it made no sense for me to write about a powerful, rich man because that's been done to death a thousand times.

So I wanted to write about a lower-middle-class woman that became a private eye to help people, solve crimes and improve lives. Then as the series goes on, she becomes powerful, extremely rich, she gets a boyfriend and she becomes a mother. And some of the series looks at how she deals with all of this, because I strongly, strongly believe that women should and can be powerful, successful and still be mothers, if they want to be.

And because this series is set in the present day, from time to time it allows me to explore more contemporary issues in a fun way that only Bettie English can deliver.

And if you like this series then you can find all the novels and novellas of the series on all major eBook retailers, you can order the paperback and hardback from online retailers and your local bookstore and library if you request it. As well as you can find an audiobook version narrated by artificial intelligence for most of the books at selected audiobook retailers.

Or just head on over to https://www.connorwhiteleyfiction.com/bettie-english-private-eye-books

So now we know more about this enthralling series, let's turn over the page and start reading some stellar stories.

AUTHOR OF THE ENGLISH BETTIE
PRIVATE EYE SERIES

CONNOR WHITELEY

CHRISTMAS THEFT

A BETTIE PRIVATE EYE MYSTERY SHORT STORY

CHRISTMAS THEFT

Walking along the small brown corridor of the university accommodation, Bettie tried to ignore the horrible brown carpet and the smooth bright yellow walls but that was hard. Too hard. Even when she went to this same university here in Canterbury, England a few decades ago, she never could appreciate the university's design choice.

As she passed more and more wooden doors with their little hotel keypads on the outside, Bettie breathed in the typical smell of university. Weed, and lots of it. She could even see smoke coming out from one of the doors and Bettie coughed as she passed it.

She knew it was normal at university to smoke weed, she never did but she knew basically everyone else did. Yet surely these university students should have more sense to smoke outside and not in their rooms.

Shaking the thoughts away, Bettie kept walking along the corridor, listening to the talking, laughing and even singing in the rooms as she went. That was something she missed about university, the community. Sure Bettie didn't like the partying aspects of it but she had made some great friends, and she supposed it was a lot easier to make friends back then compared to now.

Bettie looked ahead as she saw lots of wooden doors with dirty glass in the middle coming up ahead. She still had no idea why the university needed to separate the corridor into mini-sections but that was life.

Opening one of the cold wooden doors, Bettie thought about why she was here again after all these years. Being a Private Eye was a great job, she loved it and she loved being available to unofficially break rules time to time.

A wave of unease washed over Bettie as she remembered the panicked text message from her nephew. The text was chaotic and aggressive, he was clearly annoyed but he wasn't responding to any of Bettie's texts. So after she had calmed down and realised that the text didn't mean he was in danger, she actually read it. Her Nephew Sean wanted her to come and see him immediately.

Bettie still felt uneasy about all this yet something she couldn't understand was why he wanted to hire her. Sure, it was one thing to ask for your aunt to come to your aid, Bettie would have loved this. But Sean wanted, no insisted on hiring her, Bettie just didn't know why.

Breathing in another awful breath of weed smoke, she was starting to regret her choice and maybe thought she should have arranged to meet him outside. Bettie shook her head at that idea, she wouldn't do that. She loved her nephew and she had a feeling there was something he didn't want her sister to know about.

Just the thought of that made Bettie's stomach tighten into a knot, she hated the idea of her nephew being in trouble. But the idea of Bettie being the only one who could save him did have a certain ring to it, and it might allow her to get out of her sister's present this year.

Opening another cold wooden door, Bettie smiled as she walked into the last section of the corridor and smelt the delicious hints of ginger, allspices and cinnamon in the air. They smelt amazing.

At least that made Bettie relax a bit more, she knew her nephew wasn't smoking weed.

As she heard the buzz of a room opening she looked straight ahead smiling as she saw her nephew's little head pop out. Bettie couldn't believe how well he looked with his smooth young face and longish brown hair parted to the right.

Sean rushed over and hugged his aunt. Bettie returned the massive hug, she couldn't remember how long it had been. As Sean led her into his room, Bettie's eyebrows rose as she realised he hadn't said a word to her.

But what was more shocking was how Sean was wearing designer jeans, Bettie had no idea why. Sean was the least fashion conscience person in the world but he... looked good.

Stepping into Sean's room, Bettie had to admit it was a lot nicer than she was expecting. She remembered her room was a tiny box room covered in dirty clothes with textbooks littered around.

Sean's was nothing like that with his small rectangular room with sterile white walls and neatly arranged desk with his laptop, and a pile of neatly folded clothes. Then Bettie looked at his perfectly clean en-suite and she had a quick look in this rarer empty brown wardrobe.

A part of her started to question why her nephew wasn't asking her to stop, she checked places out on instinct, it was a terrible habit as her mum kept reminding her. But Sean was sitting there on his small blue bed that was tucked into one corner, his foot tapping rapidly.

Bettie smiled and gently sat down next to him, feeling the soft sheets take her weight.

"You want to talk about it?" Bettie asked, trying to make sure she didn't sound like an interrogator.

Sean looked at her. "Aunty, I.. I've got something to tell you,"

Bettie wanted to say something along the lines of she guessed that by the text. It was better than *No Shit Sherlock* which was her usual saying and never failed to make Sean laugh. But she behaved herself because she had a feeling Sean wouldn't laugh at it this time.

"Okay," Bettie said.

"And you can't tell mum please!"

Bettie forced a smile and nodded.

"I lost a present. I have a boyfriend. Someone robbed me. They threatened me. And-"

Bettie placed a finger on her nephew's lips and hugged him. She and her sister had had a bet for years about when Sean was going to come out and to who. Bettie smiled as she could feel the plane tickets to Antigua in her hands now. (and at least she didn't have to pay for her sister to go to Australia)

After a few moments, Sean pulled away.

"You… you aren't mad?"

Bettie's eyes widened as she tried to understand what he was talking about, then she realised.

Trying to be the supportive aunt, Bettie grabbed Sean's hands.

"Sean, me and ya mum we know you're gay. It's fine. We're both happy about it. And I have to say thank you because you just won me a bet,"

Sean cocked his head and smiled as he knew exactly what his mother and Aunt were like.

"Why would we be mad?" Bettie asked already knowing the answer.

"You know what Dad's like. He'll hate me,"

Bettie went to open her mouth but she closed it. There was nothing she could say, only support and love him.

"Me and ya mum will protect you,"

Sean hugged her again.

"Now tell me what happened about this robbery," Bettie asked.

Sean frowned. "I bought this wonderful present for Harry for Christmas. This special Christmas tree necklace, he'd love it!"

As Sean kept talking over the minor details, Bettie smiled as she realised she had never seen her nephew so happy and smiley about anyone in his life. He was full of life and honestly happy, something she hadn't seen in a long time. She couldn't even remember the last time she was full of life.

"Then I told some friends about it. I promise I kept it hidden. I know what people are like. I came back from a lecture. Someone was in here and grabbed the present. They threatened me and Harry if I told anyone,"

Bettie's eyes narrowed and her voice turned deadly cold.

"Someone robbed you and threatened you when you walked in on them?"

Sean nodded.

"Who was it?"

Sean stood up and paced around a little bit.

"My friend Danielle next door. She was wearing a mask but I recognised the voice,"

Bettie stood out frowning, how dare this criminal target her nephew. Why the hell would she do it? There was no reason for it, Bettie tried not to scream in rage but she couldn't let someone threaten her family.

With her eyes narrowing, Bettie asked:

"What does *that* girl look like?"

Sean closed his eyes. He clearly hadn't seen Danielle in a little while.

"She has blond hair, nose piercing, round face, white and… Aunty she has a horrible burn mark on her right hand,"

Bettie nodded. She could work with that, a part of her couldn't believe that rather vague description was better than the normal ones she got. Maybe her nephew was better at this crime thing than she thought.

But there was one question still bothering her.

"And why *hire* me?"

"I wanted to hire you because I know… mum's always talking about how tight money is for you. I… I wanted to help,"

As soon as she heard that, Bettie gave him a massive hug. Her sister definitely wasn't perfect but she did know how to raise great children.

"You really are such a kind boy. Make you a deal, give me twenty and we'll call it square," Bettie said.

Sean smiled and got out his wallet, giving Bettie the money.

As she walked out the small room, Bettie said: "I'll call you when its done,"

She realised how bad that must have sounded but no one ever

threatens her family. No matter who they are.

***

Walking back into the awful corridor with its horrible brown carpet and bright yellow walls, Bettie turned to the wooden door next to Sean's room.

The smell of delicious Christmas spices filled the air and the warm heat coming from an overhead vent in the ceiling made Bettie smile a little.

As she looked at the small keypad in the front, Bettie tried to decide what to do next, she wouldn't do her normal Private Eye stuff that involved unofficially smashing down doors. She didn't want Sean to see her doing that nor did Bettie want the university to blame Sean for the damage.

So she decided to do what she always did in times like this, Bettie knocked on the door three times, surprising at the warm feeling of the door against her hand.

No answer.

She knocked again.

"Danielle House Keeping," Bettie said.

Still nothing.

Placing her ear against the warm wooden door, Bettie tried to listen out for any sign of her inside but there weren't any sounds. Bettie took a step back and slipped out a small black device she always carried, a little gift from a black market friend a few years ago. It made electronic keypads a breeze to crack.

She was about to press it against the pad when she heard another buzz of a door opening. Turning around Bettie put the device back in her pocket as she saw a tall, slightly overweight girl walk out of the kitchen covered in flour.

Bettie walked up to her. "Excuse me, I'm looking for Danielle, the library sent me to get her to return a book,"

The girl rolled her eyes. "That sound like her. Always useless ain't she. She still owns me a score for last Saturday,"

Bettie was starting to get a much better picture of this Danielle girl, she didn't like her. Not one bit.

"Do you know where I might find her please? The Librarian won't be happy without that book," Bettie said.

"I know that Librarian so moany. Soz girl, Danielle left for the station half an hour ago,"

"Thank you. Merry Christmas," Bettie said.

Bettie stormed over. She wasn't going to let this Danielle person escape with that present. She had no right to do that, and no right to steal from her family!

***

Bettie knew some things never changed in university towns and thankfully the train station was one of them. As she walked into Canterbury East train station, Bettie smiled as the memories of her getting the train home returned to her.

Her eyes narrowed on the wide grey platforms with the dirty white pillars that supported an old tiled roof shelter that was over the platforms. It might not have sounded much but Bettie remembered more than enough times of when the shelter provided welcome relief from the rain.

Bettie listened to the talking of parents, students and everyone else as her eyes narrowed on the shop that smelt of rich bitter coffee on the other side of the platform. There weren't any trains yet but Bettie wasn't taking any chances.

As Sean reminded her as they raced down here in her car, Danielle could have grabbed a bus half an hour ago and be on a train already. Yet there was something about Christmas time that made her doubt that, a girl like Danielle wouldn't be scared or think any retribution would come for her. She wasn't going to make a quick getaway, she was going to walk down, take her time and enjoy the Christmas markets.

Looking around, Bettie couldn't see Sean, which didn't concern her that much as she had sent him to look in the little subway tunnel that connected the two train platforms but she would be amazed if Danielle would that easy to find.

The heat of strangers pressed against Bettie as the train station got busier and busier with all the students hoping to grab a train home, most of the international students were heading to London for the Eurostar. Bettie so badly wanted to join them and see the continent, she loved Christmas in Paris a few years ago. But she had to focus.

Taking another rich coffee scented breath of the air, Bettie saw a small blond-haired girl with a (horrible) nose piercing a few metres away. There was something familiar about her, Bettie closed her eyes as she tried to remember what Sean had said about her.

Bettie opened her eyes when she remembered the detail about the burn mark on her right hand, she knew she had to get closer. So gently gliding through the crowd, gently pushing past students deafening themselves with bad music.

She kept her eyes focused on Danielle.

When Bettie got closer, she noticed Danielle was playing music as she touched her EarPods with her right hand. Bettie smiled as she saw the blistered skin and bright red burn marks.

Bettie supposed she would normally feel bad for Danielle, she must have been in a terrible accident but in this moment she didn't care. This Danielle girl had threatened her family, her nephew no less.

Placing a hand on Danielle's cold shoulder, Bettie stood next to her. Danielle took out her EarPods and frowned at her.

"What ya problem woman?" Danielle said.

Bettie frowned. "You have something that belongs to my nephew,"

Danielle laughed and looked away.

Bettie stuck her finger in Danielle's side.

"Don't move. I want the item back now or I'm not afraid to… well you can guess," Bettie said.

She never ever liked using these sorts of tactics but she would do anything for her family.

Danielle snorted and shook her head.

"That just a finger. Fuck off," she said.

Bettie couldn't believe how disrespectful she was being.

"Give me back the item and I will leave. I won't report you to the police,"

"Bitch, I got friends in police. My mother's an officer. So go fuck yourself,"

Bettie shook her head. "What's your problem with my nephew? Maybe I can help you,"

Danielle turned to face Bettie.

"That little boy. He ain't a man. He's a gay. I wanted him, asked him out, no guy rejects me so yea when he confessed he was a gay. I got pissed. No one rejects this," Danielle said, pointing to her body.

Bettie tried not to laugh but this was ridiculous. So Bettie tried her ultimate card.

"You might think you're safe but you aren't. I can do a quick search on the deep web. Learn all your secrets, learn your passwords, credit card numbers. I can own your identity, I can own you,"

Danielle's eyes widened. "You won't. My mum's a cop bitch, she'll-"

Bettie smiled. "I wonder how many crimes has she fixed for you. I wonder how will you do without an officer for a mother. I could find all her secrets, get her fired. I've done it before,"

Bettie wasn't lying, she never enjoyed it but she hated dirty cops, thankfully they were always rare.

Danielle frowned as she took off her black backpack, open it up and gave Bettie a small wrapped up present in the shape of a thin jewellery box.

The sound of the train pulling in almost deafened Bettie as Danielle started to walk away. Bettie grabbed her arm.

"If you bother my nephew again. All my promises will come reality,"

"Fine. Now fuck off!" Danielle said, walking away.

Bettie frowned as she watched that horrible girl walk onto the train and disappear. She really didn't like making threats but after decades as a Private Eye, Bettie sadly knew it was a needed part of the job.

Yet she was still telling the truth, if Danielle did come after Sean again. There would be hell to pay.

***

Stepping outside the train station, Bettie took a deep breath of the fresh Canterbury air with hints of delicious Christmas spices from the markets nearby. She missed the delicious Christmas markets, she missed a lot of things about Canterbury.

Looking around, Bettie watched the odd taxi drive past as students ran into the station and other students smoked normal cigarettes (thankfully) as they leant against the dirty brick walls of the station.

As she looked dead ahead Bettie focused on the amazing view for a moment, it wasn't much compared to other parts of Canterbury, but for a train station it was amazing.

Her eyes narrowed on the remains of the Roman walls that littered the horizon as it mixed with the urban shops and more white modern buildings. Then in the distance she could only just make out the spire of the cathedral, that amazing cathedral she loved exploring.

Bettie just stood there for a moment holding the perfectly wrapped gift in her hands, Bettie knew she said she would call Sean when it was done but she just wanted to enjoy those strange moments of peace between the completing of the job and reporting to the client.

The sound of talking and goodbyes behind her reminded Bettie of all the people she had left behind since her university days. Sure she missed them, she really missed her international friends but she was a completely different woman now. It still didn't make her loneliness feel any easier.

"Aunty!" Sean shouted behind her.

As soon as she heard Sean, Bettie realised she was never ever alone. She had a family, a nephew and everything she really needed. Of course her sister drove her mad at times but that's the magical thing about family.

Focusing on Sean with his designer jeans and massive smile, Bettie cocked her head as she realised there was someone attached to his arm. It had to be Harry.

Bettie's mouth dropped as she focused on Harry, she couldn't believe how attractive he was, he was honestly like a movie star with his strong jawline and perfect smile. and she knew it sounded awful but she couldn't exactly understand how Sean landed a guy like that. Even Bettie couldn't back in the day and she had had tons of comments about her looks.

"Thank you!" Sean said as Bettie passed him in the gift.

Bettie stared at both the boys as she was waiting for some sort of official introduction.

"Sean aren't you going to introduce us?" Harry said, his voice deep with a slight accent.

"Oh yea sure. Aunt Bettie, this is Harry and…" Sean said before he looked away.

Bettie knew exactly why he didn't look at her. She had been wondering how long until Sean finally realised it was the Christmas season and he would have to come home. Well, Bettie wanted him to come home and so did her sister.

"Harry, going home for Christmas?" Bettie asked.

Sean looked at her, a puzzled expression on his face.

"No Miss. I'm afraid me and my parents can't afford it. I…" Harry said.

Bettie knew he had worked it out and both the boys smiled at each other as they realised what Bettie was doing.

"Come on boys. We'll go back to the uni, grab your stuff and you can stay with us for the holidays. Grandma won't mind,"

"Thank you!" both the boys said as they hugged each other and walked off to Bettie's car.

As Bettie watched the boys both happy and deeply in love, she couldn't help but smile. That's all she had ever wanted for Sean and her family, to be happy, safe and loving life. And watching those boys deeply in love, that was all Bettie needed to see.

She had done her job today and that made her feel damn proud. Bettie had helped her nephew, she got paid and she was even a helper in the romance department. Sure her brother-in-law wouldn't be happy but Bettie never liked him anyway. She could and would handle him like Danielle if the need arose.

Because like as Bettie always said, she would protect her family to the end and do everything to protect them. But at this magical time of year, Bettie knew love would prevail, she would make sure of it.

And she would hope the new year bought some of her love along with lots and lots of business.

But until then, it was a magical time of year. A time for gifting, thieving and sharing but most importantly- family.

AUTHOR OF THE ENGLISH BETTIE
PRIVATE EYE SERIES

CONNOR WHITELEY

TROUBLE IN CHRISTMAS

A BETTIE PRIVATE EYE MYSTERY SHORT STORY

TROUBLE IN CHRISTMAS

Bettie felt her stomach twist as she looked at her small silver watch and realised her sister Phryne would be meeting her soon. She loved her sister, she really did but Bettie would have preferred to wait a few more days to see her. She had no idea what could be so important her sister would want to see her before Christmas.

As she attempted (but failed) to push those thoughts away, Bettie leant on the cold concrete railings that run along the cold riverbanks with the lustrous green grass under her feet.

Bettie remembered sailing on the large river below as a child with her family but none of them were into sailing anymore.

She still loved it here in Rochester, England. As Bettie looked across the large river to the other side, she tried to count all the cars driving into the retail park with the cinema and bingo halls and even a few restaurants.

Listening to the playing of children in the playground behind her, it bought a few happy memories of her playing with her younger brother a few decades ago but... but that was before he died.

Bettie still managed to smile as she listened to them laugh, play and live. She just wished her brother would have been like that.

With the freezing wind howling, Bettie tightened her black woolly coat and hoped her sister would come soon, she didn't want to be in the cold for too long. At least the air smelt amazing with the delicious hints of Christmas cake, mince pies and puddings filling her nose from the Christmas markets inside the castle behind her. She could taste the amazing flavours on her tongue now, she definitely needed to grab a pie at least later on!

Blowing on her cold hands, Bettie tried to figure out what her sister could want so urgently and before Christmas. She knew her sister loved her and Phryne did love seeing her, well she didn't always act like it. Especially when she said Bettie was being silly for being a Private Eye.

But from what Bettie remembered Phryne was still doing exactly what she always did. Working, working, looking after Bettie's amazing nephew Sean and more working. Bettie loved the sound of Phryne's job, she worked for the Crown Prosecution Service but the details of everyday life hardly interested Bettie.

She felt a shiver ran down her spine as Bettie struggled to think how she would ever work in an office. She was a woman of action, investigating crimes and hunting down bad guys, she wasn't the sit down at a chair type of person.

Hearing the typical tapping of high heels, Bettie took a deep breath and turned to see her beautiful sister walk towards her. Well, walking was an understatement, more like strutting her stuff, with a massive black designer handbag. It was clear Phryne wanted everyone to know she had money and power, if she was on the other side of the river in Strood Phryne wouldn't have wanted to do that. But Bettie knew her sister wouldn't care if people saw her as a good target.

As Phryne stood next to her, the two sisters looked out over the river and Bettie tried not to cough or gag at the smell of her sister's perfume. It was so flowery and strong, Bettie hated it. It was disgusting!

"Phryne," Bettie said.

"Oh honey, come on now. We're haven't seen each other since last Friday. Thanks for bringing Sean home from university and his boyfriend's nice. Isn't he?" Phryne said, each word exaggerated and posh.

Bettie smiled. "Yes they're both great. How's my brother-in-law dealing with it?"

Phryne frowned and Bettie turned to look straight at her sister. Bettie hated to see how sad and wet Phryne's eyes were, she knew something was very wrong.

"Bettie darling. I... I need your skills,"

Phryne couldn't help but smile. "Are you admitting Private Eyes have skills you don't?"

"Oh honey of course not. I'm still better than you but I need you,"

Bettie rolled her eyes and they both turned back to the river smiling. She knew her sister would never admit she was good at this, but Bettie was going to prove her wrong.

"What's wrong?"

"Oh honey, I... think John's cheating on me,"

Bettie tried not to smile because she knew this was going to happen sooner or later. Her brother-in-law was not exactly the nicest of people in the world, he was a racist, a homophobe and Bettie wasn't exactly comfortable with Sean living with him now he was out.

But she was a sister first, she had to be supportive.

"I'm sorry. How you doing?"

"Honey I didn't come here for a sister. I wanted you for your skills as a *Private Eye*. I need my sister later,"

Bettie could respect that. Phryne hardly needed anyone to support her if her jerk of a husband wasn't having an affair, but Bettie did look forward to proving it. Her stomach relaxed at the idea of getting rid of her brother-in-law.

After the basic questions Bettie always asked she started to understand what was happening and why her sister was so concerned. Her husband was working late at night but friends had seen him in the high street, at restaurants and some of the lies didn't make perfect sense. And yet there was something eating away at Bettie.

She knew she didn't like her brother-in-law but she never ever made it clear in front of him or to the rest of the family, except behind closed doors, because Bettie always respected how he had treated her annoying, brilliant sister and Sean. So the idea of him cheating was odd.

"Oh honey, do you think he is… you know cheating on me?"

Bettie wasn't sure what to say. "As a *Private Eye*, I don't like to judge the outcome before I investigate. Did you bring his phone or anything?"

As Phryne dug through her handbag, Bettie smiled as it wasn't surprising her sister had bought something of him along. She didn't quite know (or care to remember) what part of the Prosecution Service Phryne worked in, but it was always a good guess to know Phryne would know what evidence Bettie might need.

After a few moments, Phryne passed Bettie a small black smartphone and smiled.

"Honey, I stole it!"

Bettie wasn't exactly sure why she was so happy about it, then she remembered this was probably the worse thing Phryne had ever done in her life.

Not caring enough to comment on her sister's theft, Bettie wiped the cold phone, rolled her eyes that it wasn't password protected and swiped through his calls and texts.

There was hardly anything remarkable on it. Just a bunch of work things, a few calls to some restaurants and jewellery shops. All in all not very exciting and exactly what Bettie expected from a man who worked in hospitality, she thought he worked in a hotel thing or other. But she didn't know.

All she did know was how much he boasted about having the chance to talk to film stars and models in London as he got them tickets and whatnot.

Bettie hardly cared.

As she continued to swipe the cold screen, Bettie checked his GSP data which all phones had and so many people didn't know about. Then she sighed as that data was about as interesting as watching paint dry.

Except for one piece of data, Bettie's eyes narrowed as she saw her brother-in-law had got to somewhere in Chatham, the next town over and... it wasn't exactly the nicest of areas.

"Phryne where's John working now?"

"Oh honey, he's been showing someone around the Chatham Dockyard all week. Something about a movie director. I didn't listen,"

"Director?" Bettie asked.

"Yes some new male one,"

Bettie wanted to roll her eyes as she knew that was another dead end, knowing how homophobic John was Bettie knew he wasn't seeing the director. Bettie couldn't understand the mismatched lies, the late working and everything else there was something odd about it.

Bettie just had to find out what.

***

Watching her sister walk away with her massive black handbag, Bettie took a deep breath of the Christmas spiced air as she could almost taste the mince pies and delicious puddings. She supposed her sister could just be overreacting and making accusations out of nothing, but she would like to think she knew her sister a little better than that.

So listening to the children playing, laughing and talking on the playground behind her, Bettie got out her warm blue smartphone and dialled a number of an old friend.

With the phone ringing, Bettie felt a drop of sweat run down her spine as she remembered who she was calling. A very hot attractive man, an old flame but still a very sexy blond cop she used to know.

"Bettie, how ya doing?" a man said, his voice middle age and full of energy. (Something Bettie wished she felt)

"Hi Graham, good thanks. I need a favour?"

Bettie could hear his disappointment through the phone, she felt bad. She felt bad for a lot of things but now wasn't the time.

"Glad to hear ya okay. Go on, what ya need?"

Bettie smiled whilst her stomach slowly twisted. She felt bad as she knew Graham would do anything she wanted, Bettie hated to think of herself as using him, she wasn't. She was simply asking a friend she hadn't spoken to for years for a favour.

That sounded bad.

Bettie felt bad, she needed to make it up to him. Yet deep down she already knew she was only acting like this because of a whole lot of other issues from the past. Issues she had to fix.

Right now though, she needed to focus on her sister.

"Thanks Graham. Do you still have that friend in John's company? You know my sister's husband?"

Bettie heard him chuckle through the phone.

"Checking out ya own family, Bet. Isn't that unethical?"

Bettie opened her mouth.

"It's fine Bet. I still love ya so sure I have that friend. Great guy. Want me to ask him something?"

Bettie paused as the words of love still rang in her ears. As the wonderful Christmas spiced air blew past, she pulled herself together.

"Um yes. What does he know about John's late night activities lately? And anything odd about the Chatham Dockyard thing?"

"That all Bet?" Graham asked.

"Yes. Thanks Graham. I'll... I'll come and see you soon,"

The phone went silent for a moment.

"That'll be great Bet. At the same place. I'll call back in a minute with your info,"

Graham hung up.

Pressing her back against the cold concrete railing of the riverbank, Bettie closed her eyes and just listened to the howling of the spiced air and the children playing. She supposed she really had missed Graham but that was years ago. Surely she was over something she had ended, she wasn't even sure why she ended things. His job? her job? Bettie didn't know.

Walking off Bettie felt the soft mud move under her weight as she walked along the river bank back to her car, she still wasn't sure if

Graham's friend would have the information she needed. So she needed to try another angle, and what better angle than her nephew.

Bettie learnt a long time ago that Sean was far more observant than he ever let on.

***

Bettie loved the cold rough stone as she ran her fingers across the waist high wall on top of Rochester castle, it was amazing. Bettie had always loved it up here, she was able to look out from miles around.

Looking at the large river Medway as it rushed past, Bettie smiled as she watched all of it from the up high, the little houses, the cars driving across the bridge. It was all wonderful.

And Bettie finally got to see the Christmas Markets in the Castle grounds, all the rows upon rows of amazing white stalls. Some selling Christmas rubbish, others selling good Christmas decorations and some selling the most amazing food ever.

As she breathed in the amazing smell of roasted nuts, Bettie could taste their rich crunchy flavours on her tongue. She was going to enjoy the market afterwards that was for sure.

"Aunty!" Sean shouted, his voice young and manly.

Bettie smiled as she turned around and saw her amazing nephew with his perfectly straight brown hair parted to the right and his black designer jeans, as he walked across the smooth stone floor.

He gave her a massive hug and Bettie almost coughed at his strong aftershave, before they both leant on the cold stone wall. Bettie kept smiling for a moment as she actually realised she wasn't glad to see Sean for him, she was glad to see he was okay and his father hadn't hit him or anything for being who he wanted to be.

"Where's Harry?" Bettie asked.

"He's shopping in the market. He's actually getting you something, it'll be a surprise. Why you call?"

"I don't need a reason to call my favourite nephew,"

Sean smiled. "I'm your only nephew and you're seeing me in a few days for Christmas,"

Knowing there was no delicate way to put his, Bettie knew she just had to tell him straight. Well, a version of the truth anyway.

"How's dad?" Bettie asked.

Sean frowned a little. "He wasn't happy if that's what you're asking. He doesn't like Harry but I don't know if that's because he's foreign or gay,"

Bettie nodded, she hadn't expected anything different.

"Has he been home at night at all?"

Sean's eyes narrowed. "Did mum hire you or something as a *Private Eye*?"

Bettie playfully hit him. "Yes I'm a very good *Private Eye* I hope. So has he been home?"

Sean shook his head. "And he's been deleting his internet searches too but Harry managed to find some search for private hotels with… discretion,"

Bettie wasn't exactly sure what to ask next, did she ask about Harry's skills, why Sean was digging about or if there was anything more about the searches? Bettie decided on the question she was getting paid for.

"Anything else about the hotels?"

Sean shook his head. "Sorry Aunty. I still did everything you taught me,"

Bettie's eyebrows rose, she didn't think she had taught him anything about being a PI, she hoped not. Phryne would have her head!

Her phone rang. "Thanks I'll let you get on. Tell Harry I said *hi*,"

Bettie answered her phone as Sean gave her a quick hug and left.

"Bet I got great news. Interesting gossip at John's work. Everyone is gossiping about why he was asking about discretion hotels in private,"

"Doesn't he work on getting whatever the directors or VIPs want?"

"Yea but Bet, he was asking everyone to keep it quiet. It wasn't work related. Everyone's gossiping about who he's having an affair with,"

With the delicious smelling wind picking up, Bettie went silent for a minute as she tried to work out another explanation for what was happening. Now there was some sort of proof of an affair, Bettie didn't feel good, she felt sick. She hated what this would do to her sister.

"Is there any proof Graham?"

"Na sorry Bet. I tried,"

"I know Graham. Thanks. I'll call you later," Bettie said hanging up, she wasn't sure why she said she'll call him later. It was more of a reflex rather than a conscientious thought.

Looking out over the castle wall and staring at the stunning beauty around her, Bettie knew there was only one way to settle this once and for all. It was something she never would do normally but it was Christmas, the sun was starting to set and she didn't want to chase John for the next few days trying to get proof.

She had to go to the source.

She had to talk to John.

***

One good thing about keeping John's phone was all it took to find him was a quick check of his calendar and thankfully he was at an *interesting* restaurant across the river.

Of all the places John could have gone for a meeting, Bettie couldn't understand why he wanted to go to the retail park, there were much nicer places to go to.

Inside the Hungry Horse, Bettie looked around, studying all the little brown booths, brown tables and the ugly red, brown and yellow carpet. Bettie never did like the décor but the food was great in here, as were the staff.

Walking straight ahead, Bettie stood at the slightly warm, brown bar that wrapped itself all around the centre of the restaurant with spirits and all the beer on tap neatly arranged. The air smelt thick of alcohol, beer and delicious food. She thought she could even smell rich barbecue sauce from their delicious ribs.

Bettie listened carefully to the people in the restaurant, all she needed was to hear John's voice and she could find him easily enough. Of course she could just walk around but she wanted to be a little more stealthy than that. Yet all she could hear was the talking about Christmas from spouses and the high pitch talking of young kids with their grandparents.

"Did you like your meals?" a woman said.

"Oh yes it was amazing. Thank you," John said, his voice smooth and posh like he was still working with high end clients. Bettie hated how fake his voice sounded to her, and she hated how she couldn't change her voice like that.

As she turned, Bettie walked over to the brown booth in the far corner and sat directly opposite John. She admitted Phryne knew how to pick attractive men, John was quite the looker with his smooth square face and stunning smile. His bright green eyes were great too.

Bettie frowned as she saw John turn around.

"What? Am I not the one you're looking for?" Bettie asked.

John stared into her eyes. "What?"

"Seriously John. She's my sister,"

"What are you talking about?"

"The hotel searches. The mismatched lies. The gossip from work,"

John rolled his eyes and placed his face in his hands.

"She actually hired you. Really?"

Bettie's eyes narrowed as she realised there wasn't disappointment or guilt in his voice. There was concern or something like that.

"Does she have a reason to hire me?"

"Come on, I knew I was acting careful but I wanted to surprise her and Sean," John said smiling.

He searched his pockets trying to find his phone. Bettie passed it to him.

"Really? Phryne grabbed my phone,"

Bettie smiled. Maybe her sister was more like her than she realised, devilishly light fingered.

John swiped his phone a few times, did a quick Google search and showed Bettie something. Bettie didn't know what it was at first then she read something about a hotel for four people in Hollywood or somewhere else in Los Angeles.

Bettie looked at Sean indicating she wanted some sort of explanation.

"Bettie, I wanted to take us on Holiday for the new year and until Sean went back to Uni. That new director wants me to help him for a couple of weeks in LA. He's letting Phryne, Sean and... *Harry* come to the set and stay if they want,"

Bettie's eyes narrowed. "Why discretion hotels?"

John leant closer. "Because that's where all the non-acting VIPs stay. Insider secret there,"

Bettie leant back in her chair as she tried to understand it all. So there was no affair, all this was was one husband trying to surprise his family and give them the trip or experience of a lifetime.

Her mind switched to think about this as some sort of lie but Bettie knew it was the truth. This was honestly the first time John had been down in Rochester for months, he was too busy in London for his job to come down more often. He was damn good at it so Bettie wasn't really surprised a client had taken a shining to him.

"Last question, why the Hungry Horse?" Bettie asked.

John's eyes widened as if it was a stupid question.

"Because the food's good and I need to eat,"

Bettie nodded. "Why class it as a meeting?"

John rolled his eyes. "Do you know what my bosses are like? The second I have a free moment, they have me booked in with another client. I need a break,"

"Oh. Hence why friends saw you in restaurants when you were working,"

"Bettie, I do love Phryne. I just love my job as much as she loves hers, I need a break sometimes,"

Bettie couldn't argue with that logic so she ordered herself some food and let John tell him more about his amazing job and how he was the go-to guy for the VIPs in London.

She wasn't sure how much of it was true but she loved the stories John could spin.

***

Before she returned to her car, Bettie leant against the cold concrete railings that overlooked the stunning river Medway. Even with the playground silent with all the kids going home and even the smell of the Christmas cakes, mince pies and other amazing puddings starting to fade. Bettie still loved it.

Watching the little boats sailing and powering across the river, Bettie just watched them for a moment, enjoying the peace and quiet with only the sound of cars and wind joining her.

The river continued to flow just like Bettie continued to move, solve cases and love her life. But it didn't mean something wasn't missing, she still needed someone else. She had really learnt that in the past week, first with her nephew finding a beautiful boy of his own, then seeing how much John loved Phryne.

So knowing John would tell Phryne, Sean and Harry about their present in a few days on a cold Christmas morning, Bettie knew her job was done. The case was solved but the great thing was, there was no case at all.

Pushing herself off the cold concrete railing, Bettie waved like a child goodbye to the river, just like she, Phryne and her little brother used to do as children and she walked back to her car.

Christmas was still a few days away so she had time to disappear before she saw her family again. And she fully intended to use that time to reconnect with a very old friend.

Walking back to her car, Bettie got out her phone and dialled John. She looked forward to seeing him again, she wanted him but most of all, she wanted to see what the new year would bring with Graham. Bettie hoped the new year would start off brilliantly, and continue for years to come.

AUTHOR OF THE ENGLISH BETTIE
PRIVATE EYE SERIES

CONNOR WHITELEY

SMELL OF THE LAKE

A BETTIE PRIVATE EYE MYSTERY SHORT STORY

SMELL OF THE LAKE

If Bettie wasn't working then maybe she could have smiled, but she was working and there was no reason to smile.

Bettie stopped walking and dug her feet into the soft muddy ground as she stared out over the large Lake. She kept staring, studying every little detail of the Lake from the thick groups of trees that lined the edges of it with their large roots digging into the water, to the sheer glassy stillness of the water.

The air was perfectly calm and cold, freezing in fact. Bettie wanted to pull her thick fake fur coat over her more to keep her warm but that would take some of her attention away. She couldn't have that.

She had no idea how big the lake was but considering this was Leybourne Lakes in Kent, England and one of four. Bettie had a suspicion it was easily the size of a football pitch.

The perfect place to hide a body.

Well, Bettie wasn't sure how true that fact was but as she listened to the spooky calmness of it all with only the main road and cars rushing past in the far distance. Bettie knew no one would find a body for days.

Especially as all the sailing, swimming and everything else that happened on the Lake had been cancelled for the winter months. So Bettie raised an eyebrow as she realised a body could easily remain here for another 3 months until April. But by that time Bettie had no idea what would be left of the body, maybe the chest and a head, but even they would be badly rotten by then.

Bettie had to find the body.

Her drive only increased as Bettie remembered all the tears and crying and screaming she heard from the mother of a lost boy (Alex Malt) who ran away from home after a massive argument. Bettie still couldn't believe the story of how the mother had lost a finger. Some sort of farming accident.

The parents didn't agree with the son hanging out with certain people because they were too posh for the family. (They weren't. They made Bettie seem like the Queen) but the parents hated them anyway.

At first Bettie had no idea if she would take the case or not because the mother said outright she couldn't pay Bettie. But she was a sucker for a mother in need so she agreed, fully intending to get paid from the mother afterwards. Or Bettie had a suspicion her cop friend/ boyfriend/ whatever-he-was Graham could find something on the mother.

Staring at the Lake Bettie found this all strangely peaceful with the sun starting to set and shining a gently orange beam on the glassy water. Bettie had no idea how to find the body, she hadn't done this before but she had to try.

After investigating for a few days, Bettie had tracked Alex's past whereabouts to friends and drug dealers and well… Bettie started to understand that this new group of friends weren't the ones causing Alex any harm. Alex seemed to know that so he made these new friends, got clean and left his old friends.

Bettie wanted to smile but didn't feel like she had in it her when she remembered how one of the posh (compared to his family) friends had said Alex wanted to become a doctor now. A future only possible now he had left his old friends, and a future worth living.

A part of Bettie knew the mother and old friends knew Alex was getting a better life and wanted a life worth living with these new influences. But she still couldn't understand why they didn't support him. Alex was happy, his teachers said a lot happier than he's been in years.

So the idea of his *friends* and family not supporting him made no sense to her at first. Then as she talked to them more and more, Bettie realised they were all connected to the local drug rings around Kent and London and they apparently needed Alex. Bettie didn't find anything quite connecting the mother to it all but Graham probably could.

After all that Bettie partly didn't want to find Alex, she actually considered calling it quits and letting Alex escape it all. But one question kept pounding in her mind.

What if he was in trouble?

The second Bettie realised that she was back on her laptop and managed to find a street camera showing Alex going into Leybourne Lakes, but he never left.

Remembering the Suicide Awareness Classes from PrivateEyeCon, Bettie felt her stomach twist as she realised she needed to come to the lake and she hoped she was wrong.

Returning her attention back to the Lake, Bettie felt her stomach twist into an even tighter knot. She had to find him, she had to find him now.

Bettie was about to walk off and follow the muddy ring path around the lake when the cold wind picked up. She gagged.

Covering her nose, Bettie gagged as the overwhelming smell of rotten flesh came over her. She couldn't smell anything else, not her perfume, not the fresh lake air.

Everything stunk of rotten flesh.

Tears started to stream down Bettie's face as the smell kept growing and growing in intensity. She hadn't smelt anything like it before, this was far worse than rotten eggs. Maybe a million times worse.

A tiny part of Bettie wanted to leave and never return but she had to find the body, and she knew her clothes would be smelling of dead body for months.

She frowned at the idea of having to get rid of her clothes, Bettie had only bought the fur coat yesterday.

Bettie's eyes narrowed as she tried to think about where the smell was coming from. Considering she had only smelt it when the cold wind started to blow, she deduced it was coming from ahead of her.

Turning around, Bettie started to walk along the soft muddy path that went around the lake but with each step the smell of rotten flesh got worse and worse.

She was definitely getting hazard pay!

After twenty steps, Bettie was forcing her eyes to stay open but even then her vision was so blurry she could barely see. She was also fairly sure she'd only be able to smell odour d'dead body for weeks to come.

After a few more seconds of walking, the smell started to drop in intensity and Bettie smiled a little. Her eyes became slightly clearer and she was certain she had just missed the body.

Walking closer to the edge of the muddy path, Bettie's eyes narrowed as she focused on all the twisted muddy roots of the trees. Large chunks of plants stuck out of the mud and Bettie was sure the mud would have smelt disgusting. But only the smell of rotten flesh filled the air.

Her eyes covered each and every centimetre of the muddy edge of the lake but she couldn't see anything. Bettie felt her stomach tighten even more, she wondered if her stomach was about to burst. She couldn't give up, Bettie had to find that body.

Knowing she was going to have to throw her clothes out anyway, Bettie took a few steps off the muddy path and stood on the edge of where the muddy lake met the shore.

Her black high heels sunk into the mud slightly but Bettie couldn't care less. Bettie's eyes kept scanning until she saw exactly what she didn't want to see.

About two metres from her was a little bunch of hair exposed with something much larger covered in mud. The smell couldn't get any stronger now as Bettie's nose felt as if it was dying from the intense odour d'dead body.

Bettie knew with 100% certainty she shouldn't have done what she was about to do but she did it anyway. She walked further into the mud, her body sinking until she was waist deep in mud. She could feel the suction of the mud form around her and her high heels broke on sharp rocks, but in that moment she didn't care.

Reaching out Bettie's little hand touched the little bunch of hair, it felt freezing and wet and Bettie pushed some of the mud away from the person's face.

She was surprised it was so easy but after a minute or two of pushing away the mud, she thought she was almost going to collapse as the worse, most intense wave of odour d'dead body hit her.

Once she regained her composure she stared at the young smooth face of Alex Malt. Bettie gently rubbed his freezing cold, deadly pale cheek with her hand.

No one should ever have to deal with this and Bettie wasn't going to let any of his family and friends get away with this. It was their fault he'd killed himself, all Alex had wanted was a better life and they didn't love or support him.

Outrageous.

As Bettie rubbed his cheek a final time, her eyes widened as she saw his cold lifeless eyes move slightly. A memory of a class at PrivateEyeCon came into her mind, it was something about a smashed skull and the brain pressed against the eye.

So without really knowing what she was doing, Bettie took a careful step closer to the body, and stuck her hand into the freezing mud, and she pressed her fingers against the back of his head.

Bettie gasped as the skull moved and cracked ever so slightly, she couldn't believe what she was feeling.

Her mouth dropped as she took her cold hand out of the mud and wiped it clean. She couldn't believe someone had actually killed him, someone had killed Alex Malt.

Why?

She couldn't believe it, why on earth would someone want to kill anyone so kind and only wanted a better life for themselves.

Remembering not to panic as she slipped out of the mud to combat the suction power, Bettie took out her slightly muddy phone and called the only person who could help her.

"Hi Bet-" Graham started.

"Graham I have a body for you,"

***

Sitting on the cold, slightly frozen grass with a blanket wrapped round her, Bettie took slow deep breaths as columns of vapour formed in front of her. She suspected herself to be shivering but she was glad she wasn't.

As Bettie focused on the large shingle car park packed full of police cars and even some black cars she didn't recognise, Bettie's eyes focused on the group of white covered crime scene techs who pushed Alex's body into the Coroner van.

That simple fact still left Bettie in shock, her entire body felt cold and numb. Of course that could have just been from the cold but it didn't make Bettie feel any easier.

The sounds of cars driving past, police officers talking and the gentle wind howling made Bettie feel useless and unwanted as she sat there waiting to be released.

A part of her knew she could go home whenever she wanted because Graham would cover for her anyway. Yet Bettie didn't feel like going home anyway, she didn't want to have to tell the mother her findings.

After a few moments, Bettie smiled as her handsome, fit friend/ boyfriend Graham walked over with his stunning smile and longish brown hair parted perfectly to the left. He was beautiful and utterly perfect. What Bettie couldn't have given in that moment just to kiss him.

When Graham sat next to Bettie, she loved the smell of his rich earthy aftershave that reminded her of Sunday dinners with her family.

"Ya still shouldn't have gone in the mud Bet," Graham said.

Bettie playfully hit him. "You have your crime and we need to solve it,"

Graham's eyes narrowed.

"Bet this is a police investigation not a Bettie investigation,"

Bettie rolled her eyes and took out her phone, bringing up security camera footage of both the Lake's entrances.

"Where did ya get that?" Graham asked.

Bettie smiled. "You can get the footage through your methods, I'll get it with my methods,"

Graham smiled and rested his chin on Bettie's shoulder. Bettie loved the feeling of his body warmth.

"Now when I was finding Alex I only checked the camera towards the houses probably because at the time I was only looking for him,"

"Okay,"

"But if we look at the other camera towards here, the car park. We can fast forward it," Bettie said as she fast forwarded the footage for the past few days.

As it was January, there weren't many people. Only the crazy runners who thought it was a brilliant idea to go running in shorts in freezing conditions.

Bettie stopped the footage.

"What is it?" Graham asked.

Bettie zoomed in on the footage when she saw a tall middle aged woman wearing a black coat. She could have sworn it was the mother so Bettie zoomed in on the woman's fingers and the picture was blurry, but a finger was almost certainly missing.

"That's Alex's mother," Bettie said.

"But ya said ya were hired to find him,"

"I know,"

"But why hire ya if she found him?"

That was the question and Bettie didn't have an answer in the slightest. Graham gave her a quick kiss and ran off in his police car.

Bettie looked around but everyone was gone. There was no one to take her home. Some thanks!

***

As Bettie returned to the lakes the next day, admiring their stunning beauty as the large lake churned and returned to life with swans swimming about and talking with each other, she couldn't help but smile.

Leybourne Lakes might not have been the most sort after lakes to see in Kent or the UK but they had their own special beauty to them. Even the soft muddy path wasn't that bad after all, the mud had hardened to create a harsh bumpy landscape for Bettie to walk across.

She still loved it compared to yesterday, the air was still chilling her as she breathed it in but Bettie preferred it. Yesterday the cold was just annoying and bitter, yet today it seemed to be refreshing and revitalising.

Bettie didn't know why she felt so good, it could have been because she had helped to catch a killer or some other reason.

Listening to the sound of swans talking and splashing and people walking, chatting and laughing, Bettie couldn't believe the difference a simple day can make in the Lakes.

Bettie breathed in the chilling fresh air with hints of fresh pine that reminded her of delicious roasted lamb on holidays to the New Forest as a child, she knew that was probably her favourite difference for today.

She frowned as she remembered throwing away her clothes after yesterday, her fake fur coat was binned along with the rest of it. Bettie hated throwing it all away but it wasn't like she had a choice, they smelt horrific.

Taking a step closer to the cold water's edge, Bettie smiled as she finally got what she wanted. She had to admit she was surprised when she got the phone call from Graham earlier in the morning that he had arrested the mother for Alex's murder. She confessed to the entire thing and just as Bettie had suspected, it all was about drugs.

It turned out the entire family and friendship group was some

41

gang that supplied weed and stronger drugs all across Kent and London. Then Alex met these new people, wanted a better life and left the family.

Bettie shook her head as she remembered what Graham had told her next. It surprised her the mother was the gang leader and killed her own son to send a message across the gang and county that no one messes with or leaves the gang.

But Bettie loved the best part of it all and she definitely needed to make Graham feel appreciated later, apparently he had found a pile of cash with Bettie's name on it as payment when they arrested her.

Of course Bettie knew he was probably lying, she knew the mother was never going to pay her. But considering how risky it was for Graham, Bettie knew he cared about her and probably loved her. That meant a lot, it didn't mean she wanted him to do it again. But another thousand in the bank account is hardly something to moan about.

Turning around and walking back along the cold muddy path back to her car, Bettie wondered what would of happened if Alex was allowed to simply live out his life and become what he wanted. Maybe he would have saved lives as a doctor, maybe he would have become an office worker in some company and develop something, or maybe... Bettie didn't know. But that didn't matter.

What did matter was that other children and vulnerable teens could have some sort of meaningful life.

Bettie rolled her eyes as she promised herself that she would keep at least £200 as she honestly needed that for food and living stuff. But the rest of the money she didn't need that, and if this case had taught her anything. It was how badly other people needed it, Bettie knew of a few charities that would use the money properly so that's where it would go. Bettie would make sure of that when she got back home.

After a few minutes of walking, Bettie got back to her car and placed a hand on the cold plastic door handle. Before she pulled it,

Bettie took one final breath and smiled at the beautiful freshness of the smell of the lake. It was a stunning smell, so fresh, so full of life, so perfect.

And Bettie had done her job, the crime was solved, the money was paid and the smell of the lake was gone.

AUTHOR OF THE ENGLISH BETTIE
PRIVATE EYE SERIES

CONNOR WHITELEY

PROBLEM
IN A CAR

A BETTIE PRIVATE EYE MYSTERY SHORT STORY

PROBLEM IN A CAR

When Bettie opened her eyes, she didn't see anything. Everything was black, actually she wasn't even sure if everything was black or if she was blind.

She couldn't see a thing.

Bettie forced her eyes to open but as she felt her muscles strain, she realised her eyes were wide open and she still couldn't see anything.

A headache corkscrewed across her head and she hissed with pain as she felt pain radiate from the back of her head. Bettie tried to remember what had happened but she couldn't.

In fact she couldn't remember anything.

Her body jerked as it felt like she was moving forward but after a few seconds she realised she wasn't moving, it was what she was in. Bettie realised she must have been in some kind of vehicle.

As she closed her useless eyes and focused, Bettie frowned as she heard the distant sounds of honking, driving, screaming, talking, shouting and banging.

Bettie was hardly impressed with all this, she knew she was a Private Eye who might have been hired. Maybe this was connected to a case, maybe it wasn't, maybe-

Maybe Bettie just had no idea.

As she tried to move she felt something move on her face, Bettie's frown deepened when she realised she had some sort of thing over her face. It wasn't tight but it was good at blocking her sight, it could have been a blindfold, a bag or anything for all Bettie knew.

Bettie tried to move and stretch out then she realised she was stuffed into something small with her knees pressed into her chest. She rolled her eyes. She was stuffed into the boot of a vehicle!

Bettie didn't know if the criminals or whoever did this to her was stupid or brave. Kidnapping was serious, Bettie felt her stomach churn as it dawned on her whoever did this to her probably weren't some normal crooks.

She tried to roll over but stopped and hissed. Tight ropes sliced into her wrists and ankles as she tried to move.

Bettie tried again. She froze when she felt something tighten around her neck.

Swearing under her breath Bettie didn't doubt for a moment the criminals behind this had tied a restrictor knot around her. In other words, Bettie knew the more she struggled, the tighter the rope would get around her neck.

She was trapped.

A part of Bettie wanted to congratulate the criminals because this wasn't an easy thing to do. A knot like that took skills, it took even more skills to kidnap someone like Bettie.

But the more she thought about it the more the cold fearful sweat dripped down her back, Bettie hoped she'd survive. She tried to cast her mind back but there was nothing.

Bettie was relieved to remember her beautiful, annoying sister Phryne. Her sexy, drop dead gorgeous friend/boyfriend Graham but she felt like there was someone else she needed to remember.

She tried to remember, the person felt like the centre of her world, someone she loved like her own child. Did she have children? Again, the memories weren't returning.

Taking a few deep breaths, Bettie's frown deepened even more as she breathed in the thick polluted air of London.

She cocked her head at that idea, why was she in London? Sure she sometimes worked here and did a few cases for high power companies, Bettie knew that. But she lived in Kent, she remembered wanting to spend more time there to see what happened with Graham.

Bettie went to nod to herself but she remembered the knot around her neck. None of this made sense but-

She tried to think about the case or anything that might explain why she was kidnapped but another headache corkscrewed across her mind.

Bettie hissed.

Yet the headache passed she remembered something and Bettie instantly smiled. She remembered her amazing, beautiful nephew Sean and his boyfriend Harry. Bettie felt her stomach relax as she focused on Sean and his amazing smile and how happy he was with Harry. He truly loved him and-

The case!

Bettie gave a quiet cheer as she remembered something. They were all working on a case together, it was something to do with an accounting company who had hired her. The boss thought someone was stealing from the company and he only trusted Bettie to do the job right.

Bettie smiled more and more as she remembered what had happened. She was looking over the accounts in her office when Sean and Harry had popped in after a date. They wanted to know if Bettie wanted to go see her sister with them. (Also known as drive them home)

She remembered agreeing because she would do anything for Sean, and she wanted to hear about his degree as he was home for a few weeks from university.

Bettie curse under her breath as she couldn't remember anymore, but it was a start. The case had something to do with stealing from a company.

Her body jerked as the vehicle ran over a speed bump. Bettie curse.

Casting her mind back, Bettie tried to consider what she

normally did in these cases. Considering she must have involved Sean and Harry, the books must have been uneventful but there must have been something computer related. Bettie's eyebrows rose as she remembered a few fragments of memory of Harry's computer powers being useful in the past few months.

Her hands ached and the tips of her fingers felt numb so Bettie carefully moved her fingers.

The rope tightened around her neck.

Another memory popped into Bettie's mind as she remembered Harry suggesting she checked the employee's finances and start from there. She normally did that first but perhaps the Client had made her start with the company accounts.

Bettie couldn't remember that clearly.

Her body moved forward as the vehicle braked. Bettie's heart jumped to her throat. She relaxed when she heard the beeping of traffic lights.

But her panic was realised as she knew sooner or later the vehicle (probably a car actually) would stop and she would be dealt with.

Dealt with.

Bettie's eyes narrowed on the darkness as she remembered the entire case now. Those words were what she had found, they were the key to everything. They were the words she heard before she was kidnapped!

Fully remembering what happened, Bettie remembered Harry helping her check the finances and all the criminal records of the employees. She couldn't believe how quick of a job it was with two people. It turned out the records and finances were clear.

But Sean found something in the books that Bettie had missed (She wasn't too pleased with herself), he found there was a weird charge every month to an international company. Bettie knew Sean had a few friends doing Law and Business at university so she didn't know why she was surprised when he told her all the strange ways companies used to hide money. Bettie remembered there was a former Fraud Investigator at the university too.

Bettie jerked forward. Her head hit something. Pain flooded her head.

The car sped off.

Bettie swore repeatedly as the pain cleared and she knew she had to hurry up and remember everything.

Retracing her steps she remembered looking into that international company. Yes! She smiled as she remembered breaking into the building in London the company was registered to.

The car turned violently.

Images of documents, people and rooms filled her mind. Bettie remembered finding a name, no not a name, an organisation.

Then it hit her.

Bettie's eyes wetted as she remembered every little detail in the clearest detail. When Bettie was looking through the office of the international company, she found some photos and she recognised them all. It was a photo of the office's Christmas party a few months ago and an entire Syndicate of human traffickers were there that Graham had been hunting down in the last few months.

The Syndicate were trafficking people through the Port of Dover, there were bodies everywhere this group went, and now tears dripped down Bettie's face.

She knew she was next.

Then she realised she couldn't remember where she was when she was kidnapped. But there was a fragmented memory before everything went black. She remembered a smooth sexy voice of a handsome cop, Graham.

Well she hoped it was Graham, she didn't know, she could have been hoping. It could have been her would be killers for all she knew.

The car stopped. Door slammed.

Bettie's heart pounded into her throat.

The boot door opened.

Someone grabbed her face.

They pulled off the bag.

Bettie forced herself not to scream as she stared at a tall middle age man in a tight black suit and a black face mask. It wasn't expensive like the suit but the mask covered his head. But Bettie would never, ever forget those cold dark eyes.

In that moment, all Bettie wanted was for Graham to save her.

The man pulled a knife.

Bettie screamed.

He cut away the knot around her neck and Bettie moved a little. Feeling returned in her fingers but she still didn't feel safe.

Then her Private Eye training kicked in, she needed to focus, she needed to survive. Her eyes narrowed on everything except the man, the man wouldn't be any use to her.

Bettie focused on the cold concrete ceiling and bars of flickering white light that ran across the walls. She heard other cars in the distance, maybe there were several floors up and the air stunk of urine and weed.

She hated it.

At least Bettie knew she was in a multi-storey car park. Her eyes widened as she realised what that meant, it meant the criminals were moving her into another car.

Her mind screamed at her to do something, the logical part of her knew if Graham was coming for her it all depended all on him being able to track this car. Perhaps the police had satellite or camera footage and they were following the car.

The police couldn't afford for a change of vehicles.

Bettie's eyes narrowed on the black suited man as she knew exactly what she had to do.

The man pointed the knife at her and cut her legs free. A small part of Bettie wanted to kick him but there was a chance the man didn't see her as a threat yet. She needed to keep it that way for a long as possible.

"Can I sit up?" Bettie asked calmly.

The man nodded.

Stretching herself as she moved Bettie sat up inside the car boot and dangled her legs over the edge. She wasn't going to dare get out yet.

"You know who I am, who are you?" Bettie asked.

The man cocked his head for a moment.

"Come on. You're going to kill me. I might as well know my killers are,"

The man nodded at that and took a step closer to Bettie. She breathed in his rich earthy aftershave.

"The Syndicate is who we are. We are the ones who plague nations. Build up countries. Tear them down,"

Bettie smiled. "A bit overdramatic,"

"Agreed. We always deal with more impressive people but the Syndicate sends me when they have a you sized problem,"

Bettie frowned. "A me sized problem?"

The man smiled. "I'm sorry. A small fish problem. No one will miss you. You kill a cop, diplomat, intelligence asset. You get a nation after you. Kill an everyday person…"

Bettie nodded. She was about to say something when she thought she heard footsteps. Even if she had heard them, they didn't sound like normal footsteps, they were heavy, armoured and more than one.

She pushed those thoughts away. Bettie was being silly.

"What's going to happen to me?"

Oddly enough the man looked sad and gently rubbed Bettie's hand.

"I don't want to kill you. You intelligent. Nice. A good person even,"

Bettie wasn't sure how to take that.

"But I'm getting paid. Normally I love the killing of stupid low lives who cross the Syndicate. But you missy…"

A part of Bettie wanted to try to stupidly talk him out of it, but she wasn't sure if that would anger him or not.

She opened her mouth but closed it slowly when she saw a very small flashing light behind some cars tens of metres away.

Bettie smiled. "Tell me when did you start working for the Syndicate?"

The man started playing with his knife. "I don't know maybe a few years back in Paris. Beautiful city, ever been?"

"Sadly not. Would love to go. How many Syndicate members have you met?"

The man pointed the knife at Bettie's throat.

"I know all six members. They know me and they pay me enough to kill you,"

The man pressed the cold blade against her throat. Bettie stared at him. Their eyes locked.

"Do I have to make him say names!" Bettie shouted.

Armed Response Units stormed out.

Guns raised.

They prepared to shoot.

Graham rushed out.

Grabbing the knife.

Throwing the man to the ground.

Bettie breathed. She was safe. Her Graham had found her.

***

A few hours later, Bettie allowed the warm toasty blanket to cover her entire body like a tight cocoon. She loved the warm feeling of safety it provided, Bettie gently moved her fingers over the soft baby blue fabric of her sister's three-seater.

The air smelt delicious of warm hot chocolate and cheese toasties as everyone was in the kitchen making a fuss over her. When Graham had bought her back everyone cried in happiness as they saw her.

Bettie almost cried herself, she didn't know the man had been that wrong about no one missing her. Her family loved her so much, and she loved them.

As someone moved her head, Bettie smiled as her focus returned to the love of her life and the only person who wasn't in the kitchen. Looking up Bettie blew Graham a massive kiss, and she stared into his warm eyes as she admired his smooth handsome face.

The sound of her family in the kitchen trying to make sure everything was perfect for Bettie's dinner and hot chocolate made her laugh a little. It still hadn't sunk in how much her family loved her, even Harry who was basically family now had wanted her back.

Continuing to stare at Graham's beautiful face, Bettie struggled to believe what she had found out today. Graham gave her a massive snog for helping him and his task force, there were whispers of major arrests going to happen now and Graham expected even more was going to happen after the Intelligence Service had interrogated the man.

Graham was even grateful for Bettie's client agreeing to tell the police everything he knew about the stealing.

But Bettie wasn't interested in that.

As Bettie breathed in the delicious chocolate, felt the warm blanket and her amazing boyfriend and heard her amazing family in the kitchen. She realised she had everything she cared about, she was perfectly happy lying here and she felt safe.

Happy and safe.

Two things she hadn't felt for years, but she had always had. Especially now with Graham in her life.

So as Bettie's eyes grew heavier, she smiled as she realised she had everything, she loved everything and this all started with some problem in a car and how she was saved by the people who loved her.

Now that, Bettie could happily live with.

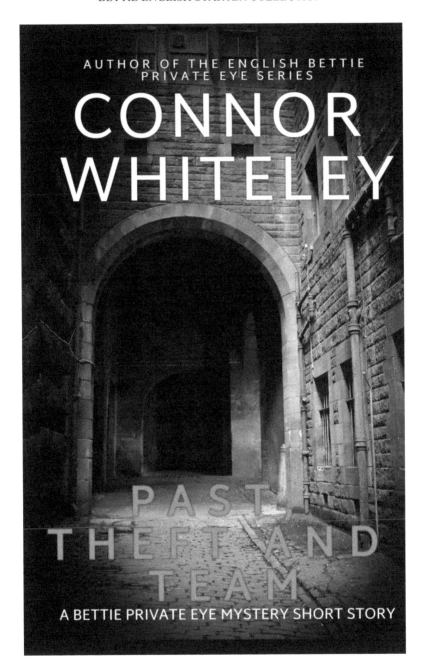

AUTHOR OF THE ENGLISH BETTIE
PRIVATE EYE SERIES

CONNOR WHITELEY

PAST
THEFT AND
TEAM

A BETTIE PRIVATE EYE MYSTERY SHORT STORY

THEFT, PAST AND TEAM

Bettie was hardly impressed her old university friend Alice had called her out of the blue during a lunch with her sister, Phryne, she wasn't exactly sure why she was bugged by it. It could have been because this lunch was a rare chance for the two sisters to talk without family around.

As Bettie walked down the grey cobblestone high street of Canterbury, England, she felt a wave of energy pulse through her. There was something great about walking in a student town.

All around Bettie there were tens or maybe even hundreds of university students of all different ages, weights, colours and heights walking up and down the high street. They were all laughing and talking and chatting with one another.

For a moment Bettie missed how she and her old friend Alice had spent hours talking each day. Sometimes about boys, sometimes about horrible lecturers, sometimes about the future.

Bettie had no idea what Alice did nowadays, their friendship had ended quickly enough when... actually Bettie wasn't sure why the friendship had ended. They were friends one evening but not the next morning, and Bettie never knew why.

Continuing to stroll down the high street, Bettie loved all the little shops and restaurants that were infused with the stunning architecture of the buildings. They were lovely in Canterbury.

Bettie loved it how even the most posh and expensive brands had managed to keep their elegance but add nicely to the stunning history of the high street.

As she walked past Hotel Chocolate, Bettie had to resist the overwhelming temptation to go inside. The smell of rich dark chocolate and other intensely sweet combinations, hints of nuts and fruits scented the air too.

It was delicious. Bettie could almost taste the amazing chocolate in her mouth.

Continuing to walk down the high street, smiling to herself as she walked past more impressive buildings from the Tudor period with their white walls and intense black beams of wood. Bettie looked forward to seeing her friend, all this amazing architecture and the youthful energy of the students had made her excited.

On the phone Alice had said something about a theft or robbery but over the background noise of cathedral bells and the singing of hymns, Bettie couldn't make it out.

Turning her head Bettie saw the immense spire of Canterbury Cathedral, it stood there like an imposing guardian over the city. Always watching to make sure everyone was safe, no matter who they were.

As much as Bettie wanted to believe that, she knew that wasn't the truth, crime could and would happen anywhere regardless of what religious figures claimed to watch over the city.

As Bettie passed a few side streets that were packed with seating from more amazing specialised cafes, Bettie breathed in more stunningly scented air that was rich in bitter coffee and sweet cakes.

Bettie really wanted to stop in one of them and have a slice of cake as her and her sister didn't even get to that portion of their lunch. She wasn't impressed.

A part of Bettie wanted to stop and cock her head and focus on the passing crowd. Alice had said she would be walking up the high street and they would meet in the middle. But Bettie was easily three quarters of the way down the high street, there was no sign of Alice in the slightest.

After a few more moments, Bettie stopped walking and moved over to the side of the high street, feeling the hard cobblestoned ground under her feet, she was about to call Alice when she saw a large woman in a poorly fitting black coat walked towards her.

It took everything Bettie had not to smile at her friend, not because she was being (or wanted) to be horrible. But because all throughout university Bettie had been a lot larger than she was today and Alice had always bullied her about it.

So seeing Alice was about twenty stone and it looked like she was struggling to walk up the high street, Bettie didn't know what to think.

To help put Alice out of her misery, Bettie walked up to her, hugged her and tried not to gag when she smelt Alice. It quickly became clear to Bettie that she was the one who ended up better in life.

But she couldn't understand how, at the end of university it was Alice who had been headhunted for her amazing skills at accounting and computers. It was Alice who had all the top grades and it was Alice who had all the lecturers dying to give employers *their* letter of recommendation.

Bettie never quite understood why it mattered who the recommendation came from, sure some of the lecturers were the best in the world, but at the end of the day it was just a recommendation.

A part of Bettie wanted to learn what had happened to Alice. This was not the Alice she remembered, but she'd be lying if there wasn't a hint of smugness in her over landing on top.

"Hi Bettie girl," Alice said.

Even the way she spoke had Bettie puzzled, when she was at university Alice only spoke *proper* English. She didn't speak *common* (Alice's words) or slang.

"Why you call me?" Bettie said sounding a lot more direct than she meant.

"Come on Bettie. No hi how are you. you haven't seen me for years,"

And that was the point. Bettie realised she didn't want to be here, she wanted to be having dessert with her sister, a person who was extremely annoying and judgey but a person who still phoned her from time to time.

"I'm sorry but you haven't called me in years. Why now?"

"You haven't called me either,"

That was a fair point and one that Bettie didn't have an answer for. She tried to think up some kind of excuse, an idea or an outright lie to make up for it. But she knew she didn't need to justify herself to Alice.

"Alice I'm sorry but I have client meetings today. Please tell me why you called," Bettie was lying but she didn't care at this point. She was mad.

"Fine Bettie girl. I got robbed by some punk kids back there outside Weatherspoon. I saw ya social and saw ya close by,"

Bettie cocked her head. Alice was checking her social media, she didn't know if that was creepy or not. Especially as Bettie never used it, her Facebook wall was only filled with things she was tagged in.

"What did they steal?" Bettie said.

A part of her wanted it to be something so small and minor she would easily forget about it and make up another excuse for not helping her. But she doubted it would be that easy.

"Bettie girl they stole ma phone!"

"I need more,"

Bettie tried not to shake her head or sound judgemental but she really failed, and she knew it.

"Bettie girl, I need ma phone. It has pics of my dead hubby and my parents,"

Her eyes narrowed on Alice. She had no idea she had a husband now and as far as Bettie knew her parents were alive. But that meant nothing in the real world, considering she hadn't spoken to Alice nor her parents for years.

So she needed to play it cool.

"I'm... sorry to hear that. I always liked them,"

That was a half truth at least, Bettie did like how they treated her and they were funny people. But Bettie had learnt the hard way to never even joke that Alice wasn't perfect or a perfect student.

With that memory in mind, Bettie remembered she wasn't here as a friend. She was here as a Private Eye and that meant she needed information and money.

"What did the kids look like?" Bettie asked.

"I donna know. They were tall, wearing black, they were white and young. Maybe uni students,"

"Any logos, tattoos?"

Alice smiled. "Yes! They all had a university logo on their black things. Maybe hoodies. The logo was a large dragon,"

Bettie rolled her eyes, Alice was hardly the best witness but at least Bettie knew the logo. Her wonderful nephew Sean had told her how him and his boyfriend had flickered through the sport societies at their university and somehow the conversation had moved onto their weird logos.

The weird dragon head on a black background was one such logo.

"Ya wanna know about money?" Alice asked.

Bettie nodded.

"Pay ya hundred for finding my phone,"

Bettie looked at the hard cobblestone ground for a few seconds as she considered her offer. A part of her wanted to charge more for her, maybe it was a little revenge, maybe it was for interrupting her lunch.

Bettie nodded. She couldn't be nasty to a client, she was a professional first and foremost. No matter her feelings towards the client.

Integrity sucked sometimes!

"Thank you, I'll be in touch," Bettie said, walking away.

Bettie wanted to walk away quickly and get rid of Alice, but before she could she heard Alice shout something.

"They died in a car accident. All killed. I knew ya were wondering!"

Bettie stopped for a moment, she didn't know what to do. should she stay and comfort her friend, do her job or, or, or...

There were too many questions or possibilities for Bettie to think about so she did the thing that felt natural to her.

"I'm sorry. I'm really sorry for your loss,"

Then Bettie walked away, disappearing into the swarm of university students.

***

Of course Bettie felt bad for leaving Alice after she told her about her parents' death, but Bettie was still processing everything that was happening.

After all the bullying, name calling and digs at Bettie for not being a good enough student, too fat and too lazy. Bettie was mad that Alice had ended up like this.

Now Bettie was a fit, perfectly in-shape Private Eye who always solved her cases and Bettie loved her job. She loved not being an accountant and dealing with all that rubbish and pressure.

But after seeing Alice today she didn't know what she felt. She was mad and rageful she knew that for sure. Maybe she hadn't left the Alice skeletons in the closet like she thought.

Trying to push those thoughts away from her, Bettie focused on the task at hand. She didn't at first know or at least fully understood why the phone was so important, but if anything happened to her precious Graham, annoyingly perfect sister or her beautiful nephew, then Bettie would definitely want photos of them. So she might not have liked Alice and how she was now, but she was a Private Eye. There was a case that had to be solved, and Bettie had to solve it.

So Bettie focused on the massive green park in front of her. The park was filled with thick lustrous green grass and the smell of it filled her senses. Bettie loved the smell of freshly cut grass so she was perfectly happy here.

Looking around Bettie didn't particularly care for all the dirty houses and their bright red fences that lined the edges of the massive park, but at least there was a few football pitches for the students and societies to train on.

And that's why Bettie was here.

Her eyes narrowed on the men in their black sportswear with the dragon head logo on their chests. All the men were fit and in perfect shape, she understood why Sean had told her the girls would come and support the team from time to time. Also known as the girls wanted to look at the men.

Bettie couldn't blame them.

She was even sure Sean would have wanted to come but being the only guy in the group might have given away what the girls were doing. Bettie definitely remembered that from her university days.

The blowing of whistles made Bettie focus on a tall muscular man about her age who was running across the pitch, and pointing his finger at some of the players.

Bettie had no idea what was going on, but he was in charge so she needed to talk to him.

As she walked over to him, Bettie's eyes widened as she recognised the man. She recognised that fit muscular body, she knew there was a six-pack under that sportswear.

Bettie stared at into the amazing eyes of her boyfriend as he turned around to see her.

Surprised was hardly the word for it. She had no idea what Graham would be doing here, Bettie knew he did some kind of training during lunch time and he had mentioned he was working somewhere in Southern Kent for a few days.

She clearly hadn't shown enough attention.

But the real question was, why was a police officer training a university sports team?

"Hello beautiful," Graham said, kissing her quickly.

Bettie loved the taste of his soft lips against hers.

"Why ya doings here Bet?"

"What are you doing here?" she asked.

"Ya know Bet I'm covering a friend for a few days then I'll go back to training at my normal place,"

Bettie smiled as he finished lying. She knew he wasn't lying to her because Graham had made sure to speak loud enough that the other players heard it.

That meant only one thing to Bettie and she would have done the exact same thing if she was him. Graham was clearly lying to maintain some kind of cover.

With the sound of men shouting and cheering like they always did at football games around them, Bettie decided as much as she wanted to know what he was really doing here. She did have a sort-of client that she was working for.

"What players are missing today?" Bettie asked.

Graham took a step closer and smiled. "Bet, I love ya but I can't answer these questions here. They can't get suspicious,"

Bettie smiled back. "I have a client,"

"I have a criminal to catch,"

Bettie smiled deepened. She had been waiting for this conflict to come up and she loved it.

"The players?" Bettie asked.

For a moment Bettie thought she saw a tall blond man stare at her and Graham. His body looked like he was playing but he wasn't. He was moving on the spot, looking busy but he wasn't.

In case he was the suspect Bettie looked away. The man went back to playing.

"Bet, you okay?" Graham asked, his voice concerned.

Bettie smiled and nodded. "Yes, the players?"

Graham rolled his eyes. "All the players are here Bet. The entire team is here because they have a match at the weekend against the two other Canterbury unis,"

Bettie frowned.

"Please go," Graham said.

Bettie gave him a quick kiss and walked away. Clearly she needed to think bigger, but there was one question that kept repeating in her mind.

Where did the thieves get the logoed hoodies?

***

After a bit of research on the internet, Bettie found nothing that remotely answered her question and it was really annoying her now. Nowhere, not even the university societies themselves, sold the black hoodies with the dragon logo on. That was ridiculous to Bettie considering how much money university societies made off merchandise so it was beyond her why this particular football team didn't sell.

A part of her wanted to give up but there was something interesting and exciting about this case. She had to get the phone back so Alice would remember her dead husband and parents, but she didn't know how.

Bettie pressed her back against the cold glass window of one of the many shops along Canterbury high street, breathing in the nutty scented air from a nearby seller of sweet roasted nuts.

She watched the hundreds of university students that talked, laughed and shouted as they walked up and down the street with their friends.

That's when Bettie realised why she was really mad with Alice. It was partly because of the bullying and all the nastiness that she'd mistaken for true friendship. Bettie was annoyed that Alice had left her.

They were a team, a duo with another few friends. They were a team that did everything together, shopping, talking, studying and more. Bettie loved them all, they were her team, her family.

So when they all abandoned her, Bettie knew she had lost too much. That was properly why it had taken her so long to get with Graham, she needed time to recover and learn how to be with a group again.

A team?

Bettie smiled as she remembered she was part of a team, an

64

unofficial one but still a team that loved her, if anyone knew how to get university wear outside of proper channels, who better to ask than a university student.

As Bettie phoned her nephew Sean, she considered hanging up in case he was in a lecture or something, but she was on a case. Nothing else mattered.

"Hi Aunty, in a study group. Make it quick," Sean said.

"If I wanted a uni sports hoody with a logo without anyone knowing. How would I do it?"

"Easy. Go to a team member, pay them. They say they lost theirs and they get it for you,"

Bettie didn't know how Sean knew the answer without thinking, but she had her information.

"Thanks, see you soon," Bettie said, hanging up.

As she breathed in the nutty-scented air, Bettie tried to think about it. She didn't have time to interview all the players on the team, and Graham wouldn't let her question them again.

She wasn't even sure she wanted to, Bettie loved her work but even she knew when to draw the line between her case and police work.

The sounds of students walking and talking made Bettie smile as she remembered a tiny detail. That blond man from earlier, he was watching her, he was interested.

Bettie stopped her thoughts immediately. She knew she had to talk to that man but if he was the criminal Graham was after, she couldn't cross that line. She hated the idea of Graham losing a case over her, she didn't want to be that sort of Private Eye.

At PrivateEyeCon, there were always stories of Private Eyes putting themselves and their cases over their loved ones. They all ended in breakups, divorces and even fights. Bettie swore she would never do that to herself.

She had to talk to the blond man though.

Dialling her phone again, she had an idea. Graham was mainly a homicide detective but because he worked drugs for a decade, he sometimes got asked to help because of his connections.

Maybe him and Bettie could help each other.

***

About an hour later, Bettie was amazed her phone call had gone so well, she was expecting to be moaned at and told to back off. But Graham was interested in Bettie's plan.

Yet Bettie wasn't keen on Graham's plan. Especially after she pressed Graham a little harder and he mentioned how this blond man player had turned up later to practice. Bettie couldn't believe how Graham could have missed it, but at least she was sure this player had time to commit the theft. He probably had a few friends help but Bettie was only interested in him.

Walking up a cold stretch of tarmac path with thick trees lining it, Bettie had to admit she hated this, she hated walking in the dim light as the sun started to set with nothing but her wits as her defence.

The air smelt fresh and crisp with hints of delicious nuts that someone had probably dropped on the path earlier.

As the cold engulfed her, Bettie hoped this wouldn't take long. Graham's plan was for her to call up and ask for a package for a party. She hated drugs, she hated everything to do with them, but Graham was firm this was the only way to help him.

It wasn't that Graham was being unfair, Bettie knew she would be the same if she was Graham. It still didn't make her feel any better, she had seen the damage drugs did to her friends and other students.

She didn't want anyone else to suffer, that's why she had to help take this guy off the streets.

The sound of heavy footsteps coming from behind made Bettie smile as she knew this was game time. Excitement filled her as she prepared herself and switched on the recorder app on her phone.

A disgusting smelling man came up to her, Bettie wanted to gag at the horrific smell of weed that assaulted her senses. Even though the guy had the same blond hair as earlier, he was different. His eyes were bloodshot and he was clearly using something.

Bettie took a deep breath in some failed attempt to stop her panicking, this wasn't for her. It was for Graham and Alice. She had to get the phone back.

Her slight panic stopped the moment she focused on the man's black unzipped coat. As the coat flapped around as he moved, Bettie saw the large dragon head logo on a black background.

Bettie stopped. "Got the package?"

The man's eyes turned crazy. They narrowed, they were becoming more bloodshot.

"Got the cash bitch!" he shouted.

Bettie frowned at him.

"You think I'm kidding. Give me the cash bitch!"

Bettie smiled. "Give me back the phone,"

The man manically laughed.

"Ya stupid bitch. Ya think you goanna out smart me,"

Bettie was completely lost now. If she wasn't doing this for Graham then she might actually consider flooring the guy and taking back the phone. He had to still have it.

As Bettie grabbed a lump of fake cash from her pocket, she saw the man's crazy high eyes wide and he smiled.

Bettie closed her hand.

The man frowned. "Give. It. To. Me!"

"Do you have the drugs or not?" Bettie asked.

This guy was so high he probably didn't even think she might be recording him.

"Yea bitch, I got ya drugs. Coke, hero, whatever. I wanna my money!"

Bettie smiled and took out her phone. She stopped the recording and sent it to Graham.

The guy's eyes widened and Bettie started to walk away.

The man screamed.

He charged.

Bettie sighed and stepped to the right. She shook her head as the guy ran past and Bettie stretched out her foot.

Tripping the guy over.

The man slammed into the ground.

Bettie stood on the back of his neck.

"Now I don't like people who call me bitch. I don't like drug dealers, I don't like you. You've made me walk all around Canterbury today,"

The man shouted something but Bettie couldn't make it out.

"As I'm a good Private Eye, I'll give you two choices. One. Give me the phone you stole earlier and I'll release you. You can run before the police show up. Two. Be silent and the police can take you,"

The guy went silent.

Bettie wanted to taunt him some more but there was no point, Graham would take him in and charge him with drug possession or whatever the police called it now.

They would find the phone too on him.

If Alice wanted to press theft charges, Bettie knew she could easily persuade her not. The theft would mean the phone would have to go into evidence and knowing the state of police evidence rooms, those photos would almost certainly get lost.

Just the thought of that made Bettie tense. She couldn't fail her client.

Against her better judgement and knowing Graham would show up any moment, Bettie did something she always hated.

She kicked him in the head.

With the man out cold, Bettie cursed herself as she hated using violence of any sort. But she was doing it for her client, that was okay, wasn't it?

Trying to forget about her minor assault, she started to search through his pockets. She searched his jeans, hoody then his coat. Bettie smiled as she went through his coat pocket.

As she pulled out two things, she immediately frowned at the small package of white powder she pulled out. Bettie put that straight back in his pocket, but Bettie smiled at the large black smartphone in her hand.

Bettie pressed the power button on the side and let out a long breath as she saw Alice's face on the lock screen. This was her phone, her job was complete and she was going to get her money.

***

Closing the large front door to her sister's house, Bettie gently ran her fingers along the smooth wooden door with strange carvings on the inside. It looked like something from a fantasy film but Bettie loved their cold texture.

As Bettie walked inside the little porch area that was nothing more than a small box room with a steep step of carpeted stairs and a massive white door. She didn't know how to feel.

She heard the talking and lovely sounds of her sister, nephew, his boyfriend and Graham inside the living room. But she didn't want to go in just yet.

Bettie lent against the cold white walls of the porch and pressed her head against them. Sure she was now a hundred pounds richer but after talking to Alice, she didn't feel any better.

After Bettie had run all around Canterbury for Alice and took down a drug dealer so she could get her stupid phone back, all that Bettie wanted was a thank you and maybe an explanation.

Maybe an explanation for why Alice had subtly bullied her for years and then abandoned her.

Bettie wanted to chuckle as she now knew how stupid she was. She was just another naïve pathetic version of her younger self, she just wasn't as large as she once was.

She was still as stupid though.

Bettie's hands formed fists as she remembered how Alice had laughed at Bettie's face as she asked for a thank you and an explanation.

That had hurt. No one wanted to be laughed at and even though Bettie had partly expected it, it still hurt.

Bettie did like how she reacted, she loved how demanding she could be. Bettie's throat still hurt a little from shouting as loud as she could at Alice for an explanation.

She really, really wished she hadn't now.

Bettie closed her eyes and tried to suppress the tears as she recalled how much of a pathetic loser Alice had called her. Apparently she never liked Bettie, she only used her as a friend because she felt sorry for the losers.

That still broke Bettie's heart. All those years of so-called friendship was only because she was a charity case, a bad one at that.

Then the more Bettie remembered, the more she realised how often she had been the one to suffer during university. Bettie was always the driver, the one who had to stay up late before an exam because her *friends* were out.

Bettie hated herself. She never considered herself stupid but she supposed she so badly wanted friends, she blinded herself to the truth.

She didn't even know how to respect herself again.

The sound of laughter, hugs and even kissing followed by silence reminded Bettie of what truth she needed.

She heard her family mutter and whisper as they wondered why she wasn't coming in, was that really her, where they being robbed.

She loved her family.

At last it hit her, Bettie did not need a single person from university. She had been hanging onto old memories and skeletons for far too long. This was her team, her family, the people who loved her.

They're all she needed.

As Bettie stood up she heard Sean and Harry kiss before the precious little face of Sean opened up the door and smiled at her.

She knew she was just an aunty, but she really did love Sean. Like he was her own. In fact she loved all her family and extended family like they were her own.

They were her team.

So as she walked into the living room, she forgot about the past and looked to the future and her family. Whatever team she thought she'd lost, she had more than made up for.

And that was more than fine by her.

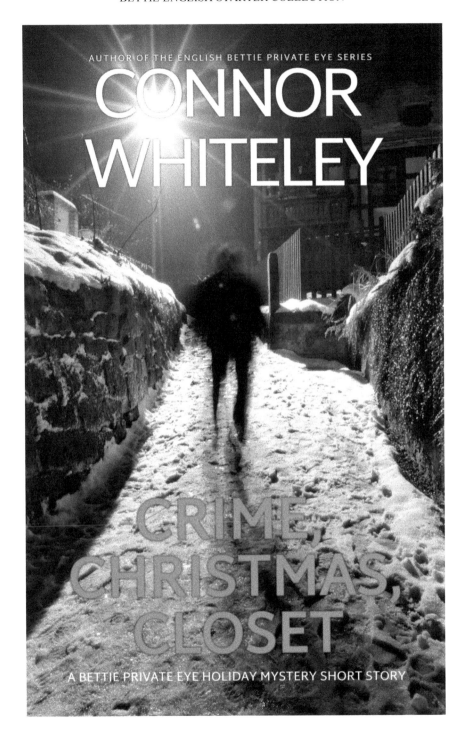

AUTHOR OF THE ENGLISH BETTIE PRIVATE EYE SERIES

CONNOR WHITELEY

CRIME, CHRISTMAS, CLOSET

A BETTIE PRIVATE EYE HOLIDAY MYSTERY SHORT STORY

CRIME, CHRISTMAS, CLOSET

Bettie English, Private Eye, opened her eyes only to realise, she couldn't see. She even strained her eyes forcing them to open as wide as she possibly could. It didn't matter. She could only see darkness.

As she tried to move, Bettie felt something cover her skin, hold her tight and constrict her movements. She wasn't going anywhere anytime soon.

Knowing she was trapped for a moment, or the foreseeable future (she didn't know), Bettie pressed her back against the smooth cold surface of something. For a moment Bettie wondered if it was even worth trying to guess where she was, but that's when she felt something.

She hissed a little as a headache corkscrewed across her head and sent a wave of pain over her. Bettie kept hissing for a few seconds before the headache passed and Bettie knew something bad had happened.

Breathing in the musty air of wherever she was, Bettie tried to focus on what she remembered. She couldn't. She felt as if there was something she was meant to remember, but she couldn't. The smell of mustard started to chip away at her concentration, it was so strong, so ugly, so awful.

But Bettie smiled because even that was a clue of sorts, lots of objects and places and perfumes didn't smell musty so she just needed to figure what places did smell musty.

Trying to ignore the awful smell, Bettie focused on everything else, but she was really focusing on sound. If she could hear something, music, cars, whatever. Then she might be able to figure out where she was.

After a few moments of listening, Bettie heard some Christmas songs, some children playing in the snow (maybe) in the distance and something else. Someone opening, searching and banging cupboards nearby.

Bettie was sure they were all the clues she needed to figure out what was going on, but she hissed a little more as the headache returned for a few moments.

Taking a few deep breaths of the musty air, she tried to stretch her fingers in case she could feel something on the walls or maybe even a door or light switch. But her fingers were covered in something too.

In some attempt to find out what she was covered in, Bettie rubbed her fingers as much as she could (which wasn't a lot) against the material and Bettie frowned. She was sure she had concussion but Bettie swore she was feeling tinsel or something.

Bettie shook her head at the stupidity of her being tied up with Christmas decorations and tinsel no less, but as a private eye she couldn't say she hadn't seen weird things.

Pressing her head against the smooth cold wall (?), Bettie focused on remembering what had happened. She was a private eye so she had to be here for a case, she just couldn't remember what case. It could be civil, kidnapping or theft for all Bettie knew.

But a fragment of a memory reminded her about something. It was new and Bettie hadn't done very many of these cases but she had recently got her bounty hunter license.

At first Bettie hadn't wanted to get it because no one uses bounty hunters in the UK but Bettie always liked a challenge.

But Bettie still felt as if there was something she was meant to remember. Something about what happened. Something… she just didn't know but it felt important.

She cocked her head and felt something tinsel-like brush against her cheek as she wondered if she was here as a bounty hunter.

Bettie had no idea, it was possible. Her boyfriend Graham had suggested a few targets for her but she hadn't listened, she was too focused on… relationship things whenever she spoke about it. She still wasn't sure if she wanted children like he did.

The sound of opening, searching and banging cupboards nearby stopped and now it sounded like someone was walking up some stairs.

Then it hit Bettie and she felt some sweat drip down her back, neck and hands as it dawned on her she was in a closet. It made sense to Bettie and there were worse places to be tied up, she knew all about that from the time she was tied up in a car and driven around London.

But this was something else.

With sweat continuing to roll down her back, neck and hands, Bettie needed to think about what to do. If there was a dangerous bounty target walking up the stairs to finish her off, she had to be ready.

She wished there was some light for her to see, maybe she would have been able to see something sharp or something thing to break her tinsel prison with. Yet there was still no light.

Pushing herself up, Bettie pushed her weight forward, fell and landed on something soft. She was glad it wasn't something hard.

Using her head, lips and cheeks, Bettie managed to rather impressively (if she did say so herself) feel that it was probably some kind of mattress that someone had stuffed into the closet.

Bettie swore under her breath as she really wanted something to help break free, she didn't want to be tied up, constricted or someone's prisoner. She had to be free and she had to solve the mystery of what happened to her.

A part of her wondered if she had been gone long enough for Graham to come back from home, notice she was gone and start searching for her. But Bettie remembered he was working late tonight because of an operation with the French.

The idea of her being gone for days briefly went through her mind but she quickly dismissed it. Partly out of utter terror that it was true and her friends and family couldn't find her, but she knew her family loved her too much to let her stay missing for so long. Especially her nephew.

Rolling over on the mattress, Bettie almost gagged as a massive whiff of mustard was kicked into the air.

The lights turned on.

Bettie blinked rapidly as her eyes adjusted to the bright light bulb hanging from the ceiling.

Looking up, Bettie's eyes narrowed on the little rectangular closet she was tied up in. She swore again as she felt her blood boil at herself for letting some criminal get the better of her.

Bettie looked at the white walls, door and mattress in the closet and wondered why someone wouldn't put more in here. It was almost like someone had either emptied it or made it just to trap her.

Her mind quickly started to come up with silly ideas about her being trapped by a serial killer, a trafficker or a kidnapper. But Bettie realised there was a much more pressing question.

Why did the lights turn on?

Bettie looked at herself and nodded as she saw she was tied up with blue, red and green tinsel that she hated. As much as Bettie loved Christmas she didn't like green tinsel, it wasn't an attractive colour and as for when her boyfriend got dressed up for Christmas, Bettie made sure he didn't wear green.

The sound of Christmas songs, children playing in the snow in the distance and someone walking right outside the closet made Bettie smile and her eyes narrow.

She knew normal people would be scared in this moment, but Bettie wasn't. She was excited, thrilled, ready for action. She wanted, needed to confront this criminal who dared trap her. Her plan was simple. Scream to scare the criminal.

The door opened.

Bettie screamed.

Someone else screamed.

Jumping back.

Bettie wormed out of the closet.

Climbing onto the other person.

She headbutted them.

Then she realised it was her nephew Sean. Bettie instantly recognised him from his black designer jeans, smooth face and long white coat.

As she stared wide-eyed at her nephew, she felt her stomach tighten and her spirit drop as she had just attacked her nephew. Her sister was going to shout at her that was for sure and as for his boyfriend Harry, Bettie didn't even want to think about that.

"Aunty want to get off me?" Sean said.

Bettie rolled off him as she heard Sean get some scissors and cut her free.

"What were you doing in a closet?" Sean asked smiling.

"I thought I would try it. You know what being in a closet is like," Bettie said.

Sean playfully hit her head.

"Seriously Aunty. Mum's been worried sick," Sean said as he finished cutting.

Bettie smiled as she stretched and felt joints, muscles and bones pop as they moved for the first time in hours.

"I don't know. Someone hit me from behind,"

"You don't remember do you Aunty?"

Bettie's eyebrows rose. "What?"

"You got Harry to ran a background check on a cop friend of Graham's. He sent you the results and we didn't hear anything of you,"

"What's the time?"

"Six,"

Bettie nodded as her memory started to return to her and remembered it all. She met Detective Inspector Lawrence two days ago at some awards ceremony. The food was nasty, cheap and awful so Bettie didn't taste too much and Graham avoided it all.

But when she met Lawrence there was something about him, the way he spoke, moved and acted. It was strange and then there was a rumour that Graham had mentioned in passing about him taking brides for politicians.

At first Bettie knew she was being paranoid but there weren't any cases that she was working on so she had the time. A quick internet search alone revealed a lot of good information about Lawrence. Lots of accusations, some evidence, no charges.

Returning her attention back to Sean, Bettie's eyes narrowed.

"How did you find me? And who was banging the cupboards?"

Sean looked to the floor. "I know you're with a cop, but you won't tell would you?"

Bettie smiled and shook her head. She didn't really want to hear his next sentence.

"Me and Harry pinged your phone,"

A part of Bettie wanted to chastise him for doing something so illegal but she could hardly talk these days. Bettie just hoped her sister wouldn't find out, she would burn Bettie alive for corrupting her son.

"The cupboards?" Bettie pressed.

"What about the cupboards?"

Bettie's eyes narrowed. "Before you found me. I heard someone opening, searching and banging cupboards. Was that you?"

Sean shook his head and they both smiled. If that was the criminal then they had just made a very stupid mistake. There were plenty of cameras round the house, so Bettie and Sean rushed out and went to find their criminal.

***

Sitting on the cold brick wall outside the house she had just been trapped in, Bettie looked up and down the snowy road that looked rather magical with the white snow against the black sky, as she wondered who had kidnapped her. It made sense for it to be Lawrence but she needed proof.

As Bettie felt the cold wintery wind blow gently past as Bettie focused on all the semi-detached houses with their large drives and neatly arranged front gardens that were all covered in snow.

Whilst she was waiting for Sean to come back with his laptop, Bettie just sat there listening to the Christmas songs from inside the houses, children playing and the distant sounds of cars driving.

Returning to a thought from earlier, Bettie wondered if she was ever going to have children (she really didn't have anything else to think about), she loved Christmas with all the food, presents and family, but she wasn't sure if she wanted her own little family. Graham had spoken about it but she wasn't sure. She loved her job, she was a private eye through and through, and Bettie had seen the terrible things humans could do.

So the idea of being a mum… it terrified her.

The smell of the piney air and sound of Sean returning made Bettie smile as she saw Sean walk up, sit next to her and pass her a black laptop. She hoped the answers she needed would be on the security cameras, which she didn't have access to but Graham did.

And after one passionate night between them, Graham had given her his passwords for anything she might need. At first she had made sure to forget them so Graham would never get in trouble, but Graham had unofficially cleared it with his boss.

The rule was as long as no one knew, Bettie had results and she didn't interfere with cases, it was okay.

Opening the laptop, Bettie clicked on a few buttons, swiped the mouse and tried to ignore the cold numbness that was starting to infect her fingers.

It didn't take long for her to access the security footage from a camera that looked at the house directly and Bettie played it, only to hear Sean laugh a little as they watched Bettie in her massive coat, thick trousers and messy hair go into the house.

As much as she was tempted to give Sean a gentle elbow in the ribs, she knew he was right. From this camera angle she hardly looked attractive and it was true. The camera definitely adds 10 pounds (or more likely 100 pounds for Bettie).

Bettie swiped the mouse a few more times as she fast forwarded the footage and there was no one there until Sean went into the house later on.

Cocking her head, Bettie tried to understand how this camera that had a wide open view of the house and most of the road didn't manage to see anyone come or go.

"Aunty, any other cameras?"

Bettie looked at the choice of cameras that the police had access to and there was only one other camera she could look at. She clicked on it, sped it up and smiled.

After a few moments of looking, Bettie found a tall man wearing nothing more than a tracksuit, a black hat and black boots. Bettie stopped the footage and she zoomed in.

"Isn't that-" Sean said.

"Yes it is,"

Bettie recognised those boots, body and face anywhere. She never thought of Detective Inspector Lawrence as an attractive man but Bettie recognised his face anyway, and even his body was an odd shape, large in the chest, thin at the waist. All making it easy to identify on camera footage.

"What now Aunty?"

Bettie opened her mouth but she wasn't sure. She saw snow was starting to fall once more so she knew she had to be quick, she didn't want Sean driving in a snowstorm.

But what could she do?

Bettie knew she couldn't declare Lawrence guilty because the footage showed him going into a house and Bettie didn't need to check again to know who owned it, it was his own house. But there was something odd about it all.

"Could Graham use the footage?

Bettie shook her head. "I don't know but if Lawrence is the man who attacked me then-"

She remembered!

"Sean! I remember something about the man. I know it was a man for starters. He had a..." Bettie said as she did a circular motion on the back of her hands towards Sean.

"What? A tattoo? A Burn? A Cut?"

That was it.

"Yes a cut. Quite large. I remember it from when he was tying me up. I must have regained consciousness for a few seconds."

Sean nodded thoughtfully to himself.

"What?" Bettie asked.

Sean took out his phone. "In bed last night, me and Harry were looking at some of the pics from the ceremony,"

Bettie went to nod but she was a bit caught on the fact her nephew and his boyfriend were sleeping together.

Shaking those thoughts away and breathing in more of the piney air, Bettie took Sean's phone, looked at the ceremony's website and scrolled through the pictures.

She knew it wasn't a perfect idea as people only shook with their right hand but it was the best idea she had.

There were tons of photos. Bettie had no idea that there was an official photographer, then she remembered that skinny boy that was probably Lawrence's grandson taking photos. Bettie shook her head, she would have thought the police would pay for a proper photographer for an official awards ceremony.

"Here," Sean stopped Bettie scrolling and zoomed in on the photos of Lawrence shaking hands with the different police officers.

Bettie flicked through them, frowning as in each photo Lawrence's right hand was clear. But there was one photo with an officer with a broken right arm so Lawrence couldn't shake it. So he had to shake it with his left hand.

Sean zoomed in. "And we have it,"

Bettie smiled as she took a screenshot of the photo, edited it with a red circle and sent it to Graham. There was a large cut in Lawrence's hand that was going to be his downfall.

***

A few hours later with her family talking, laughing and playing Christmas songs, Bettie allowed the soft sofa to take her weight as she sat down. For a moment Bettie just wanted a few seconds of peace so she focused on the amazing smells of Christmas pudding, cake and mince pies.

Her sister definitely knew how to make great mince pies, Bettie could almost taste their sweet fruitiness on her tongue.

Bettie looked around at all her amazing family from her tall beautiful nephew who saved her to her mini-helper Harry to her knight in shining armour, her beautiful Graham. They all sat on the sofa next to her and talked and laughed with each other.

Because it was that time of year.

It was the time of year for laughing, loving and joy and that's what they were doing here tonight. After what happened to Bettie, everyone wanted to have a practice (an excuse) Christmas dinner with all the trimmings and everything.

Bettie still thought it was an awful fuss over her just because she got kidnapped (again) and it was already past midnight. But then her nephew and sister reminded her that she was important to them, and she mattered.

As she listened to everything going on around her (and tried to ignore the crashing, banging and bubbling of her sister in the kitchen), Bettie stared at her beautiful Graham's face as she remembered how he told her about the official investigation that was launching into Lawrence and if she was willing to testify.

She was.

And so that case was done, Bettie wrapped her arms around her family and Graham as she knew she had proved Lawrence was corrupt, she had solved who kidnapped her and most importantly she had got to have a Christmas dinner early with the people she loved.

All because of a crime, Christmas and a closet.

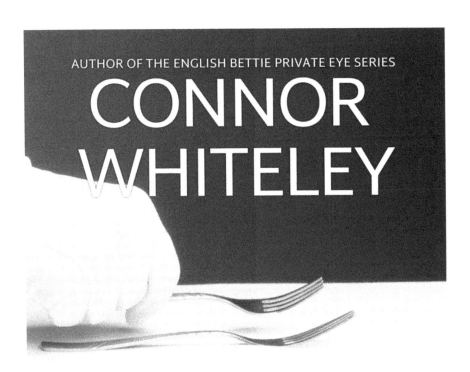

AUTHOR OF THE ENGLISH BETTIE PRIVATE EYE SERIES

CONNOR WHITELEY

CHEATER AT DINNER

CHEATER AT DINNER

Surrounded by rows upon rows of stunning white tables with their perfectly pressed napkins, posh cutlery and people sitting there dressed in stunning suits and dresses, Bettie English, private eye, turned her head and focused on her table.

As she breathed in the amazing smells of rich meats, expensive fruity wine and freshly steamed vegetables, Bettie couldn't help but smile as she stared at the most amazing plate of food she had ever seen.

She loved how the traditional British Christmas dinner looked like an expensive painting on the plate with its golden crispy roast potatoes, stunningly sliced juicy pork and Bettie's favourite the succulent, vibrant colours of the vegetables on the side.

Bettie could almost taste how crispy and vibrant the vegetables' flavours would be from here, their amazing sweetness would be sheer perfection against the juiciness and meaty flavours of the pork.

The sound of people talking, chatting and laughing all around Bettie made her force her attention away from the amazing, stunning food and on the equally beautiful person she was with.

As she looked up from the plate (longing to taste the delicious dinner), she saw her cop boyfriend Graham smiling at her as he poured a fruity red wine into her glass.

A part of her wondered if she should get him to stop, but she was here as a private eye and a girlfriend, so she might well blend in.

Watching her beautiful boyfriend with his perfect hair, jawline and body, Bettie took a few shallow breaths of the amazingly scented air as she knew this was going to be a perfect evening. She had a delicious dinner (that she really wanted to eat) and the love of her life, which she hadn't seen for a few weeks.

When Graham put the wine bottle down, they both just stared at each other for a few seconds and Bettie loved that. She knew it probably looked weird to other people but she loved all the time she spent with (and admiring) Graham.

The sound of cheering filled the restaurant so Bettie turned, smiled and her eyes narrowed as she looked at a couple who were hugging and kissing and everyone was clapping around them.

She knew they had just gotten engagement and a part of Bettie admired the man was being so ballsy and proposing in public. Bettie was still getting used to the whole relationship thing with Graham, but she loved him and he her.

Marriage might have been a long time away, but Bettie wanted it one day, one day far from now.

Then Bettie saw Graham cross his arms and smiled.

"So why ya wanna come here?" Graham asked.

Bettie gave him a massive smile. "What do you mean? Can't a girl take her man out on the town?"

"A girl or woman can. You don't,"

Bettie pretended to be offended and they both laughed.

That sole reason was why Bettie loved him and she would give anything to always see that amazing smile of his.

But he did have a point she supposed, they were always working, busying and helping others so much that they often forgot to work on each other, in more ways than one.

And tonight was no different.

"Look my left and tell me what you see," Bettie said.

She watched Graham carefully as he subtly turned his head and his eyes narrowed on a table.

"What the two dudes in the business suits?" Graham asked.

Bettie looked left and shook her head. "No,"

As she subtly pointed with her eyes at another table, and when Graham smiled she knew he had seen what they were looking for.

Mr Nero Alessandria was apparently some hotshot new businessman in London but Bettie had seen some of his speeches and companies, she wasn't that impressed but given that his wife had paid her a few thousand pounds to follow him, Bettie didn't really care.

It was even better that the wife had done almost all of Bettie's hard work by giving her all his contacts with pictures, addresses and phone numbers.

Bettie bit her lip a little when she remembered some of the rumours she had found online about him, apparently he was a ruthless man capable of horrible things but she hadn't seen any proof of that. It still worried her though.

And when Bettie had found possible evidence of an affair with Mr Alessandria and the mystery woman meeting at a fancy London restaurant tonight, Bettie knew she wasn't going to refuse. Especially when her terms of employment always being the client pays for all needed costs. A fancy meal or two for getting evidence sounded like a needed cost.

Granted Bettie knew she would have to have a more compelling reason when she sent the invoice to the client.

The amazing smell of those beautifully golden, crispy roast potatoes made Bettie return her attention to the utterly stunning dinner in front of her. Bettie wasn't sure how much longer she could contain herself with that perfectly sliced juicy pork just staring at her.

"I presume ya hear for photos?" Graham asked.

Bettie nodded and subtly turn her head to focus more on the person sitting opposite him.

From where she was Bettie couldn't see too much about the woman, but it was definitely a woman. Bettie noted the woman's long blond hair, slim body and large assets. But she couldn't remember seeing anyone who matched the description in the information the wife had sent over.

"What ya waiting for then? Take some pictures?" Graham asked.

Bettie smiled, shook her head and rubbed his warm hands.

"I can't just take photos. Right now it is just a man and a woman sitting together. A lawyer would simply say it's a friend, a missing daughter or even his good looking mother,"

Graham's eyebrows rose at the last two.

"I'm not kidding," Bettie said.

Releasing Graham's hands wonderfully warm hands, Bettie picked up her posh knife and fork and sliced into the pork.

Just the ease of which the pork was cut got Bettie excited, her pork was normally rough and tough, but this... this was something else.

When she popped the pork into her mouth, she thought she was going to faint at how amazing it was. The succulent juices with their rich meaty flavours flooded her senses and the meat dissolved in her mouth.

This was going to be a night to remember.

As Bettie continued to eat the best dinner she had ever had with those golden crispy potatoes being her true favourites, she constantly flicked her eyes over to Mr Alessandria and the mystery woman.

The more Bettie focused on them, the more she couldn't understand what was going on. Even her and Graham who were working but still a loving couple, they were laughing, smiling and talking whenever they weren't eating.

But Mr Alessandria and the mystery woman weren't.

Bettie couldn't understand how they were looking at each other and barely speaking. It was almost like they weren't on a date but something else was going on.

After a while of subtly looking at them, Bettie put down her cutlery, finished off her amazing golden crispy potato and looked at Graham.

"You aren't a cop tonight are you?" Bettie asked.

Graham's eyebrows rose. "No. Why would ya ask that?"

Bettie smiled, took out her phone and dialled a number.

"Cos I'm doing something questionable,"

"Who ya calling?"

Bettie smiled at the thought of hearing her wonderful nephew Sean who should still have been at her office with his boyfriend. She had said to him just to do her filing but Bettie knew he would have done other stuff too, which was why she hadn't cleaned her office in the past week.

"Calling Sean,"

"He and Harry wouldn't be in the office?"

Bettie smiled and just looked at him. "Two young boys alone in an office together. Away from my sister and her husband. They aren't going to be there. Seriously?"

Graham nodded and went back to eating.

Sean answered sounding a bit out of breath. "Hi Aunty,"

"Sean I'm going to send you a picture and I need you to try and find out who it is. Check the information the wife gave us first. I might have missed something,"

"Okay,"

"Thank you," Bettie said as she hung up, took a picture and send it to him.

When she turned back to Graham he had his normally ruggedly handsome cop face on.

"How you goanna identify it?"

Bettie rubbed his hand gently. "It's perfectly legal. I always save the questionable software from the dark web as a last resort,"

Graham gave her a sort of nervous chuckle and he went back to eating his dinner. Bettie felt her body relax and tense and relax again as she realise she had just basically lied to him. As much as Bettie loved that dark web software from time to time, she knew it was 100% illegal.

But worth every penny.

Pushing those illegal thoughts away, Bettie picked up her cold glass of wine, breathed in the fruity hints and pretended to slip it.

When her eyes flicked back over to Mr Alessandria, Bettie put the wine glass down and her eyes narrowed. He was waving his finger at the woman like an angry parent would at a child.

He was clearly mad and probably struggling to keep his voice down.

Bettie wondered what he was talking about, he was a business owner so maybe it was something to do with that, but then Bettie remembered all the financial records and everything looked okay. Mr Alessandria had plenty of new investors too so he was set financially.

She had to get more information.

"Graham," Bettie said her eyes moving back to him. "Want to do a bit of acting?"

Graham frowned and Bettie smiled.

"I was wondering why I was here," Graham asked.

"Oh darling you're here because I love you. And Sean's too young to play certain roles and her sister would kill me for getting him involved too much in the Private Eye world,"

Graham shook his head. "Fine, what do you want me to do?"

"Easy. We get into a fight. I storm off towards the target. We both take a glass of wine. We spill over them,"

"Then they go to the loos and follow 'em,"

"Exactly,"

Graham filled up the wine glasses again and giggled like a little schoolboy.

"Please Graham. Act serious," Bettie said laughing herself.

Both of them took a deep breath, made sure no one was watching and blow each other a kiss.

"You what! You sold my car!" Graham shouted.

Bettie was a bit taken back. "Well. You're useless. Lazy! I work all day and you do nothing!"

People were starting to look.

"You didn't have to sell my-"

"It isn't your car Graham. I paid for it,"

"It's our money. We're married,"

"Maybe we shouldn't be. Your mother is a such a nob too!" Bettie said.

Everyone was watching now.

Bettie shot up and grabbed the wine glass.

"Don't ya dare talk about my mother!"

"She's horrible. She hates me!" Bettie said.

She started to storm off.

"She's right Bet. I hate you too. You are so controlling!"

Bettie glided through the rows of tables.

She was almost at the target table.

Mr Alessandria stared at her and Graham.

"I wouldn't have to be so controlling. If you were useful. You gold digger!"

Graham grabbed her.

Bettie turned around.

"That's right Graham. You're a gold digger. A dickhead. I'm leaving you!" Bettie shouted.

Throwing her wine glass.

The wine covered Mr Alessandria.

"Fine then nob!" Graham said throwing his wine over the other woman.

"You idiots!" Mr Alessandria shouted.

Bettie and Graham turned around and their hands covered their faces.

"Oh my god. I am so sorry sir," Bettie said, grabbing a napkin off a table and helping him clean it up.

Graham did the same for the woman.

"Go away. I need to clean up," Mr Alessandria said as he stood up, marched off and went into the toilets.

Bettie nodded at Graham and he left.

As she watched him go into the toilets, Bettie stared at the tall slim woman at the table and saw her just stare into space, she didn't even bother trying to clean herself up.

It was about this time Bettie realised that she hadn't needed to get wine over the mystery woman, but there was something off about her.

Sitting down on the horribly warm chair, Bettie looked at the woman and waited for her to ask why Bettie was sitting there, or how was she after the fight.

But the woman just stared.

Feeling her phone vibrate in her pocket, Bettie took it out and smiled when she saw it was a message from Sean telling her the woman was actually a new investor called Lady Penelope Bishop, some rich daughter of the English nobility.

"You don't look like a Penelope," Bettie said.

Penelope looked up at her.

"What were you two arguing about?" Bettie asked.

Bettie wondered if the woman was going to leave when her eyes kept switching between the door and Bettie, but after a few seconds Penelope stared into Bettie's eyes.

A part of Bettie felt as if Penelope was borrowing down into her soul, yet Bettie was surprised that this clearly fierce capable woman would allow Mr Alessandria to moan at her.

"Are you police?" she asked.

Bettie shook her head. "No but that is all you need to know,"

Penelope stood up. "Then whoever you are, I do not need to speak to the likes of you,"

"One scream from me and a police officer runs out of that bathroom," Bettie said coldly.

Penelope stared at her.

"I will scream. You know the lengths I go for my acting," Bettie gestured to the red wine stains on Penelope's dress.

"Fine. I am investing millions of your pounds into his company for a favour,"

Bettie's eyes narrowed, she wasn't from here and the way she said *your pounds* wasn't right, it sounded evil, dark and mysterious all at the same time.

Then the more Bettie looked at the woman, the more she

realised that the woman definitely wasn't British and probably had ties to overseas crime.

"Who are you?" Bettie asked.

"I am just a businesswoman the same as you. But unlike you I presume you own your pockets. I do not. I have all the money in other pockets that I can play with,"

Bettie partly wanted to explain how her client was paying for all of this tonight, but this didn't seem like the real moment for accuracy.

"What is this favour?"

Penelope smiled and stood up. "Miss whoever you are, I urge you to go back to your table and finish. Tell your client…"

Bettie stepped forward. "How many Private Eyes have come for you?"

Penelope placed a gentle hand on Bettie's shoulder.

"So, so many. But you should know that your London is filled with opportunities and criminal gangs. So many wonderful opportunities for me and my kin to spread, work and love,"

Bettie felt a shot of icy coldness wash down her spine as she watched Penelope gather up her things and prepare to leave.

"What do I tell my client?"

"That man rejected us tonight. Don't do everything. She'll be rich soon enough,"

Bettie smiled and felt her stomach churn and tighten.

"Don't come for her," Bettie said bitterly.

Penelope stopped and stared Bettie dead in the eye. Again Bettie felt as she was having her soul burrowed into.

"You have yourself a deal. But I will call on you one day. I will find out who you are and you will do a single case for me,"

Bettie stopped and wondered if this was the only way to keep everyone safe, it didn't sound unreasonable. Her client would soon be rich but… Bettie hated the feeling of sitting back whilst something terrible happened.

Bettie knew this woman spoke perfect English, but there was more to it, a much darker side that a part of Bettie didn't want to get involved in. She wanted to tell Graham about it, but this was out of his jurisdiction and she remembered what these gangs were like.

She had to protect Graham.

"Fine. One case. Don't come to my client for help," Bettie said then realised something. "How did you know my client was the wife?"

Penelope started to walk away but she said a final message to Bettie in perfect Russian. "We always watch,"

As Bettie stared at Penelope (or whoever she really was) walk out of the restaurant, she felt her entire stomach tighten into a knot and even the amazing smells of the perfectly sliced, juicy pork couldn't relax her.

The sound of Graham and Mr Alessandria walking up behind her made Bettie tense even more as she knew she couldn't warn Mr Alessandria in front of Graham. As much as Bettie loved him, she knew he was far too good of a cop and the last thing she wanted was him investigating the Russians.

And something deep, deep inside her knew everything would be okay in the end. The client would be rich, the questionable businessman dead and Bettie only had to do one case for a potentially dangerous Russian woman.

Bettie smiled at the craziness of it all so she shook Mr Alessandria's hand, bid him good night and walked back over to her table.

As she sat down, Bettie stared at what was left of the golden crispy potatoes, perfectly sliced juicy pork and the most amazing vibrant vegetables she had ever seen.

Picking up her cutlery, Bettie knew the food would be cold but it would still be amazing and worth every single bite.

At the sound of Graham pouring them another glass of the rich fruity wine, Bettie stared wide eyed at him as she admired his beautiful hair, face and body.

"Merry Christmas Bet,"

Bettie gave him a schoolgirl smile. "Merry Christmas Graham,"

AUTHOR OF THE ENGLISH BETTIE PRIVATE EYE SERIES

CONNOR WHITELEY

PRIVATE EYE, CONVENTION AND CHRISTMAS

A BETTIE PRIVATE EYE HOLIDAY MYSTERY SHORT STORY

PRIVATE EYE, CONVENTION AND CHRISTMAS

"What's EyeFoodCon aunty?"

When Bettie heard her nephew Sean ask her that simple question, she wasn't really sure how to answer it. As a private eye she had just known what it was for as long as she could remember.

Bettie looked at her tall slim nephew and tried to think about how to answer such a strange question, that she knew what it was, she just didn't know how to explain it to someone who wasn't a private eye.

The sounds of people talking, chatting and laughing on the awfully cold December night made Bettie shiver. She hated the cold so she pulled her long black overcoat tighter and ignored her nephew.

As much as Bettie loved him, she wanted, needed to buy herself a few extra seconds so she could think of an answer to his question.

Bettie watched the little families walk around with the occasional parent moaning at their overexcited kids and other people were weighed down with their Christmas shopping in Bluewater shopping centre in southeast England.

She was glad her and Sean hadn't bought that much stuff tonight but she did need to press on with their shopping. That was probably the only downside to the Christmas season, even more so as a private eye, there were so many cases at Christmas time that it made Christmas shopping in advance impossible.

Bettie bit her lip as she wondered how many more presents she needed to buy. There was her sister, her boyfriend and more.

As she pushed those panicked thoughts away, Bettie watched the busy crowd around them go in and out of shops like their lives depended on it, it seemed them too needed to get lots of presents before the big day.

The smell of rich Christmas spices filled the air as Bettie and Sean kept walking on, gliding through the crowd and walking like they were on a mission. Because in a way they were, Bettie had to get all the presents tonight considering the all the private eye parties started soon.

With the smell of the Christmas spices getting stronger with hints of sweat that made her mouth taste of Christmas cake, Bettie kept gliding through the crowd as her eyes narrowed for the next shop she needed.

"What's EyeFoodCon aunty?" Sean asked again walking next to her.

Bettie smiled. "It's hard to explain Sean. It's a little private holiday for private eyes,"

"Is it like a Christmas party?"

Bettie stepped out of the way of a big family of shoppers and saw a massive wonderful sign in the distance of a perfume shop she needed to go to for her sister. She had no idea why her sister wanted some expensive perfume that she was never going to wear, but Bettie just wanted to keep the peace, love her sister and get on with the rest of the shopping.

The only problem was the sea of busy (grumpy) shoppers in her way.

"Aunty?" Sean asked.

Bettie took Sean's hand like she did when he was a toddler and guided him through the sea of people.

"In a way yes," Bettie said. "It was started a few years back by the Jewish and Muslim private eyes,"

Bettie gently knocked a shopper out of the way so her and Sean could continue through the crowd.

"They heard all their private eye friends were busy and missing over Christmas as they were celebrating with the family. So the Professional Private Investigator Society created EyeFoodCon as a secular celebration for everyone,"

"Ah," Sean said.

After making it through the massive sea of grumpy, busy shoppers, Bettie loved the amazing smell of the sweet flowery perfume in the massive shop she entered.

Bettie cocked her head for a moment as she didn't remember the shop being this big before, but she loved the long white walls of colour perfume bottles in all their different shapes, sizes and prices.

She wanted to shake her head when she saw Sean walk over to the unisex (but more feminine) perfume as she knew for a fact that he was getting it for himself.

The smell of the sweet flowery perfume kept getting stronger but Bettie knew something was off. It was too strong for someone just spraying.

Bettie stared at the horribly shiny white floor and her eyes widened when she saw a smashed bottle of perfume a few metres from her.

She walked over and had to cover her nose with her hand, Bettie normally loved that perfume but it was way too strong when she was breathing in a whole bottle of it.

"You're going to have to pay for that Miss," a woman said.

Bettie looked at the tall business-like woman who had said that, and she shook her head. It was silly that this woman thought Bettie had done it, she had only just got here.

"I found it like this," Bettie said.

The woman shook her head. "They all say that. Come with me and you can pay for it at the tills,"

"I didn't break it. I'm innocent. Check your cameras,"

The woman frowned. "I know what I saw,"

Bettie couldn't believe how silly this woman was, she supposed the woman could be fed up with all the stealing and breaking that normally happens at Christmas, but Bettie wasn't guilty.

"Aunty?" Sean said walking over.

"Sean how are you?" the woman asked. "How's Harry? We have a new stock that aftershave he likes,"

Bettie wanted to shake her head so badly, trust Sean to walk into a scene and instantly know how to calm it down. That was probably why she had bought him just in case.

"Thank you, I'll take a bottle. What were you talking to my aunty about?"

Bettie couldn't believe it when the woman looked at her and explained everything to Sean like Bettie was the worse criminal ever.

Sean nodded. "I know my Aunty seems shifty, criminal and a bit crazy but she's safe,"

How Bettie didn't playfully hit him she didn't know.

"I can assure you my Aunty didn't break anything. She's honest and she could help you,"

Bettie felt like she was going to regret this for sure, maybe she should have bought her boyfriend Graham like he had suggested.

Bettie stepped forward. "Help you how,"

"Your nephew mentions you're a Private Investigator,"

As much as Bettie wanted to correct her as she loved the more playful term Private Eye, Bettie knew this probably wasn't the time considering whoever this woman was still thought she was guilty.

"Bettie English Private Eye at your service,"

The woman nodded. "Our cameras aren't working at the moment and… my boss isn't happy with me. If I hire you to watch the store for a couple of hours-"

Bettie's mouth dropped. "Wait! I have Christmas shopping to do. I have a mini-convention to buy food for and… it's Christmas soon,"

"Aunty I can do the shopping for you,"

Bettie wanted to protest but she supposed she loved Sean too much and he was being nice, but Bettie didn't want to do this.

"How much?" Bettie asked.

"We paid the last security person a hundred pounds for the night,"

Bettie didn't know whether to be shocked, pleased or horrified that a security person is actually given that much money for a few hours of work. But the sound of a hundred pounds for two little hours, it did sound good.

It was technically her turn to host and pay for most of EyeFoodCon so that money would easily pay for it.

"Hundred pounds for the night. Extra twenty for false accusations," Bettie said.

The woman frowned.

"And throw it two bottles of whatever Sean wants since you hesitated," Bettie said smiling.

"Fine. I trust you know how to look innocent and like a random shopper,"

As she watched the woman and Sean walk off so he could choose what he wanted, Bettie looked around the massive store and rolled her eyes. Some days it really sucked to be a private eye but a hundred pounds was a hundred pounds that she didn't have before, and maybe she could find a nice present for Graham to buy her.

The advantages of borrowing his credit card earlier!

Walking up the rows of perfume bottles, Bettie didn't know how these two hours were going to go, surely a perfume shop didn't see that much crime at Christmas.

***

After an hour and forty-five minutes, Bettie couldn't believe how brilliant this actually was, at first she thought she was going to hate it with a passion, but she didn't.

Bettie had already found some great new perfumes that she loved, she found the foul smelling one that her dad loved and she even found a new special one for herself that she might wear on Christmas day.

But Bettie still didn't want to buy any of them because as much as they were great perfumes, they weren't cheap and a hundred pounds was not going to cover it. Not by a long shot.

Bettie ran her fingers over the cold white shelves as she looked at all the perfume and aftershave bottles in all their different sizes, shapes and colours. The bottles were beautiful but Bettie remembered from her business study classes at school that was all part of the visual appeal. It did nothing practical, except from increase the prices.

The sound of customers talking, trying on perfume and judging the smells echoed all around the massive shop as Bettie waited for her two hours to be up.

Yet Bettie could have sworn there was another sound she was hearing, it was like the low quiet voices of two people conspiring to do something.

Bettie had hated the idea of people stealing from the start, it was Christmas for crying out loud, this was not a time for stealing, it was a time for love, giving and caring.

Walking to the end of the shelf she was looking at, Bettie's eyes narrowed on the two young women that were close together and trying on different perfumes.

To other people they may not have looked like criminals or would-be shoplifters, but Bettie recognised the closeness, quiet voices and the long expensive coats of the two girls.

It reminded Bettie of her own troublesome streak when she was a teenager, if that was the case with these two women then Bettie supposed she could get rid of them without any major problems.

But these women weren't teenagers, they were fully-fledged adults who were looking like they were going to try and steal something.

After a few moments of watching, Bettie noticed that one of the women had got out her phone and was pretending to take a phone call. Bettie shook her head as she watched the perfectly clear black screen of the girl's phone, if you're going to pretend to take a pretend phone call you need to make it a bit more convincing.

Bettie wondered if she should get the woman or the manager to deal with them, but she wasn't going to risk losing her hundred pounds for simply *failing* to do her assigned job. She wasn't risking any comments like that.

As the woman with the phone pretended to nod, promise the person on the other side of the call she'd take a picture and check the surroundings (completely missing Bettie). Bettie knew that this woman was an amateur, there was no way these two had done shoplifting before.

If Bettie was doing this she would have been in the car park driving home by now.

Then Bettie watched in horror as the two women did a final check of the store, missed Bettie and just picked up the perfumes like it was nothing and placed it in their coat pockets.

Bettie walked towards them. The two women pretended to act normal.

"I know what you just did," Bettie said.

"We ain't steal nothing," the pretend phone caller said.

Bettie shook her head. "I finish my 'shift' in two minutes. I do not want to be here any longer than I have to be. Just apologise, pay for the perfumes and go,"

"We ain't steal nothing," they both said together.

Bettie hated this entire thing, she had Christmas shopping to do, EyeFoodCon to plan and buy for and on top of all of that she no longer wanted to be in some perfume shop.

"Empty your pockets," Bettie said firmly.

The two women ran.

Bettie ran after them.

Her feet pounded the floor.

The two women were fast.

Bettie couldn't let them leave the shop.

She looked around.

The women were close to the exit.

There were a sea of shoppers.

Bettie was going to lose them.

Bettie panicked.

Picked up a perfume bottle.

Threw it.

It smashed on the woman's back.

She fell forward.

Catching the other woman.

There was something oddly satisfying around that Bettie realised as she walked over and stood over the two injured women were who frowning and probably wished they had tried another shop.

The tall business-like woman ran over to Bettie.

"Miss English! What have you done?"

"These two women were stealing. I stopped them. You own me my hundred pounds,"

"You damaged my store! You broke a bottle of perfume! You…"

Bettie shook her head. "My hundred pounds and extra twenty please. Or I will call your head office and tell them you hired a private eye on company time and money without approval,"

Bettie couldn't help but smile as the woman looked so shocked and panicked as if this was the first time ever she had been challenged.

"Fine Miss English," the woman said giving Bettie her money.

"Let's do this again some time," Bettie said leaving the shop.

"Let's not," Bettie heard the woman muttered.

The moment she left the shop, Bettie glided into the sea of busy grumpy shoppers and called Sean. As the phone dialled she was slightly surprised how good she was feeling after all of that, it felt great to be out in December, doing her shopping and stopping crime at the same time.

But now she had to get on with the most important event in the Private Eye calendar, EyeFoodCon.

Sean picked up his phone.

Bettie smiled. "Hi Sean, want to come to EyeFoodCon with me?"

***

A few days later Bettie sat on a terribly cold chair on the head of a long, long oak table with wonderfully decorated Christmas decorations covering the entire walls.

Bettie loved all their baubles, tinsel and the wreaths that covered the walls of the business room that she had hired especially for the convention.

And as she watched all the different Private Eyes in all their different ethnicities, sizes and heights eat the beautiful golden, crispy food in front of them, and the rest of the juicy meats and other sweet treats that covered the entire length of the table, Bettie realised something precious.

The sound of happy Private Eyes talking, chatting and laughing with one another reminded Bettie how EyeFoodCon should be explained to anyone.

Bettie looked at Sean who was laughing with a young woman at the table and he saw her.

Bettie leaned closer to Sean. "You see all this,"

Sean looked around and nodded.

"This is what EyeFoodCon is all about. No matter your race, religion, preferences, whatever. You are always welcome in the Private Eye community. We are all a family,"

Sean smiled at that.

"So what is EyeFoodCon you ask," Bettie said.

Sean leant closer.

"EyeFoodCon is about community and the secular side of Christmas. I love all Private Eyes no matter who they are and I welcome them all. This mini-convention is a reminder of that at this time of year,"

Sean looked around a final time.

"Just because we don't all celebrate Christmas doesn't mean we can't love, give and support each other at this time of year,"

Just saying that made Bettie feel all Christmassy and merry because she knew that was all the truth, and that's why she loved being a Private Eye because it truly was a community.

A loving, supporting and amazing community for all.

Bettie was a bit surprised when Sean kissed her cheek and held her hands.

"Merry Christmas Aunty,"

Bettie stood up and said to everyone: "A Merry Christmas, New Year and all the other celebrations to everyone,"

AUTHOR OF THE ENGLISH BETTIE PRIVATE EYE SERIES

CONNOR WHITELEY

GREAT GIVE AWAY

A BETTIE PRIVATE EYE HOLIDAY MYSTERY SHORT STORY

GREAT GIVE AWAY

Bettie English, Private Eye, loved her mother's birthday. It was always an amazing day filled with laughter, love and plenty of tasty food. But as she stood on the pavement of a long road with little houses lining each side of it, she was hardly impressed.

She had told her boyfriend, who was currently bent over the engine of her red car, to take a right then a left. That wasn't hard. It was easy, she had done it hundreds of times and her sister had done it drunk even more times.

But no. Her boyfriend Detective Graham had to take left then right, leading them to this God forsaken little road (Street?) with pretty little houses far away from her mother's house and then the car broken down.

Bettie was not impressed!

She didn't even know if Graham knew anything about cars. He was a detective, he was amazing at his job, but as she had learnt way too many times recently if she told him to put his mind to anything else, he was sexy and hot as hell, but next to useless.

Bettie had to admit watching Graham in his tight jeans, white shirt and blue shoes bend over her car was probably the only upside of the situation. Yet Bettie was starting to realise that they were going to be stuck here for a while and she hoped, prayed, whatever-ed that her mother's birthday cake wasn't going to spoil.

Granted it was cold enough. Late December was always cold in southeast England and all the little houses were covered in a thin layer of ice, frost and even a little snow, but Bettie didn't like how her breath condensed into long columns of vapour.

The smell of wonderfully warming spices filled the air and Bettie loved those smells as she remembered the buttery, luxurious mince pies she had eaten all over Christmas along with the fruity, boozy cake and yule logs. It really had been the perfect Christmas with her family and now she wanted to top it off with the perfect birthday for her mother, but that clearly wasn't going to happen within the next hour.

The sound of panicked voices in the distance made Bettie wonder what was going on. It was clear the voices were coming from further down the street, and considering Bettie had nothing better to do and Graham would never call the breakdown services, she had no other choice than to check out the sound.

And it meant Graham wouldn't be able to spring up the conversation of having kids on her again, like he had accidentally done that morning.

A conversation she really didn't want today. Especially as her mother was going to ask about it a thousand times already.

"Gra, I'm going down the street to check down the sounds. Be back soon. Love you," Bettie said, walking down the street.

"Love you too Bet," Graham said.

Bettie actually looked at the houses as she went down the street, they were more beautiful than her quick glance had showed her earlier. Each house still had up their wide range of Christmas lights in all their different stunning colours. They were rather beautiful. Each one could probably be described as an art piece with how each house had shaped, decorated and sequenced their lights.

But why were the lights on at nine o'clock in the morning? It was hardly dark.

"The Gift is stolen!"

Bettie stared at the man who kept shouting the same thing over and over. She wasn't sure what to make of the man, he wasn't very tall, but his (hideously) bright Christmas jumper and trousers spoke volumes.

"Bettie English, Private Eye, can I help you?" she asked.

"Oh yes, you can," the man turned towards the rest of the street. "Everyone! The Great Give Away is saved!"

Bettie really didn't understand what was going on. At this rate she'll have to charge a confusion fee to these people.

As more and more people walked out of their houses towards Bettie, she couldn't believe how they all looked so different. Each person was a different height, weight and class. That alone was different from the rest of England.

"Miss? Who are you?" a little old lady said pulling on Bettie's arm.

Bettie introduced herself and wasn't sure what to make of the little old lady as her face lit up like a Christmas tree.

"Miss, the Great Give Away is lost without you?"

Now Bettie wished she had had that second mug of coffee like Graham had wanted her to. Damn him for being right!

"Sorry. What is the Great Give Away?" Bettie asked.

Everyone in the street gasped and looked at horror at Bettie.

"It's the most amazing time of the year!" everyone shouted.

The little old lady placed a cold hand on Bettie's shoulder.

"Miss. Every year on this day, we Give Away all our Christmas leftovers to the homeless so they may get fed through the New Year after our Christmas joy,"

That was a rather good idea actually, Bettie had never thought of that before. It made perfect sense and she was a bit surprised that no one else had thought of it. Everyone always bought too much at Christmas (that alone was disgusting) and everyone just threw it away (including her), but giving it to the homeless and less fortunate, now that was an excellent idea.

But the idea of someone stealing it was monstrous. Who in their right mind would steal from such a great idea?

It was probably as far from the Christmas spirit that you could get. Especially given the entire idea of St Nick and Father Christmas was to give the poor presents and help others. This theft was flat outrageous!

Bettie had to find out who did it.

The little old lady and everyone else grabbed Bettie and pulled her further down the street.

Bettie tried to resist but she just went along with it in the end.

Then the crowd pushed her in front of a large metal cage with red, pink and green tinsel covering it. But there was one very disturbing thing that caught Bettie's eyes, where a presumably large metal padlock should have been, there was only bend twisted metal.

"Is this where you stored the leftovers?" Bettie asked.

Another massive gasp from the crowd.

The little old lady gestured for the crowd to go away and leave her and Bettie alone.

"Miss. I'm sorry about that. For them The Great Give Away is the highlight of the year, they believe everyone should do it,"

"I do agree. Tell me what happened?"

"I run the street Miss. I own most of it and now walk up and down every morning and evening if my old body allows me. I walked past this morning to see the food was gone,"

"Was it there last night?" Bettie asked.

"Oh yes Miss. I bought some leftover… I mean The Gift of My Husband's Christmas Cake to donate,"

Bettie smiled. "It's okay. Say whatever you want to me, I won't get offended,"

"Thank you Miss,"

Bettie knelt down on the cold ground, looking at the twisted metal. It was clear that the lock had been forced off but that wasn't what bothered Bettie so much.

Now she was on the ground, Bettie saw stains of coffee, tea and syrups, but they were all going in the direction of the back of the cage. Not the front.

Bettie would have imagined if the thief had broken off the lock, then they would have pulled all the goods and leftovers through the front and presumably onto whatever they were using to transport the food away.

In fact the ground was cold, perfectly soft and perfectly intact. There were no impressions of feet or wheelbarrow marks or anything else that would suggest someone had been standing here weighted down with all the leftovers.

Something wasn't right here.

Bettie went round to the back of the metal cage.

"Here," Bettie said.

"What Miss?"

Bettie just pointed to the deep marks and the stains of tea, coffee and syrups in the mud.

"Oh Miss!" the little old lady said, her voice panicked.

Bettie tapped the back of the metal cage a few times and watched it vibrate, hum and eventually fall off.

"Someone must have carefully cut off the back part, stole the leftovers and twisted the lock off to make you think that was how the theft happened,"

"Oh dear Miss, oh dear. What will I do?"

Bettie stood up and placed a gentle hand on the old lady.

"Relax. It will be okay. I will find your leftovers for you. But can I ask a favour?"

"Anything Miss!"

Bettie smiled. "There's a little red car up the street with a hot man failing to fix my engine. Do you have a mechanic on the street please?"

Again the old lady's eyes lit up and she simply walked away.

Bettie had no idea if that meant they had a mechanic, or if the old lady had simply gone off to check out Graham. It sounded silly, but in Bettie's past experience the older women of the world did enjoy his looks. Thankfully she was younger than him by a few years.

Bettie knelt down next to the marks in the soft mud. They didn't look right or what she had seen from other thefts in her years as a private eye.

The marks were too narrow to be car wheels and she doubted anyone could get a car on the soft mud and get it off again without the car spinning out. Then again the marks were still too large to belong to a wheelbarrow.

And judging by the size of the metal cage and the odd marks of rice pudding on the top of it, Bettie was sure the cage had been stuffed full.

But the marks did go away from the metal cage towards one of the little houses who had a large brown fence.

Bettie went up to the fence and strangely enough the marks seemed to go straight under the fence like it wasn't there.

Maybe it hadn't?

Jumping out Bettie grabbed onto the top of the fence and pulled herself up, she'd forgotten how tough climbing was. In the new year she had to get back to the gym and do weight training, forget cardio, she had to do the weights!

Over the fence, Bettie didn't like the plainness of the little garden that she was looking at. All the garden had in it was a child's swing, a sandpit and a bed of half-dead flowers.

It all looked so plain and unloved. Unlike her garden, this one didn't scream love, nature or beauty. It looked like some half-ass attempt to make a garden fit for a family.

But the marks weren't in the garden.

"Can I help ya?" a woman said.

Bettie dropped down from the fence.

The woman in front of her was hardly a looker with her long twisted hair, short stocky body and black teeth, but Bettie had dealt with worse looking people.

"Yes actually. Did you-"

"Leave woman. I donna have time for ya. Go away and don't come back," the woman said starting to leave.

"Does your kid want a new bike?" Bettie said, randomly.

The woman stopped. "Go away. My kid don't want anything from a posh snob like you. Now leave,"

"How about some Gifts from The Great Give Away?"

The woman hissed at Bettie as she almost went into her house.

"Those snobs donna give me any. I might be poor, but I gotten a house. Now leave. I don't want ya charity,"

The door slammed shut and Bettie wasn't sure what to make of it. The woman was clearly annoyed at the street, snobs that lived here (even though Bettie had met snobs and these people weren't ones) and hated the Great Give Away.

But the woman had seen contempt at least a little bit to live her life how she wanted, Bettie doubted the woman wanted to do any harm to the world.

Bettie went over to the woman's door and pushed a twenty-pound note through the letterbox. At least the woman might be able to buy herself and her kids some food and maybe a nice treat with it.

The sound of a bike's bell made Bettie look at the street as she saw two young children ride around.

She still didn't know if she wanted kids, Graham definitely did, but he was a detective, she was a private eye. Full time jobs and lifestyles that didn't allow for kids, but she still had time to find out, if that's what she wanted.

Then Bettie looked at the tyres on the bikes, they were narrow, smaller than a car and wheelbarrow. They might be able to make the marks in the soft mud.

Bettie went over to the side of the road and knelt down.

"Kids," Bettie said, waving them over.

"Mum said don't talk to strangers!" one of the kids said, he was probably about ten.

Bettie rolled her eyes. "I'm a friend of the… little old lady, owns some of the houses,"

She had no idea if they would know who she was talking about.

"Mrs Birchwood!" the younger kid shouted, he was certainly six years old.

The ten year old kid got off his bike and walked over to Bettie, keeping at least three metres between himself and her. Very clever, Bettie was going to have to remember that if she had kids. Three metres was more than enough space to run away if she wanted to kidnap him.

Of course she didn't, but still.

"Are you two the only ones with bikes in the street?" Bettie asked.

"Na. Jonny boy has a big bikey for big boys,"

"Has he ride a lot?"

"Ya. Saw him riding last night after Birchwood did her walky. I donna think she was gotten make it back home, I was gonna ride her home but mum said no,"

Bettie only just realised that there was something amazing about young children. They always wanted to love, help and support others no matter what, if she was going to have kids, she had to teach them that. And then make sure they didn't lose it when they grew up.

"That's very good of you. Well done. Now where do I find this Jonny Boy?"

The kid shrugged, jumped on his bike and they both rode off again.

***

When Bettie returned to her little red car she was expecting to stare at her beautiful Graham bent over the engine failing to fix it. Instead she found the little old lady bend over and hammering away at the engine.

The wonderful smell of the warming Christmas spices filled the air as Bettie went up to Graham who had a few dark smudges on his white shirt and tight jeans, but he was still the sexy, most beautiful man Bettie had ever seen.

"At least you tried," Bettie said, rubbing Graham's muscular shoulder.

"You clearly didn't trust me," Graham said, pretending to hit her cheek.

The little old lady climbed down to the ground and out of the car and turned to Bettie.

"Miss, your car should be working again in no time. Cars advanced a lot since the war but it will work,"

"You worked in the war?" Bettie asked, doubting the old lady was old enough to serve during World War Two.

"Oh no Miss, me dad served and I was born later. He taught me a lot about cars, trucks and planes from the war. I was quite the fixer in the neighbourhood. Have you found the Great Give Away?"

"The Great Give Away?" Graham asked.

Bettie just waved Graham silent.

"That's why I came to find you. One, thank you for your father's service. Two, who is Jonny Boy?"

The Little Old Lady shrugged.

"I met two kids who called him that and said he had a bike for big boys. Maybe he's an older kid or a young adult?" Bettie said.

"Oh! Miss, you mean Jonathan Bodie,"

Now Bettie shrugged. She didn't know anyone on the street, and yet this woman was acting like Bettie was a local.

"Um yes. Where is he?" Bettie asked.

The little old lady started to walk down the street.

"Come on Miss English. I'm waiting for a part from my garage. My Husband will find it soon. I'll show you where he lives,"

Bettie gestured Graham to follow and they both followed the little old lady down the street. Even with the sun high in the sky, Bettie couldn't believe how cold and dark it was, but that was the strange thing about English weather, it never seemed natural.

The days were meant to get brighter after the Winter Solstice but they seemed to be getting darker and darker and darker, and even at ten O'clock it wasn't what Bettie would call bright.

But the strangeness of the English weather was something she loved about it though.

After a few more minutes of walking down the street, the little old lady pointed to a bright red and green door with a large wreath on it.

Bettie went up to it and knocked three times.

"Mr Bodie," Bettie said.

A tall man opened the door and Bettie was immediately taken by the amount of aftershave he was wearing, she had to focus on not passing out of its strength. It wasn't even a nice aftershave, not like the earthy, sexy one Graham was wearing.

"Merry Christmas!" Jonathan Bodie said in a happy manly voice.

"Um, Happy Christmas. Did you ride your bike last night?" Bettie asked.

She wanted to start off easy and at least place him at the scene of the crime before outright accusing him. Yet the man seemed too happy and filled with the Christmas spirit to want to steal and ruin the Christmas Season for others.

"Oh Yes, I love cycling. It's wonderful. Especially seeing all the amazing lights. Have you seen them! Have you seen them!"

Bettie nodded. "They are wonderful. Did you go to the Give Away… cage last night?"

Bodie's expression changed to a solid frown and his eyes flicked towards Graham.

Bettie clicked her fingers at him. "Yes he is a cop. But I'm not. Confess to me and nothing can happen to you. I won't tell him, you have my word,"

Bodie's eyes flicked between Bettie and Graham and a few times at the little old lady.

"The homeless peeps can't have the food. We need it. Well, my daughter's charity needs it,"

Bettie shook her head. "You're telling me. You stole the food for the good of others?"

Bodie's eyes widened and he frantically nodded.

Bettie looked at Graham and the little old lady.

"We're going to need a cup of tea for this one," she said.

"Bodie, let the Miss and Graham come in," the little old lady said.

Bettie looked at Bodie who slowly nodded his head and stepped out of the way.

***

The living room of Bodie's house was a lot nicer than Bettie had imagined. She loved his bright blue three seat sofa, chair opposite it and coffee table in the middle.

The living room was definitely small and minimalist but Bodie had managed to make it comforting and cozy and rather lovely despite its size.

There were a few pictures of his wife and presumably his three children on the walls and seeing all those pictures and the happiness of the family made Bettie just stare at Graham.

He was happy, sexy and beautiful, a perfect man who would make an amazing dad. Then she would make a great mother she supposed, Bettie loved her nephew Sean like her own child and had raised him (sometimes) a lot more than his own parents.

So maybe she could have children.

"Please sit down," Bodie said gesturing towards the three seat sofa as he sat down on the chair opposite them.

Bettie sat down. "Your daughter works for a charity?"

Bodie looked at the little old lady. "I'm sorry Margaret. I didn't mean to steal it. My daughter... my daughter just wanted a little help,"

"It's fine deary. But why didn't you just ask?"

Bodie looked to the ground. "I was embarrassed,"

"What is the charity?" Bettie asked.

"It's brilliant Miss. I love it. It's a new charity that helps the homeless, vulnerable youths and even the elderly,"

"My daughter wanted a little help. I didn't want the Great Give Away to only go to one type of person," Bodie said.

Bettie could agree with that. Her nephew could have been one of the vulnerable youths if her (idiot) of a brother-in-law had kicked him out when her nephew said he was gay. Sure Sean would have been homeless but he was still a vulnerable youth, it wasn't fair that he wouldn't necessarily benefit from the Great Give Away, just because he was young.

And most homeless in the area were older.

Bettie leant forward. "Graham I don't think there's a crime here if we reach an agreement,"

Graham smiled and Bettie loved that sexy movie star smile.

"Me either Bet, but what sort of agreement?" Graham said.

"Well why don't you Mr Bodie and... Margaret agree to support your daughter's charity with the Great Give Away so she can help even more people?"

Both Bodie and Margaret looked at each other and smiled.

"Oh Miss that is a wonderful idea. That way we can all help the homeless, young and the elderly! That is marvellous!"

Bodie nodded too and judging by his face he was trying to hold back some tears.

Bettie stood up and looked at Bodie. "Just to check I presume the food is all in the garage safe and sound,"

Bodie nodded.

"Good. We will leave you both to sort out the details," Bettie said with a smile.

Graham started to head out the door and Bettie went to follow him when Margaret grabbed her arm.

"Thank you Miss! Thank you. You've saved the Great Give Away. What do I owe you?"

Judging by the look on Graham's face as he looked outside, her car was fixed and there was something wonderful about the little street.

Unlike the normal streets of southeast England, this one actually had soul, character and love in it. All these people no matter their background all loved each other in their own unique ways and wanted to help others. Hence the Great Give Away, Bettie wasn't going to charge people who wanted to help out others and help make the world a better place.

"Nothing," Bettie said smiling and walking out of the house. "Merry Great Give Away and A Happy New Year,"

Bettie heard Margaret and Bodie laugh, talk and being happy as she left, and her and Graham walked back up the street towards her car that was working perfectly.

There was a little old man walking away covered in oil and black smudges. He had to be Margaret's husband and the one who fixed the car properly.

She really wished everyone on the street, in England and the rest of the world had a great day and in some small way benefited from the Great Give Away. Because for some reason, a reason even Bettie didn't understand, she truly believed that every little act of kindness helped to make the world a better place.

Bettie wrapped her arm around Graham's waist and buried her face into his shoulder.

"When we get home tonight, we're so doing two things," Bettie said.

"What?"

"We're going to empty the house of the leftovers and take it down to the food bank,"

Graham smile and nodded at that.

Bettie stopped and pulled Graham close. "And we're going to

make a baby,"

Graham's face lit up, they kissed and Bettie loved the soft feeling of his lips.

"Merry Great Give Away Bet,"

As Bettie pressed her lips against his, the entire world felt right as she had saved a made-up holiday for people, helped a charity and now she was going to be something she never thought she had wanted.

A mother.

And she had done that all before Eleven O'clock in the morning. A great, brilliant, perfect start to an amazing day.

AUTHOR OF THE ENGLISH BETTIE PRIVATE EYE SERIES

CONNOR WHITELEY

CORRUPT DRIVING

A BETTIE PRIVATE EYE MYSTERY SHORT STORY

CORRUPT DRIVING

Private Eye Bettie English sat at her perfectly organised oak desk inside her tiny office in the heart of Canterbury. She loved the amazing little City with its ancient architecture, wonderful students and there was always something going on.

With the weather thankfully starting to warm up after one of the worse winters Bettie had ever experienced, Bettie had the window open and she listened to the tens upon tens of students walking, talking and laughing as they went along the high street.

When she first got the new office, she definitely wasn't impressed with all the noise and it only got worse if she was working late on a Friday, Saturday or Sunday night. She always made sure she went early (or what normal people call on time) on a Friday. She didn't want to have to dodge drunk students, grabby men and people throwing up.

She didn't need that.

As she stared at the open window wondering about all the different students out there and if her nephew Sean was coming to see her at some point (he should be), she almost expected to smell one of the best smells in the entire world. Strong fresh coffee.

Then she realised she couldn't have that amazing drink for another six months.

If Bettie had actually remembered what you were and you weren't allowed to drink, eat or do when you were pregnant (something she was still terrified of), she might have said no. But as her mum and sister said the first three months are the worse.

Thankfully Bettie had managed to more or less sail through them. Minus her longing to drink coffee and meat again.

Because what annoyed her more than anything else about pregnancy and she knew for she was unique in this, was she actually couldn't look, smell or eat meat anymore. No bacon, no pork and most importantly no barbeque.

Bettie couldn't understand it but her body just flat out refused to eat meat, and her body wasn't too sure on eggs and cow milk either.

So for the next six months Bettie was more or less vegan. Which she really didn't mind because compared to what was available to her friends when they all went to university, the vegan stuff was so good she couldn't tell the difference anymore.

And just to test it, Bettie gave it to her boyfriend, partner, Bettie really wasn't sure what they called themselves, if he was being annoying.

He never seemed to mind or he never called her out.

The sound of someone walking up the stairs made Bettie smile as it would finally give her a break from all these damn background checks. She hated them so badly.

Sure the money each company offered her was amazing and Bettie loved that part of the job. But when Bettie had ten companies with each company wanting her to do fifty plus checks before the end of the month, she wasn't sure the money was enough.

At least Bettie only had another fifty to do. Only.

Yet Bettie could honestly say there were a few gripping ones. For example Bettie had had to actually dig into some of the darkest corners of the internet to find out that this one woman who applied for a marketing director role used to be a bareback porn star.

Bettie was rather impressed with herself that she managed to find it. That woman had tried very hard to conceal it, but nothing could beat Bettie and her skills, at least she liked to think so.

There was a little knock at the door, Bettie told the person to come in and her entire face lit up when she saw it was her wonderful nephew Sean.

Bettie wanted to stand up and hug him, but the little one inside her (that sadly wasn't kicking yet) was a bit... temperamental about her moving too much. Bettie got up every hour for some steps, food and stretch up but she didn't want to do too much more.

Bettie had to admit Sean looked good with his jeans, shirt and new hair colour. She had heard that he was going to dye his hair, but after the contracts from the companies, (as bad as it sounded) Bettie had been a tat too willing to forget about family life.

Sean did look good with his dyed blond hair with a little bit of pink running through it. Bettie was actually surprised he looked as good as he did in it.

Bettie pointed to her kettle and mini-kitchen area on the far side of the office and Sean went over and made himself a cup of tea.

But now he was here, Bettie had to admit he didn't seem his normally happy self. The entire reason why he was here was because he had just taken a driving test which he would have passed without a problem.

Bettie didn't know why he wasn't happy about it. She at least expected a smile, a wave of excitement or just something. Sean might be a young man but he always showed some sort of emotion. Bettie had taught him that much.

As Bettie watched Sean finish up and him walk over and take a seat in front of her oak desk, she just smiled at him. He wasn't smiling.

"You know as a soon-to-be mother, I guess I should get some practice at this mothering stuff. What's wrong little man?" Bettie said.

Sean managed a slight smile. "Yea, you got to practice that a bit more,"

Bettie shrugged. "Seriously beau, what's wrong?"

"I failed," Sean said, sounding more confused and slightly angry than shocked.

Bettie's mouth dropped at that. Sean was a good driver, a damn good driver who was probably the best driver in the family. Bettie couldn't believe he had failed, but he must have been here for a more... official reason instead of going home and sulking.

"Why?" Bettie asked.

Sean frowned and leant closer. "I... I think the examiner lied about my test,"

Now Bettie was going to need a lot more information because as far as she was concerned all driving examiners were grumpy old people who knew they were in a dead end public service job, and they took out their anger on everyone else.

"They can't lie," Bettie said, "that's illegal,"

Sean nodded slightly. "That's my point. The driving examiner said he had to stop me when I caused a car to almost crash,"

Bettie smiled slightly. "You? You almost causing someone to

crash. The boy who me, Graham and my sister have all refused to drive for now because you comment on our driving,"

Sean looked blushed a little. "Yea sorry,"

"Tell me more about this so-called crash," Bettie said.

The only reason she wanted to know was because she just wanted to get away from those damn background checks for a while.

"Well," Sean said, "I was driving down the Dual Carriageway between North and South Little Village,"

Bettie laughed a little as she remembered that terribly named village. She had no idea why someone had called it that, and it was actually a small town.

"Then in reality, I was driving fine. But the examiner said I was surfing in and out of the lanes without signalling or checking if it was safe to do so,"

Now Bettie was a bit confused, she had driven with Sean for a fair while and he had never done something as stupid as that before. That was just a suicidal thing to do.

"What happened when you questioned it?" Bettie asked.

Sean frowned. "Stupid examiner threatened to call the police because I was I quote 'getting physically abusive to him',"

"Wow!" Bettie shouted, and that was all she could do.

Sean was the last person who would ever get physically violent or even raise his voice. It was stupid to imagine Sean would get abusive towards someone.

"Your driving instructor?" Bettie asked.

"Doesn't care. Thinks I was wrong and wants me to rebook,"

Bettie didn't have the heart to tell him he would have to rebook whatever happened, but this was interesting. She didn't want to go back to those background checks after hearing that.

But she had to get them all done.

It wouldn't take too long. Bettie knew it wouldn't be too tough to prove who was correct, especially if she tapped into the speed cameras along the stretch of road.

But she had to be good and get those checks done. Those companies were paying her a lot of money to do it.

Bettie just looked at her nephew and saw his killer smile, and... damn it! Bettie knew she couldn't resist a good case and she did love her nephew too much.

Yet if Sean was right, then why did the driving examiner lie?

***

After checking the speed cameras of the stretch of road that Sean had mentioned (Bettie loved having her boyfriend's password for the police databases), Bettie had laughed as she saw Sean drive at the speed limit on a perfectly clear road like he was meant to.

There was no crash, no other cars, no problem.

It was clear as day that the driving examiner had lied his ass off. But Bettie wasn't happy with just the footage which she may or may not have downloaded and put her phone (that was what she was going with in case her boyfriend Graham found out).

Bettie still couldn't imagine why the driving examiner had lied. It was illegal as hell and it made no sense. Driving examiners were there to protect the roads but to pass and fail and play god when deciding who should be allowed on the road or not.

And in Bettie's experience, people who played God always used it. Just not to fail someone without cause. She couldn't help the feeling that something bigger was going on.

As Bettie rested her hands on her baby bump inside her little red car (forcing her fears away about being a mother), she had to breathe shallowly with her window wide open as Sean had been sulking on the drive to the Driving Test Centre, so Bettie had bought him a fast food burger.

A meaty burger, so Bettie was trying her best not to vomit and gag.

Bettie tried not to focus on the amazingly juicy smell of the burger and the hints of Sean's really rich strong coffee that Bettie was so annoyed that she couldn't have, and instead she focused on looking through the wire fence that separated the car park she was in and the Driving Test Centre.

The centre itself was really nothing special. It was just another white block building that the government had thrown up with a large car park that looked as unloved as Sean did as he ate his burger.

Bettie knew the examiners would be back soon from their fourth testing slot of the day, so she kept resting her hands on her bump (she had no idea how great of an armrest it was) and simply waited.

But she couldn't help but feel like she needed more of the story first.

"How was the examiner with you? Was he angry, annoyed, sad?" Bettie asked.

Sean just looked at her. "Seriously Aunty?"

Bettie just smiled. He was right. All driving examiners were the same sort of rare grumpy, moany and moody mixture that only came from working in a government job for far too long.

Then Bettie focused on the Centre as she saw cars starting to return from their test. Bettie's eyes narrowed on a large black car that had the engines roaring away as the car sat still.

The car surged forward. Braking sharply. Then spun around into a parking bay and mounted the curb.

Bettie hugged her baby bump a little more. She hated the idea of being inside that car, and that was why she always had her dashcam running, just in case a stupid driver like that drove into her.

A few moments later a tall woman got out of the black car and was smiling and laughing. Bettie saw the little pass certificate in her hand. To say Bettie was shocked was an understatement.

"That's him!" Sean shouted with his mouth full of burger bun.

Bettie nodded as a large bald man came out of the black car smiling. His smile was clearly fake but she only knew that from decades as a private eye. The man was clearly dodgy or something, that woman should have failed but she didn't.

Why?

"Know what time the examiners go for lunch?" Bettie asked randomly.

Sean nodded. "The grumpy old fart did mention he was looking forward to after the fourth test,"

Bettie wanted to shrug but she didn't really want to be rude to Sean after everything.

"Stay here," Bettie said as she slowly got out of the car.

She had forgotten that she was pregnant and the little one inside her caught her off balance sometimes.

Bettie turned back to Sean. "Actually. Come with me please,"

Sean laughed and Bettie wanted to playfully hit him. She couldn't easily do this herself but as she was expecting she didn't want to take any chances whatsoever.

Bettie locked the car and after a few minutes of slowly walking (a mixture of walking and wobbling for Bettie), they both went into the Centre.

Bettie was impressed with how cold and clinical everything looked. It was horrible. The entire place was a solid large box room with bright white walls and cheap plastic chairs. It was simply awful.

At least there was a single fake plastic plant at the entrance that was big enough to hide behind, so Bettie gestured Sean to do just that.

At the far end of the boxroom was a white desk with an elderly woman standing behind it smiling. And to Bettie's utter shock it was a real smile, this crazy woman was actually happy to be here.

Bettie went over to her and forced herself not to gag at her extremely strong perfume.

"What can I do for you madame and the little one?" the woman said.

Bettie was still getting used to people saying that.

"Hello I am Bettie English and I'm looking for a Mr..." Bettie said checking the name Sean wrote down for her, "Jackson Ploguman,"

The woman frowned. "Not another one of his bitches are you,"

Then the woman dared to point to Bettie's baby bump. Bettie smiled and tried to suppress her laughter.

"No!" Bettie shouted.

The woman smiled a little. "I'm sorry Miss. I didn't mean to offend. He's... just a bit difficult. I would love him to just retire,"

Bettie smiled a little herself. Bettie took out her Private Eye License.

"Bettie English Private Eye. Tell me where he was and maybe I can help,"

The woman looked around and frowned and she pointed to the exit.

Bettie turned out and frowned as she saw a large black car driving away. She knew instantly that Jackson was gone and Bettie had to find him.

She had to get to the truth.

***

"You're driving over the speed limit Aunty!" Sean shouted by accident.

Bettie made herself smile and take long deep breaths of the amazing coffee-scented air as she drove through a 30 mile an hour zone at 32 miles an hour. Hardly breaking the speed limit.

And if she wasn't pregnant, Bettie would have braked harshly just to make Sean spill his coffee. She did love him, but he wasn't even a real driver yet!

As Bettie kept driving through a housing estate, she was starting to get more and more glad for having slightly (majorly!) illegal access to the speed cameras of Canterbury, which she was pretty sure Graham was going to change his password soon.

As Bettie pulled the car to a gentle stop because apparently a harsh stop wasn't how you were meant to drive. She instantly hated all the houses in the estate, they all looked exactly the same with their red walls, black front doors and four triple-glazed windows.

Bettie really didn't like it here, there was no character, community or feeling. Then Sean wrapped his arms around her and at first Bettie thought he was hugging her. Then she realised he was helping her stay steady on her feet. Horrible kid!

"I'm pregnant. Not crippled," Bettie said.

Sean smiled and kissed her on the cheek. Maybe he was a great kid after all.

"Which house is it?" Sean asked.

Bettie simply pointed to the house a few doors up with a massive black car outside with an oil trail going towards it.

They both went up to Jackson's front door and knocked three times. To Bettie's surprise an elderly woman answered it with long grey hair and as soon as she saw Bettie's bump a massive smile filled her face.

Bettie elbowed Sean in the ribs to play along.

"I'm so sorry Miss," Bettie said, "but can I borrow your phone? I need to call an ambulance. The baby's coming!"

"Of course. Of course," the woman said forcing Bettie inside. "Jackson!"

Bettie and Sean went into the large modern living room with a massive television on the wall and all the modern comforts of home. But what Bettie was more interested in was Jackson Ploguman sitting on the black sofa.

He looked at Sean. "What are you doing here!"

The wife came in. "What's going on?"

Bettie smiled and looked at her. "I'm so sorry to misled you but we needed to make sure your husband was home,"

"That's it! I'm calling the police!" Jackson shouted.

"Bettie English Private Eye," she said, "and Mr Ploguman you can call the police and tell them how you're taking bribes. Or you could talk to me,"

Jackson swore under his breath and both him and his wife sat down.

"You ain't got nothing on me," Jackson said.

"Actually I can prove with camera footage that you lied about my nephew's driving test,"

Jackson sweated a little.

"Now that might not be enough for prison. But you will lose your job," Bettie said calmly, "and I have dashcam footage of how badly a person you passed drove back in the test centre. Will it be hard for me to find other examiners that disagree with you passing her?"

The wife stood up and walked away from her husband. "What did you do?"

Jackson frowned at Sean. "What does that *man* want?"

Bettie had no doubt that Sean's new hair colour annoyed some older people because that must have been too gay for them. But Bettie wasn't going to let Jackson hide something behind that excuse, she knew there was something bigger going on.

"You might not like my nephew's hair and sexuality. But that wasn't the reason for failing him, was it?" Bettie said.

Jackson swore again.

"Mr Ploguman I am very good at my job. Do I need to look into your financial records?"

The wife laughed. "Deary, I'll get 'em now for ya,"

She went to turn around but Jackson shot up. "Don't!"

Then Bettie realised it was Jackson who controlled the money and kept the house running. His wife probably worked and did the housework and looked after the grandkids. But she didn't know what was going on in the bank accounts.

Bettie went straight over to him. "How much? Who paid you? And you will agree to my terms,"

Jackson swore again and sat back down. "Ten thousand pounds a woman paid me. Some new marketing director girl, Mary-Anne Shoeton,"

Bettie coughed. That was the name of the woman who was a former porn star who she did a background check on. Why did she want Sean to fail?

"Thank you," Bettie said. "Now you will do two things for me,"

Jackson nodded.

"You will give my nephew a free driving test today. If he fails for real reasons, then fine. If he passes, you will pass him and give him a hundred pounds as… compensation,"

Jackson looked like he wanted to argue but his wife got up and jabbed him in the stomach.

"Fine," he said.

"Excellent," Bettie said as her, Sean and Jackson went out of the house and the two men drove off to the Driving Test Centre.

And Bettie went to visit someone.

She had to find out why Anne Shoeton attacked her family.

***

Annie's background check might have said she had made thousands doing porn, but she clearly hadn't used the money wisely, Bettie realised as she walked into Anne's apartment.

It was absolutely disgusting.

There were pieces of mouldy food walked into the dirty carpets, the wallpaper was falling off and Bettie dared not sit down on the furry sofas.

But Anne sat down wearing her baggy grey tracksuit, massive earrings and so-called slutty red nail varnish (Bettie thought they actually looked quite good).

"What's Your Name?" Anne asked.

Bettie just shook her head. "You know who I am and you definitely know my nephew,"

"How is Sean getting on?" she said.

Bettie hadn't expected her to cave that quickly.

"Now, now Miss English. I only did porn back in the day to pay for uni. I am intelligent. I just…" Anne said gesturing to the apartment, "cannot find a good job at the moment,"

"Hence the marketing director position?" Bettie asked.

Anne nodded. "I wanted to better myself,"

Bettie shook her head again. "It makes no sense. Why bride that driving examiner?"

Anne cocked her head. "Didn't you get my email?"

Bettie shrugged.

"Oh," Anne said, looking embarrassed. "I emailed you saying unless you confirm in the next twenty-four hours you won't tell the company about my porn days. I'll make your life hell,"

"By going after my nephew. I never got your email!" Bettie shouted.

Anne seemed to crawl up into a ball. "Oh,"

Bettie flew her arms up in the air. "Oh indeed. You brided someone just because you thought I would tell the company about your past,"

"Would You?" Anne asked

Bettie laughed. "No! The company you applied for didn't want all the little details like the others. Your company just wanted me to check for illegal things. Like racism, past crimes, etc. Porn isn't illegal!"

"Oh," Anne said.

Bettie just shook her head. She actually didn't know what to say to this woman. But Bettie would be lying if she said she didn't admire or at least like the woman a little. Anne had been willing to do anything to better herself and maybe even her future family. Bettie would like to think she would have no problems doing the same.

"Are you going to tell them about me now? I deserve it," Anne said.

Bettie stroked her little baby bump. "No. Just never do anything against me or my family or friends again,"

"I promise," Anne said.

Bettie nodded and went to the apartment door and stopped. "For what's its worth. I hope you get the job. You seem like a good person at heart,"

***

Later that night Bettie was laying on her wonderfully soft grey sofa with her head resting on her sexy beautiful boyfriend's lap as he blew her kisses and made her laugh.

She damn well loved him, he was beautiful with his slight beard, ginger hair and just perfect body. He really was going to be an amazing father and she hoped she would be a great mother to the little one inside her.

The air was filled with the beautifully hints of herbs, vegan meat and so many other great smells that made Bettie just flat out excited for a very late dinner with the man she loved. And after the truly awful experience of Sean eating that burger and Anne's messy apartment, Bettie was really looking forward to something her body wouldn't gag at.

As Bettie was slowly got up and snuggled up with Graham, she loved the feeling of his hard body and his loving hug. Bettie was proud of herself for what she did today, she exposed some corruption, got all but ten of the background checks done and most importantly she helped her beautiful nephew.

He had passed perfectly this time round without even minor faults. Bettie wished she was that good at his age, and now if she remembered correctly Sean had driven him and his boyfriend out for a good dinner together.

Bettie did love them both. Sean was just a wonderful young man and his boyfriend was great too. They were a perfect match, like Bettie and Graham.

Bettie gave him a kiss as she wondered about how she would be as a mother. Both her and Graham had spoken about how scared, excited and worried they were, but at the end of the day, Bettie knew that was what made great parents.

It wasn't about how much money, power or the physical things you had (but they weren't doing bad on those things either). It was about how much you cared, loved and tried your damned hardest to do your kids proud.

And Bettie knew for a fact, herself and Graham would do anything for their kids. Bettie had dropped everything for her nephew because of one of his theories. He could have been wrong, he could have lied, he could have done so much.

But Bettie loved him so she was going to try for him, and she was going to do that a hell of a lot more for her own kid.

And that really, really excited her.

AUTHOR OF THE ENGLISH BETTIE PRIVATE EYE SERIES

CONNOR WHITELEY

JUBLIEE TERROR CELEBRATIONS

A BETTIE PRIVATE EYE MYSTERY SHORT STORY

JUBILEE, TERROR, CELEBRATIONS
2nd June 2022
London, England

Private Eye Bettie English had never really been too much of a royalist, but as a British person she had always kept an eye on the royal family, what they were up to and listened to Private Eyes when they spoke about secrets they had uncovered in their own investigations.

Bettie walked along a very long London street with little terrace houses lining the street with not a single parked car on the road and everything had been freshly polished and cleaned for this very special occasion.

With Bettie's boyfriend Detective Graham Adams being called in to help protect, control the crowd and provide security for the Queen's Platinum jubilee. Bettie was more than interested in wandering around London and then hoping to go up to the Mall, see tons of amazing people from throughout the commonwealth and hopefully watch the Trooping of the Colours as the platinum jubilee weekend officially started.

Bettie couldn't deny how excited she was that the Queen had been reining for 70 years and she had done a great job. Given the Queen had no political power, or not much power whatsoever, she was more of a cultural icon in this day and year, but Bettie didn't have a problem with it.

And that was probably why people loved, respected and

treasured her so much. Because she had no power and she was part of the country's somewhat questionable history in the days of the Empire, people were always interested in how she had kept up with the ever-changing world.

Bettie had actually met the Queen once.

Bettie listened to the distant talking, shouting and other excited noises as thousands upon thousands of people gathered in London just hoping to see the Queen, the Trooping of the Colours and any members of the royal family.

It had been a few years ago when Bettie, some other Private Eyes and the current President of The British Private Eye Federation David Osborne had travelled to Buckingham palace to get an audience with the Queen.

And even though Bettie had expected and known she was a very kind, polite and down to earth person. She was still rather shocked by how much attention, respect and love that the Queen gave all of them.

Bettie would never forget how the Queen actually wanted to hear how Bettie found being a woman in this modern era and doing a so-called man's job.

Bettie loved the beaming hot sun on her face and her pregnant body as she wandered further down the long London street towards the sound of the excited tourists.

There was such a buzz of excitement, joy and celebration that captured all of London, and Bettie just loved it. It really was amazing how much London seemed to be alive today and united in the celebration of the Queen.

Bettie loved the wonderful smell of bacon, eggs and bitter coffee (that her pregnant body hated her to have) coming from a local café. And even though she started to feel ever so slightly sick at the smell of bacon (her body seriously didn't like animal products since she got pregnant) it was still a wonderful smell to start off today.

With Graham busy helping to police the crowds for the next few days, Bettie wasn't sure what she was going to do. Everyone had the next four days off so everyone could join in the celebrations.

So Bettie was more than looking forward to the wonderful street party that was going to happen on her road on Sunday. It would be simply wonderful seeing all her family and neighbours and friends coming together and celebrating together.

But Bettie was really just looking forward to the vegan food, the company and the non-alcoholic drinks. It might have been a time for celebrations but she was definitely not putting her unborn twins at risk.

The sound of two deep voices a lot closer than the excited crowds hundreds of metres away made Bettie focus on the long street. She had been the only person here a moment ago.

Then at the very, very end of the street were two very tall stone buildings, that there probably offices, there were a group of five men dressed in all black and they were quietly talking almost themselves.

The men were such a strange contrast to Bettie in her stunning flowery summer dress that hide her baby bump very well, her wonderfully comfortable high heels and her little black purse that only contained her phone and a credit card.

Considering the entire city was alive with excitement, affection and jubilation about this weekend, Bettie couldn't help but feel like this was something important.

Sure she knew that not everyone liked the Queen and the royal family. But even those people tended to at least acknowledge this was something to be happy about and they wouldn't dress in all black on a boiling hot day.

In the rare event that these men were going to cause trouble Bettie tried to figure out what the point of their meeting was at the end of the street would be.

Bettie noticed that the buildings were definitely tall enough to overlook the rows upon rows of houses and other London apartments in front of it. And if these men went to the very top of the buildings then they would have great line of sight.

If these people weren't dressed in all black then Bettie couldn't have cared about their great line of sight to the Mall, the Palace and other important roads involved in the Trooping of the Colours.

And in actual fact with the Queen's mobility issues in recent months (still amazing for a 96 year old), this was the only day the Palace had absolutely confirmed the Queen would be in London.

Bettie wanted to gasp and she felt her stomach tighten at the realisation that someone wanted to try and kill the Queen. Then this was definitely the day to do it.

Perhaps the only day.

Then the five men dressed in all black looked around, didn't see Bettie and they all went inside the taller one of the two buildings. Granted one of the buildings was only a metre or two taller than the other, but Bettie knew that was still important to snipers or whatever these people were.

The smart thing to do might have been to phone Graham, her handful of contacts from MI5 from a previous case or just called the police. But they wouldn't believe her.

Bettie knew from conversations with other Private Eyes that there had been a dramatic increase in terrorist (both abroad and domestic) chat in the weeks coming up to the Jubilee celebrations. And with the war going on in Ukraine, Bettie knew that Russia was also plotting to destroy the Jubilee.

So MI5 and the police would definitely have their hands full without her suspicions, and because Graham's protection assignment was classified (Bettie only knew he was in London) she couldn't contact him.

Bettie was alone in this.

Just in case this was a terrorist attack and MI5 did want to listen to her, she sent a quick message to Agent Daniels, an agent she had met on a previous case, and just hoped that he would read the message.

But if that didn't happen Bettie wasn't going to let some idiots kill the Queen, spoil her weekend and become remembered in the history books.

No terrorists deserved that honour.

Bettie quickened her pace.

She was going to go into that very tall building.

And find out what the hell was going on.

***

One of the benefits of being a private eye was definitely that Bettie made contacts with all sorts of knowledge. Including a very serious security fault in most electronic locks installed by the *Mrs Locks* company.

Thankfully the very tall building Bettie had wanted to get access into was locked as tight as Fort Knots but it had a Mrs Locks security system installed. So Bettie simply typed in *1, 2, 3* and the door opened for her.

Bettie went into a rather small black reception area with nothing more than a black desk, two black chairs and a lift door.

Bettie hated the musty smell that radiated from the chairs and it was rather clear that no one had loved this reception area for ages. But Bettie couldn't help but feel like the reception area was nothing more than a front for something.

The entire space just felt off for some reason.

Considering the building was so tall and massive from the outside, Bettie was surprised that it felt so small on the inside.

And even above the lift doors it showed the lift moving up the floors and apparently it had stopped on the sixth floor. But when Bettie placed her hand on the cold lift doors, she could feel that the lift was still moving upwards.

So why did the building or owners only want people to believe there were six floors?

Bettie noticed there were four security cameras in each corner of the reception area, so she went round behind the desk to see a very small computer screen build into the desk.

Bettie flicked through the security cameras. She couldn't even see herself standing in the reception area and apparently the lift was empty.

Someone had looped the feeds.

The door clicked.

Bettie just smiled to herself and she instantly knew that she was now locked in the building with five potential terrorists, so she definitely had a choice to make.

She couldn't break the computer screen and just hope that the building had professionally monitored security that wasn't being hacked, or she could try to unhack or unloop the security cameras herself.

Not that she actually knew how to do that in the slightest.

And it wasn't like she could call her wonderful nephew Sean and his boyfriend Harry (the computer experts of the family) because they were revising for some exams next week.

Bettie felt her twins kick inside her and she just knew that she had to press on, and try and find these potential terrorists herself.

Bettie turned her attention back to the computer screen and swiped away from the security cameras and she bought up a floor plan of the building.

As she expected there were apparently only six tiny floors in the entire building, but at least the floor plans were stupid enough to indicate the wall behind the reception area was false.

In fact there was even something about it being privately monitored and not on the main system, so if Bettie opened the wall. It would certainly alert someone.

Bettie turned and tapped the large black wall and it was certainly hollow.

Bettie couldn't believe how excited she was getting, so she looked back at the desk, saw a pair of scissors and she stabbed them into the wall.

A slight vibrating sound filled the air then fell silent.

Bettie quickly cut through the wall that was made with nothing more than very good-looking cardboard and she was very surprised to see a small dusty staircase in front of her.

This would definitely be the perfect way to sneak up the floors and past the potential terrorists.

The terrorists would probably be able to hear or feel the lift moving up after them, but the stairs would be perfectly silent.

Bettie was very glad that she could finally take off these damn high heels that might be comfortable but they were most certainly not practical for Private Eye work.

She gently kicked them off and placed them firmly at the bottom of the staircase so in case someone came in they would instantly know something was wrong.

Bettie loved the feeling of excitement grow inside her.

She raced up the staircase.

***

Bettie couldn't believe how outrageously hot it was in the little pitch black staircase. She was so hot sweat was refusing to pour off her anymore.

She had been walking or stumbling more like up the stairs for twenty minutes until her hands felt a little wall in front of her.

The stairs felt awfully musty and dusty and just awful. Bettie didn't want to be in here any longer than she had to be.

"Snipers are activated," a man with a deep voice said.

Bettie was surprised that the man sounded so close even though he was on the other side of the wall. Bettie used her hands to search the wall in front of her and she was delighted to find some kind of switch.

She flicked it.

The entire wall collapsed.

Bettie gasped as all the five men dressed in black just stared at her.

Bettie had been expecting there to be a little secret hole in the wall so she could peek through them.

Clearly that wasn't what that switch was designed for.

Bettie frowned as five guns were fixed on her.

But Bettie didn't care. She was much more focused on the very tall muscular man in the middle, the only man not covering his face, holding two military issue guns at her head.

"Military. Former soldiers," Bettie said looking each of the men up and down.

Bettie pointed to the man at the other end of the little penthouse room she was in with thick glass windows all around them and no furniture. This had to be the top floor.

"I'm guessing snipers?" Bettie asked, as she watched the man expertly cut the glass so he could have a clear shot from the window.

Bettie gestured if she could get closer and the man holding two guns nodded.

Bettie just gave the former soldiers a quick nod of respect when she noticed that the sniper was staring at the balcony at Buckingham palace where the Queen would be standing in a matter of...

The distant sound of people screaming in excitement and the royal bands playing loudly and the clopping of horses made Bettie want to be sick. The Trooping of the Colours was happening now.

The Queen would be out at the balcony at any moment.

"Why this building?" Bettie asked. "And why am I not dead?"

The man with two guns just gestured to Bettie's baby bump. That was a massive relief.

"My other question?" Bettie asked.

"Eagle when the traitor is on the balcony kill her. That is my command," the man said.

"Confirmed," the sniper said.

Then Bettie was surprised to see the other three men lowered their guns, walked behind Bettie and picked up a sniper rifle each.

With all the wall collapsing and the guns focused on Bettie, she must have forgotten to properly scan her surroundings. Then the other three men cut expertly done holes out of the class and aimed at the balcony too.

They were killing tons of the royal family.

"The building," Bettie said firmly.

The man with the two guns that was clearly the leader smiled and shook his head.

"You know what your Queen's grandfather did to our people," he said.

Bettie almost missed it but she was... she was a little surprised to hear faint hints of a Russian accent, but it was so faint that the men clearly hadn't been in Russia for decades.

In fact the men sounded so British and acted exactly like other members of the British Army Bettie had met before.

"Coming onto the balcony now," one of the snipers said.

Bettie noticed a red dot on the leader's ears and Bettie didn't know how she knew, but she just knew that she had to buy a little more time for something.

"Don't shoot yet. Don't you want the attack to be famous? Wait a few more minutes so the entire family is on the balcony, all the TV cameras and people are watching. Come on guys, this is basic!" Bettie shouted.

"Hold fire for 60 seconds," the leader said.

Bettie didn't dare let her smile show.

Bettie walked straight up to the leader. "The building and what did the Queen's grandfather do to Russia?"

The leader huffed. "Your King George the fifth could have saved Russia and the royal family. You could have save Nicholas the 2nd, he could have allowed him to come to England. But he didn't. The entire family died, even the children!"

Bettie wasn't exactly sure what to say. She had studied the first world war and the politics and history of the three grandchildren of Queen Victoria and how they waged war against each other, but what could killing the Queen do after over a century?

Again she only needed to buy time.

"What could this killing achieve..."

Then Bettie instantly realised that the Queen was never going to be the intended victim, there would be the Queen's elderly adult children, her grandchildren and her great-grandchildren on that balcony.

And what better way to make the granddaughter of King George the 5th suffer than watching her own children die. Just like Nicholas the 2nd of Russia would have to do all before he died himself.

"This wouldn't change anything for Russia. This is only…" Bettie said.

The leader held up two guns to Bettie.

"This isn't about Russia. Russia can die. This is about the British Royal Family learning what it means to suffer," he said.

There was no changing his mind.

Bettie took a few steps back and waved her hands.

Five bullets fired.

Five corpses smashed onto the ground.

Bettie's twins kicked in excitement in her stomach. She was seriously starting to wonder how much of a handful these two were going to be in a few months.

"Bet!" Graham shouted.

Bettie felt her entire body go weak when she heard her beautiful sexy Graham was coming for her. Granted he was a bit late, but better late than never.

Graham dressed in his blue Demin shorts, white shirt and black sunglasses and looked stunned as he walked up the stairs and looked at the five corpses in front of her.

"I always knew you could look after yourself," Graham said, kissing Bettie.

Bettie just nodded.

Then she smiled. She couldn't actually think of a better way to start off the Jubilee celebrations than by saving the Queen and the rest of the Royal Family.

As Bettie and Graham were about to walk back down the stairs (Bettie didn't want to be in a lift on such a hot day, not that the stairs weren't much cooler), she just looked at the corpses a final time knowing that the bodies would never be discovered.

"Long live the Queen," Bettie muttered as her and Graham went back down the stairs.

Then Bettie quickly told Graham the so-called reasoning for the attack.

"Makes sense in a strange extremist way. What better way to embarrass the royal family than on this historical occasion,"

Bettie nodded in the pitch darkness as she carefully went down the stairs.

"How did you find me?" Bettie asked.

Graham laughed. "Agent Daniels called. And I was already in the area dealing with some protesters but Daniels wanted me to ask you, do you know about the purpose of this building?"

Bettie smiled a little. She knew there was something wrong with this building in the first place, and it was even stranger than the police hadn't secured it. They had secured all the buildings that gave snipers a perfect shot of the Queen.

So why had they missed this one?

"I cannot say I do. Why?"

Graham stopped on the pitch black staircase.

"I think this was always meant to be a trap, a lure if you will for terrorists and I think this is some kind of government research facilities," Graham said.

As crazy as it sounded, Bettie completely agreed with him. This building was rather perfect in a way because it was tall enough for people to keep a look out for anyone about to invade the building, giving the government time to move their operations, and Bettie was sure the glass wasn't easy to cut into from the outside, and it would most certainly explain why the glass was so thick on the top floor.

It was so thick because Bettie wanted to bet it was bulletproof.

It had to be considering how dangerous it was for the snipers to poke their rifles out of the windows. Police officers, agents and everyone would be looking out for that sort of behaviour.

A very risky move for those terrorists.

Bettie and Graham kept walking down the stairs, and when Bettie went into the reception area she didn't even bother to pick up her high-heels again. She simply went straight out the door and back into the delightfully warm London air.

The air wasn't too hot and it was filled with the sounds of excited people and hints of sausages, eggs and bacon and it was filled with such a buzz that Bettie really felt alive.

And she couldn't be happier than she had helped to protect this amazing historical occasion.

Graham wrapped his amazingly strong sexy arms round her, and he started to kiss her neck.

"I am a plain clothes officer today. Want to help me?" Graham asked.

Bettie just smiled and pure excitement shot through her. She couldn't think of a better way to spend the day. She got to protect people, be with the man she loved and she got to celebrate with the country she loved.

And that was a perfect beginning to a perfect long weekend to Bettie.

AUTHOR OF THE ENGLISH BETTIE PRIVATE EYE SERIES

CONNOR WHITELEY

CRIMINAL PERFORMANCE

A BETTIE PRIVATE EYE MYSTERY SHORT STORY

CRIMINAL PERFORMANCE
20ᵗʰ August 2022
Canterbury, England

Private Eye Bettie English had seen some stunning performances at various theatres all over the United Kingdom. She had seen the breath-taking opera in London, amazing comedies that made her stomach hurt for days on end afterwards in Edinburgh and she had seen the sweetest little production done by children for the various charities that she gave money too.

But this performance was just criminally bad.

Bettie sat on a very comfortable little red seat in the circle of the Bluebird Theatre in Canterbury, this was probably the best seat she had ever had because its delightful softness, a black cup holder in the arm that was actually large enough to hold her diet coke and the seat was dead-centre in line with the middle of the stage.

The large(ish) black stage itself wasn't exactly grand, it was probably nothing more than some wooden blocks stuck together to give a very convincing look alike to trick people into believing it was a professional stage, but Bettie just knew better.

The smell of sweat, peanuts and amazingly rich bitter coffee filled the air, and Bettie was so looking forward to next month when she gave birth to her twins and she could finally have some of the delightful black gold again. She had really missed her coffee.

The roar below in the stalls came from tens upon tens of proud parents shouting, laughing and pretending to enjoy the performance going on the stage. Bettie wasn't sure if they were actually faking it or pretending or Bettie certainly was.

Currently on the stage were a group of 3 to 4-year-old toddlers with a pop song on in the background, and from what Bettie could understand the toddlers were meant to be dancing judging by the adult dressed in black moving around trying to encourage the toddlers to do the same.

But come on, they were toddlers. Bettie had absolutely no expectation that they were going to dance, sing or whatever.

Bettie just smiled as she heard her wonderful boyfriend Graham next to her huff. Clearly he was just as sad about the lack of performance as she was, he was probably just too kind to say anything.

Then next to the other side was Bettie's sister Phryne in her little black dress cheering, shouting and clapping at the little toddlers. Bettie wasn't exactly impressed that her sister had basically tricked her into coming along to this performance for the charity she gave her time too.

Bettie had never ever known her sister to be charitable in the slightest, hell this was the exact same sister who didn't really seem interested that her son, Sean, and his boyfriend, Harry, were living with Bettie, rather than his own mother after they were attacked and Harry had a brain injury.

"Now everyone please clap your hands together for the amazing, the stunning, the spectacular Thomas High Schools Girls," someone said over the microphone.

Thankfully the little toddlers who looked so scared and concerned hurried off, even though one didn't understand what was going on so she was walking towards the edge of the rather high up stage. An adult grabbed her and they all left.

A few moments later some 5 to 6 years olds (Bettie had no idea how they were classed as high school girls) came onto the stage dressed in rather… inappropriate clothing for that age (or any age really).

Bettie rested her hands on her baby bump. "Please tell me you two aren't going to be into this show stuff,"

Bettie almost jerked at the baby kicks and Bettie just smiled at her two beautiful babies. She firmly took that as a no, and she more than loved them for it. Of course if the twins had wanted to do this then she would have let them.

But she preferred them not to, for now anyway.

"Miss Bettie English?" a woman said in the darkness.

It took Bettie a few moments to realise that there was a middle-aged woman dressed in all black standing right next to her. It was so dark in the theatre Bettie was struggling to see her own baby bump let alone someone dressed in all black.

"Yes," Bettie said, still not being able to see the woman clearly.

"Are you the Private Eye woman?" she asked.

Bettie rolled her eyes at the sheer dismissiveness that the woman said it with.

"I am,"

"Great," the woman said and leant closer to Bettie. "We need your help please. There is a situation that we cannot call the police about. Can you please help us? My boss has authorised the transfer of a thousand pounds as compensation,"

Normally Bettie would have at least pretended to consider not taking the job because of course she was with the family she loved, watching a cute little child performance and supporting a charity she loved.

Absolutely none of that was true in the slightest.

Bettie grabbed the woman's hand and shook it hard. She was going to take any old excuse to get out of here.

She quickly told beautiful Graham was she was doing and he just stuck his tongue out at her in jealousy. Bettie didn't blame him but at least she was escaping.

But the theatre wanted to give her a thousand pounds. That was a lot of money for a few hours of work.

Bettie was more concerned about the case than she ever wanted to admit.

***

A few minutes later the middle-aged woman, which admittedly had seen better days with her oversized body that was putting such a strain on her black uniform that Bettie was waiting for the buttons to explode off, led Bettie into a bright white storage room that was a bit on the small size for a very overweight woman and a heavily pregnant woman to get into to.

Bettie really wasn't a fan of its bright white walls, musty smell of sweat and Bettie even saw a very well-used condom on the floor so she could only imagine what this room was actually used for.

Yet what really caught Bettie's attention was the makeshift desk covered in papers and the grey metal filing cabinet that had been forced open.

"This is the problem Miss English," the middle-aged woman said, pointing to the forced open filing cabinet.

As much as Bettie wanted to focus on the filing cabinet she was a lot more interested in all the papers on the desk. It was strange how the criminal or thief or whatever had gone to the filing cabinet when there was clearly so much paperwork on the desk.

"What happened?" Bettie said as she looked through the paperwork on the desk.

"This is my storage room and office," the woman said. "And my name is Miss Savannah Claire. Before every performance I exit my office, lock it before I go and meet the production crew to double check everything is ready,"

Bettie nodded as she was reading the bank account information and passwords on the desk. It was stupid that the theatre would leave their bloody banking passwords in the open, but she wasn't their investor or anything to do with them.

It was still stupid.

"I leave my office at half 1 and I checked with the production crew. Then I watched the opening performance of the show at two. I just had to leave after that," Savannah said.

Bettie couldn't exactly blame her too much. If she had been smarter Bettie would have realised then that the pointless opening of the performance with a mixture of toddlers, who didn't know what to do and were too nervous because of the crowds, and older children, looked more like a chaotic cat fight more than a so-called elegant performance.

"Then I came back to my office and found the filing cabinet open,"

Bettie could only nod as she found another cold piece of paper that detailed out the theatre's business plan, taxes and employee passwords. This was beyond stupid now and it was a wonder that the theatre hadn't been robbed before.

But why leave this information and not take it?

Bettie looked at Savannah and folded her arms. "What was stolen?"

Savannah looked to the ground. "Someone stole the scripts of a brand new West End performance coming down from London. This performance would have put the theatre on the national and international map,"

Bettie wasn't sure about that but if a little theatre like this could host such a massive performance that would have had positive reviews, be critically-acclaimed and have some great stars then it would definitely be a boon to the theatre.

And most importantly the person who worked in there.

Bettie quickly realised that this theft wasn't about money or anything like that, it was about sabotaging the livelihoods of the people that worked here.

Bettie picked up the recent bank documents off the desk and reread them, and the theatre was cash-strapped up to their necks. They had maxed out all their credit cards and the theatre probably had two months left at best.

"Can you help us?" Savannah asked.

Bettie didn't react and just went over to the filing cabinet had stunk of strawberry lube, sweat and a very strange earthy aftershave that Bettie hadn't smelt in a long time. She had bought it for Graham years ago before they broke up and he had hated it. He actually had an allergic reaction so bad Bettie had to take him to hospital.

Besides from that the filing cabinet (well that draw that had been forced open anyway) was perfectly clear. Then Bettie focused on the two marks where something had been forced into the draw to pop it open. It looked like a simple crowbar job but that was a little too simple for Bettie's liking.

"Do you keep crowbars in the theatre?" Bettie asked.

Savannah nodded and pointed under the desk.

Bettie rolled her eyes as she popped her head under the makeshift desk and saw an entire toolkit. She didn't want to know why Savannah had all of these tools but she guessed Savannah was also a part-time handywoman too.

This place was really cash strapped.

Bettie folded her arms again. She had some scripts stolen, no evidence in the filing cabinet, the breaking into the filing cabinet was done with Savannah's tools so that proved nothing and there were no clues in this storage room.

Bettie was at a dead end.

"Is it possible for people to get into the theatre during a performance?" Bettie asked.

Savannah looked a little annoyed at even the suggestion.

"Of course not. That is ridiculous. The theatre has had thefts before but I will not allow them anymore. I make sure this place is secure,"

Bettie actually believed her and at least the dead end meant she was going to be working a little longer so she didn't have to go back to the god-awful performance.

But Bettie did have a critical lead now.

If no one could get in it had to be an inside job. And that made Bettie even more curious about who it could be.

Was it one of the proud parents watching their kids in the stalls or was it a staff member?

Bettie was really looking forward to finding out.

***

The sheer dirtiness of the little box-room that apparently served as the security office only told Bettie more and more about how dire the situation was for the theatre. The security room was caked in dirt and dust and smelt like some teens had had a pizza party without bothering to clean it up.

Bettie really tried to focus on the little computer screen in front of Savannah as she showed Bettie the security footage. Bettie was going to do this bit herself but there was no chance in hell she was going to sit down in this room. And much less touch the wooden desk with the computer on, Bettie could see the grease covering the surface.

Bettie was actually starting to wonder if the theatre closing down might be a benefit to the local area. It would be at least from a public health perspective.

"This is the security camera outside my office," Savannah said.

Bettie was surprised Savannah thought these cameras would be useful. There was such a thick layer of ugly dust and grim on the camera lens that Bettie could hardly see the office door, let alone any details of the thin figures (presumably people) walking past.

This was another dead end.

Bettie was really not impressed now. It was almost like Savannah had purposefully kept the theatre in such a bad condition that it was useless to investigate if any crimes occurred.

Maybe that was the play.

"Bring up all employees in today please," Bettie said.

Savannah nodded and typed away at her computer a little. She bought up the employment records and Bettie was right about Savannah doing a lot of different jobs. She was the manager, handywoman and occasional extra if a play needed it.

Bettie admired this woman's resilience and lust to throw herself into everything that the theatre required of her. But Bettie also knew that this was where people tended to go to the criminal side of humanity out of annoyance, spite or another reason altogether.

"Where's the scripts Savannah?" Bettie asked.

Savannah huffed. "I respect you too much Miss to lie to you. You didn't know it but you were the first person in a long, long time to at least talk to me like I'm a person. And not some superhuman,"

Bettie had no idea she spoke to Savannah in a special way. She was just doing what she always did.

"How long have you been a one-woman band?" Bettie asked.

Savannah didn't seem like she could look at Bettie. At least she probably felt bad for her actions.

"Ever since last Christmas I have had to reduce staff levels by a factor of ten. I'm been repairing, fixing and cleaning believe it or not every day,"

Bettie found the cleaning comment hard to believe but to interrupt would just seem rude.

"I've been doing sixteen hour shifts every day this year. Finding stupid performances to put on, not paying myself living wage and it is just so trying,"

Bettie folded her arms. "What do the owners say? Have you told them?"

Savannah glared at Bettie. "You think I want this sixteen hours stuff. I don't. I really don't. My bosses tell me if I don't comply I'll be fired. I'll be on the streets. They own my apartment,"

Bettie gently placed her hands on her baby bump. This case was never what it had seemed in the first place, this wasn't a strictly criminal act, it was a call for help.

And Bettie actually wanted to help this poor woman.

She needed to get the cops involved. She needed Graham.

***

A few hours later, Bettie and Savannah leant against the wonderful warm brick wall of a shop on the delightfully perfect cobblestone high street of Canterbury as they watched Graham escort a middle-aged man and woman down the high street towards his police car with two uniformed officers closely behind him.

Other people, as they strolled up and down the high street on this wonderful evening, muttered and looked and spoke about what was going on. Bettie laughed at some of the guesses like drugs, murder or kidnapping.

But the truth was a lot, lot sadder.

As a Private Eye and doing a lot of charity work too, Bettie had always known about modern slavery but this was the first time she had ever encountered it and it was the last time she ever wanted to.

Despite the sensational buttery, creamy, sweetest scents coming from the various bakeries on the high street, Bettie felt so sorry for Savannah. A woman who had been kicked out by her husband because she refused to put up with his drinking and shouting anymore. A woman who had been on the streets for months before two people offered her a way to freedom. A woman who had been tricked into believing enslavement was a freedom.

As Savannah watched with cold distant eyes at Graham walking away her captors, Bettie focused on her. For the past year and a bit, her captors had forced her to live in a tiny little apartment on an awful wage in awful conditions. They controlled everything about her life but because Savannah loved the theatre so much she didn't notice until it was far too late.

Then the scripts for the best-selling sensational West End performance came down to the theatre.

Bettie fully understood why Savannah had taken the chance and stole the scripts. Her plan was logical, hide the manuscripts away until the theatre was forced to close and then Savannah was going to sell the scripts anomalously back to the West End production company.

And hopefully (and Bettie admitted this was a massive gamble) the production company would still want to host the play at the Bluebird Theatre which Savannah would buy with the money from the script sale.

It was perfect.

Which was why Bettie had instructed Savannah to put the scripts back into the filing cabinet and pretend they were never stolen. So whatever was said Savannah wasn't a criminal and the focus was purely on the captors and the charges of modern slavery.

"What will happen to me now?" Savannah asked as she forced herself to look away from the police.

Bettie gently rubbed her baby bump as the twins kicked in excitement.

Bettie was about to say something when her sister Phryne came over and hugged Savannah. Bettie was pleased that Phryne looked so happy considering Bettie had left her precious little performance.

"Savannah it is great to welcome you to the team," Phryne said.

Savannah's eyes widened. Bettie had no clue if it was out of fear or joy.

"The team?" Savannah asked.

Bettie gestured Phryne to explain.

"Of course my dear," Phryne said. "You are now the proud owner of the theatre. A certain detective made them sign it over to you before they were arrested and now our great charities get to work together,"

Savannah slowly nodded then Phryne wrapped her very thin arm around Savannah's chunkier one and started dragging her down the high street towards a restaurant for dinner.

Savannah looked at Bettie like a plea for help and Bettie just laughed. It was nice to see her sister get so excited about something for a change. It was actually nice that after all the chaos of late her sister was doing good, and she was even involved in a charity now.

As a delightful breeze of warm air enveloped Bettie, she smiled to herself and started to walk down the street towards where Graham went with the captors. She had no doubt the uniformed cops would take them back to the station to be booked and Graham had the car keys.

So Bettie needed to be quick otherwise she'll be stranded in the middle of Canterbury, definitely not a bad place to be stranded but Bettie just wanted to go home now and enjoy her wonderful boyfriend.

Bettie kept walking, the rough cobblestone under her feet, and she couldn't believe how great she felt about today. She had helped a theatre survive, saved a woman from enslavement and even given her a brand new start as the owner of a theatre.

If that wasn't a great day's work, then Bettie really wasn't sure she wanted to know what was.

AUTHOR OF THE ENGLISH BETTIE PRIVATE EYE SERIES

CONNOR WHITELEY

DANGER OF OPEN WINDOWS

A SEAN ENGLISH AMATEUR SLEUTH MYSTERY SHORT STORY

DANGERS OF OPENED WINDOWS
15th August 2022
Canterbury, England

Two months after the attack, Sean felt the anxiety afflicted him and stirred up in striking waves that seemed to smash into him for a moment before passing. He felt like the ground and the entire world would collapse around him, his chest might even explode and he was completely alone for those moments. Until the anxiety passed and everything returned back to normal. It wasn't really a way to live but at least the therapy was helping.

Sean leant against the warm wooden doorframe of his and his boyfriend Harry's bedroom with Harry an almost dangerously thin line under the thin blue silk sheets in their double bed, surrounded by some fine wooden chests of drawers, wardrobes and there was even a wooden black chest at the bottom of the bed.

Yet the roaring of Harry's snorting still managed to vibrate the spotlight-like lights in the corners of the bedroom, but Sean was just glad for any sounds coming from him. Because they all meant that the love of his life was alive, and that was all that mattered to Sean.

Sean never really did understand why his Auntie Bettie English, a private eye, had gifted them so much stuff when him and Harry moved in to help them recover after the homophobic attack. He partly supposed that it was because she felt guilty for some stupid reason, it was never her fault and it was her that had put the bastards behind bars forever.

Something rustled downstairs but Sean ignored it. It was probably just the neighbour cat after some of Bettie's tuna again.

If anything, it should be Sean's own mother and father who

should feel guilty for what they didn't do. Even after Sean's mother's meltdown a few weeks ago where she confessed that she never wanted children so early anyway, Sean had wanted them to fix their issues.

But they hadn't.

Sean actually didn't mind that too much as bad as it sounded, he loved his Auntie Bettie and it was great to help out around the massive and expensive house as Bettie and her boyfriend Graham, a cop, prepared for the arrival of their twins.

The only problem with Harry being so tired after coming back from brain therapy was that it just meant he slept alone. Sean wasn't exactly a massive fan of that, because it meant him and Harry didn't have too much time for talking, making love and catching up on their days.

Yet considering that the first six months of brain therapy was the most important in making sure that Harry made a complete recovery, it was always far better to sacrifice these months with him now, than possibly lose him forever. Not that it really mattered anyway, considering Sean would love Harry no less.

"House is empty mate," someone said.

Sean froze and just focused on the thin line that was Harry under the sheets. Someone was clearly in the house, they were probably in the kitchen and making their way towards him.

Sean couldn't have them in here, what if they were going to beat him again? What if these people would finish the job of killing him and Harry? What if…

One… two… three…

Sean forced himself to take slow breaths until he counted to ten and he needed to focus. Bettie and Graham wouldn't be back for hours yet because they were in London at some big fundraising event for a charity. It was just Sean and Harry here for a while, and Sean couldn't risk waking Harry because he had another day of therapy tomorrow so he couldn't be tired for that.

Sean was alone, he had to protect his soulmate and he wasn't going to let some criminal idiots dare defile his Auntie's house.

Sean took out his smartphone and quickly texted Bettie that people were in the house. The smart thing might have been to call the police, but considering it was two police cops that had beaten him and caused Harry's brain damage. That was a last resort.

"Mate look at these pictures. That woman might be old but she's banging. Wanna wait for her to come home," someone said.

Sean's hands formed fists. How dare they talk about his auntie like that.

Sean forced his gaze away from Harry and turned to focus on the very long bright wooden hallway with the long wooden staircase with an iron railing down at the end. There was nothing in the other rooms that shot off from the hallway that would help him.

The only thing that could help Sean now was to confront the criminals and get them to leave.

Sean carefully tipped-toed down the hallway, making sure to focus on the top of the staircase in case one of the criminals was coming up. He couldn't get caught just yet.

He couldn't entirely understand how the criminals had gotten in, granted he had left the kitchen window open because it was too hot and he had cooked himself a chicken curry, so he hated to get rid of the smell.

But surely two criminals couldn't climb in through a window?

Sean reached the top of the staircase and normally its smooth wooden features looked so stylish, calm and great. But today Sean wasn't pleased with them, they made the house look too luxurious and like the perfect target for criminals.

Sean slowly started to go down the stairs. All he needed to do was reach the bottom of the stairs and look round the right-hand corner into the living room to see what was going on.

"Mate what you wanna do if there's someone here. We got a lot of stuff to search and steal," someone said.

Now he was closer, Sean knew that the *mate* speaker (the only one he had heard so far) was definitely a young male.

"We make sure they don't tell on others. Boss wants us to make sure this bitch knows not to mess with us," a slightly older female voice said.

Sean's heart started to pound. What if they were killers? What if they were dirty cops? What if they were going to beat him so badly he was brain damaged too?

Sean's world started to spin. This couldn't be happening again. He couldn't survive another piece of trauma. Not now, not ever.

These people were going to finish him off.

Sean felt the entire house move around him like it was going to smash down on him. Killing him.

One... two... three...

This was absolutely ridiculous and Sean was going to end this now. He was not having some idiots scare his Auntie, rob her house and endanger the man he loved.

That wasn't happening.

"Well, well, well," a young woman said from the bottom of the stairs.

Damn it. This is why he hated himself and his anxiety and those stupid cops. That had made him into this incapable idiot that was useless when he was alone, and not next to his amazing Auntie.

But Sean wasn't stupid.

He didn't speak, he only focused on the young woman in front of him and most importantly how to overpower her, all whilst keeping a good few metres from her and the small pocket knife she was carrying.

She definitely wasn't the prettiest of young women with her deadly black eyes and horribly dirty blue jeans and t-shirt. She didn't look happy to be here but Sean had seen the coldness in her eyes plenty of times before.

She hated him. And he hated her.

"Get up," the young woman said.

Sean didn't react or move. She wasn't in control here and most people would focus on the small knife at this time but Bettie had made sure to teach Sean why that was always a bad idea. Focus on the person so he knew what she looked like for a description later on.

And the knife wouldn't be the first sign of trouble. It would always be the idiot holding it.

"Get up now," the young woman said.

Sean slowly nodded and he almost liked hearing the sheer amount of annoyance, rage and anger in her voice. Whoever this woman was she never wanted Sean to be here.

Sean went down the stairs and hooked a right into Bettie's beautiful living room, and normally the massive TV hanging on the white walls, the cream-coloured three-seater sofa and two armchairs centred around a brown coffee table were normally so bright and loving and comforting.

But the mere presence of the strangers seemed to make the entire room seem sadder, lonelier with a slight shade of anger. That was properly what Sean was feeling, but he was just determined to get these young idiots out of the house.

"Yo mate?" a young man said from the opposite side of the living room as he came in from the kitchen carrying real silverware.

Sean had to admit the young man was rather hot considering he was wearing tight black jeans, a loose-fitting t-shirt that highlighted how muscular he was behind it and he had longish black hair.

But now Sean had both of the idiot criminals in his sights he just knew that he had to focus and make sure both of them were captured.

"Sit," the young woman said.

Sean smiled. "I'm not a dog. What do you two want?"

Sean was a little disturbed that the young man was just staring in utter confusion at him. It was probably something to do with Sean's blond hair with stylish streaks of pink running through it, but he didn't care what this criminal scum thought of his hair. He was going to have them both suffer.

Sean felt the icy coldness of the point of a blade jab into his shoulder.

"I said sit," the young woman said. "Then I will tell you exactly what we are doing and how you are going to help us,"

Sean highly doubted that but the criminals were willing to talk so he carefully sat down on the sofa making sure to keep both of them in sight.

The young woman sat on the coffee table.

"We are here because our boss wants your auntie to leave her alone," the young woman said.

Sean was impressed that she knew he was her nephew, but given how Bettie wasn't only a private eye but the President of the British Private Investigator Federation, it was only strange that someone hired these two.

It couldn't be related to a case because Bettie had only been doing background checks constantly for the past few weeks because she was due to give birth next month.

Sean seriously doubted it was anything to do with the Federation because Bettie had been so focused on rebuilding it after all the corruption and whatnots of the last president.

"And breaking in will help you how?" Sean asked.

The young woman asked. "Our boss can get anywhere. Our boss

is superior. Our boss-"

"is prob useless little old lady takes advantage of children need love, support respect," Harry said from the doorway.

Sean's heart shot into his throat. He was impressed how much better his speech was coming along. He didn't want him down here. He only wanted Harry to be safe.

The young woman grinned. "Excellent. We have the boyfriend and the nephew. The boss will be so pleased,"

Then it twigged to Sean that they were never going to rob the house. This was actually all about him and Harry and they were probably going to take them hostage or threaten them until Bettie agreed to leave them alone.

Sean admired the stupidity of their boss because he just knew that any threats made against him and Harry would be met with rage, a man hunt and strict retribution.

But Sean admired people's willingness to doom themselves.

Sean stood up. Now that he had some idea of what the two criminals wanted he just needed to break them up and weaken whatever hold the young woman had over the other one.

If he was to act then Sean needed them not to be a team.

"I know you don't respect the boy over there," Sean said pointing to the young man. "You see him as a pointless burden that your boss made you bring along. I think he isn't the brilliant tool in the workshop,"

The young woman nodded. "Of course not. I come from a quality background not some council estate where idiots call each other *mate, bro* and *dude,*"

The young man stomped his foot. He was clearly annoyed.

Sean looked at Harry who was extremely beautiful standing there and they just winked at each other.

Sean's pretended his heart pounded. His breathing quickened. He clutched his chest.

Sean hissed and screamed and panicked.

The young woman looked shocked and panicked herself.

Sean collapsed to the sofa. Pretending to have a panic attack. Harry shouted at them.

The young woman dropped the knife.

She rushed to Sean. Leaning over him.

Sean kicked her.

Punching her in the chest.

She flew to the ground.

Sean leapt up. Jumping on top of her.

Sean pinned her down.

The young man whacked Sean in the head.

The young woman threw Sean off her.

Sean jumped up.

The moment he saw the young woman holding Harry in a headlock with the small knife kissing his neck. Sean stopped.

The young man put Sean in a headlock to (a rather pathetic one but still) and Sean just felt like he was a complete and utter failure.

He had put the love of his life in danger and for what. His own insecurities about the corrupt police that had put him in hospital, his own anxiety and God knows whatever concerns he had that made him feel like he was the only one that could protect himself and that no one else cared about him.

Then the living room got a little brighter. No one else seemed to notice and Sean couldn't understand if the bright tones of the living rooms were actually brighter than before but they just felt like they did.

Sean just knew that something was about to happen and he really needed to distract them.

"Your boss doesn't love you you know. She might have found you on the streets or whatever but she actually hates you," Sean said.

The young woman seemed furious. Sean hated the sound of the young man's breathing in his ear.

"And you," Sean said to the young woman. "If your beginnings were so great then why were you on the street to be found?"

The young woman's hand tensed. She gestured she would kill Harry but Sean knew that would only anger her boss.

"I think you were just a jumped-up child that no one wanted and you wanted to get respect from another person that doesn't even love you," Sean said coldly.

The young woman threw Harry onto the sofa. She stormed over to Sean waving the knife about.

"I am loved. The boss loves me. She treasures me and-"

The front door exploded open.

Sean jumped back.

Smashing the young man into the wall. His head cracked on the wall.

He released Sean.

Sean spun around. Punching the man in the nose.

He collapsed to the ground.

And when Sean looked at where the young woman had been standing, he saw one of the most perfect sights he ever could have wished for, because Graham in his fine black suit was handcuffing the young woman and reading her her rights.

A few moments later after Graham had escorted the young man and woman out of the house, Sean just smiled as a very pregnant Bettie English stumbled through the front door.

Sean had to admit she did look stunningly beautiful in her large black dress that managed to make her massive baby bump seem so stylish and she simply hugged Sean and Harry.

Sean loved the amazing warmth of the hug and he was glad that they had arrived when they did, and more importantly that beautiful Harry was okay.

Then Sean noticed the evil smile on Bettie's face, and Sean looked up at the ceiling and noticed a very small black camera right above his head.

"You knew this would happen," Sean said.

Bettie shrugged as she stumbled over to the armchair.

"Didn't you think it was odd that the kitchen window didn't lock properly?" Bettie asked.

Sean hadn't even noticed.

"That created the perfect opening for them to come in. I knew you two were smart enough to stay safe until we arrived and you got us the proof we needed," Bettie said.

"Proof what?" Harry asked.

"Two days ago I ran a background check for a government role and it highlighted that criminal gangs were trying to get jobs in the UK Government and someone was helping them,"

Sean just nodded. It was just getting too ridiculous with the Government for words.

"So after some investigating," Bettie said, "me and Graham managed to track down the extra help to an orphanage and homeless shelter in London and the owner, a little old lady I should note, had powerful friends in the government,"

Sean nodded. "This woman was doing favours for her friends by getting the vulnerable children she *cared* for to do her dirty work for her all to protect her criminal friends in the government,"

Bettie nodded.

Sean looked at beautiful Harry who was hugging him and Sean was slightly getting more and more concerned about how thin he was getting, but that was all part of the therapy process.

Sean kissed Harry's soft amazing lips quickly and then pointed to the stairs. It was a little gesture they both did when they knew the other needed to go to sleep.

Sean was never going to have Harry tired when he had a brain therapy day tomorrow, he just loved him too much for that.

Sean was about to follow Harry up when Bettie gently took his hand in hers.

"You did well today you know," Bettie said. "Your mum might not say it or be here, but I am proud of you and love you,"

Sean knew his auntie never understood the power of those words to him, but after hiding he was gay for so many years and all the bad mental health associated with it, being attacked by the people who were meant to protect everyone and now his own parents not seeming to care about him.

Those words meant everything to Sean.

Sean kissed Bettie on the head. "You're going to be an amazing mum,"

Bettie only nodded and she was probably holding back the tears (both in joy but also panic that her life was going to change forever in less than a month) and Sean simply went upstairs.

Sean might have done a great thing today that proved to him he was always more than his anxiety, past and the pain of what had happened. But there was always more to work on in the future.

Right now, he had a beautiful boyfriend to help, love and cherish and a wonderful Auntie to help with a pair of twins coming.

That would probably be a lot for most 21-year-olds to take but Sean honestly couldn't think of a better way to spend his time.

Not a single better way at all.

CONNOR WHITELEY

KEY TO BIRTH IN THE PAST

A BETTIE ENGLISH PRIVATE EYE MYSTERY SHORT STORY

KEY TO BIRTH IN THE PAST
15th September 2022
Canterbury, England

Being a Private Eye back in the day was a rather wonderful thing that Bettie English absolutely loved to do. There was nothing in the entire world like chasing down criminals on the cold rocky slopes of valleys in Yorkshire, smelling the sweet scent of water passing through an apple orchard in Kent whilst delivering top-secret information to a secret government base, and Bettie just loved the sweet salty taste of cotton-candy on her tongue as she watched an unfaithful husband at a festival.

But all that was about to change.

Bettie laid on a perfectly comfortable and warm blue hospital bed with some very thin (almost impractically thin) bedsheets pulled over her and the cold white metal of the bed frame rested against the back of her head. She had been a lot lower on the bed before with each contraction she had moved herself higher and higher onto the bed.

After nine amazing months of pregnancy, Bettie was finally going to give birth to her wonderful twins that had actually given her a lot of joy so far, and hopefully that would only continue.

Bettie smiled at her nephew Sean with his blue jeans, white t-shirt and blond hair with stylish pink highlights running through it. He stood perfectly straight as he rested against the sterile white walls of the hospital room, and his boyfriend Harry was sitting on a wooden chair next to him.

Bettie was really pleased to have them both with her because if anything, in recent months both of them had basically became her children. Especially with Sean's parents more or less kicking him and Harry out after they were attacked and Harry had sustained a brain injury.

Bettie wasn't sure if she was ever going to be able to forgive her sister for that, but truth be told with the twins coming, Bettie was just glad for the support.

"Don't break my fingers again babe,"

Bettie just laughed as she rested her hands on her baby bump and watched her sexy beautiful boyfriend Detective Graham Adams walk back into the hospital room with three fingers on his left hand fixed up.

It wasn't even like Bettie had meant to scream and react so much during one of the contractions. She had just focused on how the twins were acting inside her, it was only when Graham started screaming that she realised she had managed to break three of his fingers.

A very eventful start to the evening.

"Sorry I'm late everyone," Bettie's sister Phryne said as she strolled in wearing a very wet raincoat and carrying four to-go coffee mugs.

Bettie loved the delightful smell of the rich bitter coffee that filled the entire room and she was more than looking forward to the kids coming out, just so she could have a cup of coffee again.

"Auntie," Sean said, ignoring his mother. Harry just hugged Sean tighter. "I've never asked how you two met?"

Graham just laughed, and Bettie just smiled. Their love story was one of... an interesting start that definitely had a long road to this moment, but it was sort of beautiful in a way.

Bettie hardly had anything better to do with the doctors saying it was at least another 30 minutes before the babies were due. So she might as well tell her family the in-detail version of how they met.

Bettie just looked at Graham. "I'll start?"

Graham gingerly held her hand and kissed it. "Be my guest,"

Bettie couldn't believe how excited she felt about telling her family the crazy, criminal and spectacular story about how she met the love of her life.

***

12th October 2010

Hertfordshire, England

23-year-old Bettie English had only been out of university for six months after doing an absolutely awful and god-awful accounting degree. She had no idea whatsoever why she allowed that mother of hers to get her to do an accounting degree. It was rather easy in a way but Bettie hated the numbers and how the companies basically made you a corporate slave.

She wasn't a slave to anything.

Thankfully it wasn't long until she discovered the British Private Eye Federation and it did sound pretty cool being a private eye, so she went for it. Completed a bunch of impossible training and somewhat managed to get accepted.

Even now Bettie was surprised at how impossible the training was but that was why the Federation was so respected, loved and adored by the investigative community all over the world. It was so hard to get membership only the best made it.

Bettie stood outside a massive clay-red brick wall right outside an immense country estate that was just so typical of Hertfordshire in the midlands of England.

Bettie had always loved the countryside but this was a little too far for her. She was literally standing on a cobblestone road that was supposed to add an extra layer of poshness to the estate but it really didn't.

But that was about as fancy as it got, Bettie was hardly pleased with the miles upon miles of flat open fields with luscious green grass that blew so elegantly in the cool gentle wind.

When Bettie was a kid she might have liked this but she had a job to do now.

As a newly qualified Private Eye, Bettie had to complete hundreds of background checks to serve as a little probation and it was only because her checks were done quickly and effectively, and that the Federation had decided to test her with her first case.

She needed to Serve Papers to a wealthy businessman because he had apparently been involved in manipulating the financial markets, causing tons of businesses and people to lose their savings and he had ruined a lot of lives.

Easy?

Bettie was definitely going to make sure on future cases that she actually researched the places she was going to first of all. Because this place was impossible to get into and she had tried to ring the doorbell on the massive black wooden gates.

They rejected to see her.

But Bettie needed this job more than anything else in the entire world right now because if she failed, she would never be accepted into the Federation fully, she would never be respected and she would be doomed to be a poor private eye for the rest of her life.

Her professional career depended on this.

Even though Bettie couldn't see the estate because the brick walls with barred-wires on top were so tall. She just couldn't understand why someone would want to go to this extremes to protect themselves, and this house was in the middle of nowhere.

Bettie went straight over to the brick wall and ran her fingers across the cold surface. She had hoped to be able to climb it but the surface was far too smooth for her.

The sound of a car driving up slowly made Bettie roll her eyes. The last thing she needed was to get caught or something.

"Excuse me Miss," someone said.

Bettie slowly turned to look at the awfully beaten-up black car that had stopped a few metres from her and there was an elderly woman looking at her.

She didn't look good enough to have the rich and wealth of the person she was looking for, but maybe she could be useful.

"Who are you?" the elderly woman asked.

"A tourist passing through but I'm a little-" Bettie said.

"Really?" the elderly woman asked. "I think you wanna serve the master his court papers,"

Bettie was definitely going to need to become a better liar. She had so much to learn about being a private eye that it was infuriating and exciting.

"I'm sorry about lying," Bettie said, this woman seemed to be nice enough so she wanted to play it nicely.

"I'm the Master's chief of staff, Layla Winston and please leave," she said.

Bettie forced herself not to react, all she wanted to do was serve the court papers so the Federation would properly respect her. She needed this job more than anything.

Then Layla simply drove off again. No doubt she was going to tell her Master so that was just annoying.

Bettie started following Layla's car down the cobblestone road and within a few moments she watched two strong muscular men standing outside the large black wooden gates to the estate as Layla drove inside.

The two men glared at her.

Damn it. The two men hadn't been there before, this was quickly getting worse and worse.

Bettie was going to fail and she was never ever going to be able to get respect and get all the good jobs as a private eye.

She was doomed.

***

12th October 2010

Hertfordshire, England

Detective Graham Adams had never ever liked private eyes. They were the worst type of scum in the entire world because they were clueless, annoying and they were just so useless.

So when Graham had gotten the call about some woman private eye lurking around his target's estate, it just annoyed him. Why couldn't these useless private eyes just stay away and let the real police sort out the crimes.

Graham drove down the little cobblestone road that was definitely far too narrow for his large black land rover with large oak trees lining the road. Their strangely shaped leaves falling in the autumn breeze and dirtying up his windshield.

The only benefit about driving in the autumn was that Hertfordshire had a wonderful crispness to the air along with subtle hints of pine, oak and a freshness from something that Graham couldn't identify.

It didn't take long for Graham to see the massively tall brick walls of the estate, and this was why he had travelled up from Kent Police to help the National Taskforce take down this particular businessman.

Whilst the newspapers and other media reports had only cared to focus on Mr Albert Natt's financial manipulations, Graham knew that he was guilty of a lot more. Albert had also had a hand in three murders, the collapse of two major banks and had links to funding communist terror attacks all over the world.

All Graham had wanted to do was drive into the estate and arrest Albert there and then, but because of the stupid law no one could simply charge into the estate and no one could give him the legal papers.

Apparently the police and Crown Prosecution Service had tried hundreds of different ways. From delivering the papers to lawyers to Albert's family to delivering them through the post. But each time Albert's lawyers simply claimed the papers were never delivered.

It was impossible.

And there was even talk about the Crown Prosecution Service reaching out to the so-called British Private Eye Federation. It was a completely stupid organisation made up of wannabe cops that were just as clueless as the people he arrested most days.

He just hoped this stupid woman wasn't part of that awful hobbyist club, but he just knew she was.

A few seconds later, Graham slowed down his car to a stop and looked at the tall woman in her black trench coat, high heels and long black hair just stare at him as she stood in front of the black gates.

Graham took out his badge and waved her over.

The woman hardly seemed impressed but that had just confirmed his beliefs about private eyes. They were all so cocky, ignorant and awful people that had no respect for the law.

But as the woman walked over to Graham's car, he was just flat out stunned at how beautiful and sexy she was. Graham loved her amazingly soft, sexy lifeful hair that all Graham wanted to do was run his fingers through it.

Even her face looked so soft, beautiful and stunning. She looked like she needed to be on the cover of Vogue or something and not in the woods pretending to be a private eye, she was so beautiful.

And there was just something in the confidence and the way that she walked, it was like she knew exactly where she was going. She looked like she owned the entire land and Graham almost felt like he was the trespasser.

She was stunning.

Instead of the woman walking over to his side and standing outside Graham's car window, the woman had the arrogance to simply walk round the other side of the land rover and board his car.

How dare she.

Graham had to admit as she sat in the passenger seat, she looked even more stunning up close and Graham seriously loved the delightful hints of grapefruit, lemon and oranges that radiated off her.

"Bettie English Private Eye at your service detective," the hot woman said.

Graham had no idea how she had guessed he was a detective, his badge only said he was a cop, but it was just his luck. The only woman he had found attractive was a private eye, the worst sort of people.

"I presume you want to know why I'm here," Bettie said, not as a question.

Graham shrugged. "I know you're here on a little pretend mission. Leave the police work to the cops or I will arrest you no matter how beautiful you are,"

The moment those last words left his mouth he felt like such an idiot. He might have had been about the same age as this Bettie woman and rapidly rose through the ranks to Detective but he was always professional, calm and collective around criminals.

But why was he being so unprofessional in front of her?

"You aren't so bad yourself detective," Bettie said.

Graham just grinned and forced himself to look away. He couldn't focus on that sexy woman and think straight.

"You need to leave and personally just give up on the Private Eye stuff. It won't get you anywhere in life and you're just making a fool of yourself," Graham said.

He had never heard a woman go deadly silent before and he looked back over at her, and he wasn't sure as he stared into her narrow, cold brown eyes and furious looking face if he should have been scared or what.

After a few moments Bettie laughed and popped open the land rover door.

"Tell me detective if you weren't such a jackass you cops might have delivered the court papers instead of having a *bum* like me to do it," Bettie said.

Graham was about to say something when Bettie slammed the door and stomped back down the cobblestone.

As much as Graham wanted to leave she was trying to do a good thing and if she was successful then she would help him too.

He just had no idea how to help someone like a private eye.

The very worst sort of people.

***

15th September 2022

Canterbury, England

"Wait you hated private eyes?" Sean asked Graham.

Bettie couldn't believe actually hearing how much her boyfriend hated her at first. It was one thing to experience it and know of it throughout the other times they had met before they started dating the first time, but to hear it.

It was something else.

Bettie hissed in pain as another contraction pulsed and corkscrewed through her, and she was really looking forward to these twins coming out. And she was more than excited about getting off this hospital bed with the stupidly thin blue bed sheets and getting home to a real bed.

"Yea not my best moment," Graham said, blowing Bettie a kiss.

Bettie smiled and shook her head. She did love this man and he had actually proved to be a very capable helper over the years, something she had no doubt would have horrified the 2010-Graham.

And that was a funny idea all by itself.

"Let's continue," Bettie said.

***

12th October 2010

Hertfordshire, England

Bettie flat out hated stupid cops. She had heard about their stupidity on her private eye training but to actually see it and experience it in real life was beyond pathetic.

She hated cops and she was definitely never ever going to date one. They were just too stupid for words.

Bettie stood directly in front of the large black wooden gates and this was the only way into the estate house, and the two men acting as guards stared intently at her. Like she was actually a danger.

Bettie stared at them back, trying not to show them that her stomach was tightening into a painful knot and she didn't actually know what to do. Her entire professional career depended on getting inside and she was failing.

She had never been a violent person but Bettie was starting to wonder whether it might be worth attacking these two people and just breaking inside.

Bettie looked back over at the land rover that was still parked there with that cute(ish) cop with that amazing body, handsome face and stunning eyes she just wanted to stare into all day.

She waved him over.

Bettie went over to the two guards. "Let me in,"

The two guards laughed at her.

"What's going on?" Graham asked, he had clearly run over judging by the panting.

Bettie pretended to look all upset and almost threw herself on Graham for sympathy. At least her childhood acting lessons weren't going to waste.

"These horrible men won't let me in. These men were abusing me and I just want to see my father,"

Bettie almost laughed at last the comment but she didn't dare. She was hoping not to fool Graham but at least make the guards a bit more likely to let them in.

"You're Victoria Natt?" the guards asked.

Bettie stood up perfectly straight. "Of course I am and this is my friend. He's a wealthy investor,".

Bettie loved how hard Graham was trying not to look scared. It probably went against every single rule in the cop playbook, but she wasn't a cop. She was a private eye and a good one at that.

The guards looked Graham up and down, and one of them took out a walkie-talkie from his back pocket.

"Master, your daughter has bought an investor with her," he said into it.

"She isn't my daughter but the man looks rich. Just bring them both inside and he'll deal with them," a man replied through the talkie.

Bettie had to agree with Graham's concerned look that she just felt like she had dug them into a massive whole that she wasn't sure how to get out of.

She just hoped that she wasn't going to put an innocent man in harm's way.

Graham was far too cute for that.

***

12th October 2010

Hertfordshire, England

Graham was seriously impressed at this amazingly sexy woman he was walking next to. She was smart as a whip, smelt amazing and maybe not all private eyes were as silly as each other.

"Wait here for a moment," the guards said as one before they left.

But he was not impressed in the slightest that Bettie had gotten the two guards to lead them into a large spacious room with shiny brown walls with fine art, stuffed animals and other typical spoils of the rich hanging so proudly on the walls like those were the items that his judges would judge him on.

Graham just knew that Albert was that deluded. Albert would only ever be judged on his crimes, not his power and influence.

The only other items of note, not that Graham was brave enough to look into them, was an oversized brown desk with small piles of legal documents on top and a ritualistic dagger rested in the very centre of the desk.

Graham couldn't believe how much he hated this room considering it could only be described as the pinnacle of selfish richness.

"Here," Bettie said as she started to look at the legal documents.

Graham hated how private eyes just helped themselves. As a cop he couldn't just look at whatever he pleased and take it into evidence.

These private eyes were dangerous laws onto themselves.

"Stop that," Graham said going on to her.

Bettie pointed to a small pile of documents closest to Graham. It was probably a gesture telling him to start looking, but he couldn't. It was against the rules.

"If you don't start looking you might lose something for your investigation," Bettie said.

Graham loved how mischievous she was.

"How do you know I was investigating Albert?" Graham asked.

Bettie shrugged. "Everyone wants to nail Albert and you wouldn't have helped me if you weren't,"

Damn it. She was right. He had only met her less than an hour and she was already making him do things and bend rules for her, something he never would have done for anyone else before.

She was just too beautiful to say no to.

Graham started to look through the small pile of documents next to him and quickly realised that these were flight documents. They were dated for today travelling to countries that didn't have an extradition treaty with the UK.

Albert was going on the run. And he never would have known that without this beautiful woman.

Someone reached over Graham and picked up the ritualistic knife.

Graham spun around and instinctively stepped in front of Bettie when he saw a large elderly man in a posh suit was pointing the knife straight at his chest.

He wasn't going to let Albert hurt Bettie.

"You two are causing me a lot of trouble," Albert said. "Two of my drivers have already cancelled me and now I'm having to be smuggled by my mere cleaner to get to the airport,"

Graham was glad he was suffering a little, it was nothing compared to the thousands of people that were suffering because of him, but every bit of suffering helped.

Albert gestured them to move away from the desk with a few shakes of the knife. Graham complied, Bettie did not.

He loved how defiant she was but this wasn't the time.

Bettie simply folded her arms. "You are many things Albert Natt but you are not a killer, and why let us in?"

Albert laughed. "I needed to get you two troublemakers out of my hair and I want to offer you both a million pounds to leave me alone,"

Graham would have loved that sort of money, he would be able to help out his family, donate to charities and actually make a difference in the world. But he was a cop first and foremost and Bettie didn't even react.

She took a step closer to Albert. Graham did the same.

"You really think you can bride us," Bettie said.

Albert pointed the knife at her and Graham felt his stomach tense. He took another few steps closer. He had to be ready.

Bettie took out the court papers and offered them to him.

Albert just laughed. Hard.

Bettie lunched forward.

Graham rushed over.

Bettie tackled Albert to the ground.

She was going to arrest him.

Graham went to help.

Albert slapped Bettie. She fell off him.

Albert kicked Graham in the stomach.

Graham staggered back.

The two men serving as guards walked in and went towards Bettie and Graham wrapping their arms around them so they couldn't escape.

This was not what Graham needed. Especially as Graham had the most smelliest guard he had ever had.

"You're such an idiot," Graham said to Bettie, hoping to annoy someone enough that the guards' grip would weaken.

Bettie laughed. "Yea like you could do anything better you pig,"

"Typical private eye always name-calling because you're too pathetic yourself,"

"Fuck you cop. I wouldn't be here if you weren't so useless,"

Graham saw how amused and distracted the guards and Albert were.

He stomped his foot down. Bettie did the same.

The guards expected it.

They punched Graham and Bettie in the face.

They both collapsed to the ground.

Pain radiated from Graham's nose, heating up his face, this was going from worst to worst. He never should have gotten involved in stupid private eye business.

"Master," an elderly woman who was presumably the one smuggling Albert to the airport.

"One moment Layla," Albert said as he waved the guards to go and Layla just stood there behind Albert.

Albert walked over to Graham. The point of the ritualistic knife pressed against his throat. Graham didn't even react.

"All I tried to do was make myself rich. Know I destroyed a lot of lives, funded a lot of terror but that only allowed me to make more money, so your efforts to arrest me are pointless. The moment I leave this country I will be free," Albert said.

Bettie laughed hard. "Pathetic really. You claim to be powerful but if you were really you have enough money and power to buy your safety here,"

Graham didn't want to tell her that was exactly what he had been doing for the past year, but those friends within the UK Government had turned against him.

"Good bye detective," Albert said.

Graham grabbed the knife.

Albert kicked Graham in the balls. Pain shot through his body.

Albert grabbed him by the throat.

He prepared to kill Graham.

A foot smashed into Albert's head.

He fell to the ground not moving.

Graham felt Bettie hug him and help him get up. He wanted to hug Bettie back but he pulled her off him and simply looked down at Albert.

It was clear that Bettie had kicked him in the head and judging by the sheer amount of blood pumping out of it, almost like Bettie had popped a blood filled balloon, Albert was most certainly dead.

Graham just folded his arms.

This was going to be a hell of a lot of paperwork.

***

12th October 2010

Hertfordshire, England

A few hours later, Bettie had absolutely no idea if that hot sexy detective had noticed she was still here actually sitting in his very uncomfortable black Land Rover instead of going home. But she was pleased to be here, as much as she acted like she found his car comfortable, she was so lying.

And she was more than pleased as she watched the oak leaves fall off the trees lining the cobblestone road in the autumn breeze, that was still here.

All she wanted to do was talk to that hot sexy detective a final time, maybe thank him and maybe ask him to dinner.

Bettie had to admit he was a real cock about his attitudes towards so-called stupid private eyes, but she could see that he was a good man trying to enforce law and order into a wonderfully chaotic world.

The driver's door opened and Graham just huffed when he saw her.

"Do you have any idea how much paperwork you have caused me?" he asked.

Bettie shrugged. That was definitely another great benefit about being a private eye, and not a real cop, she didn't have to do even half the amount of paperwork. She could just solve cases, have fun and keep the world safe without as many forms.

"But thanks," Graham said. "I know you didn't have to save my life. Thank you,"

That was probably one of the stupid things Bettie had ever heard. Of course she had to save his life, he was a good man, an innocent and it was just normal to save people. She wouldn't let a hot man die for love or money.

"Do I need to travel back to Kent with you for a statement?" Bettie asked smiling.

Graham threw his arms up in the air. "You searched me or something?"

"Of course," Bettie said. "There is only so many background checks a woman can do in a Land Rover with bad internet whilst she waits for you to come out,"

Graham just laughed and it was such a cute laugh.

"No you can go and I'm sure I'll see you around," Graham said, extending his hand.

Bettie took his soft warm hand in hers and kissed it. Graham looked excited but in case she never did see this wonderful man, she just wanted one kiss to remember him by.

Bettie got out of the Land Rover but before she shut the door, she just smiled at him.

"I hope to see a lot of you about detective," Bettie said.

"Feeling's not mutual," Graham muttered.

Bettie just laughed and really looked forward to seeing this hottie again.

**

15th September 2022
Canterbury, England

"And then she stalked me down in Kent, ran into each other two more times and then we started dating the first time," Graham said.

Bettie just smiled at the beautiful love of her life as he gingerly held her hand in fear of her breaking any more fingers.

Thankfully the hospital bed sheets were wonderfully toasty and warm now that she had been lying here for so long, and as another contraction corkscrewed through her, she just knew that the babies were coming soon.

But the bright lights of the hospital room against the bright white sterile walls were becoming blinding now, and Bettie was seriously looking forward to going home with her new additions to her family and starting her journey as a mother.

That was scary but going to be amazing.

Pure excitement, joy and relief filled her as she stared at her beautiful family round her. Her wonderful nephew and his boyfriend who had loved and supported her through so much, her sister that could be a piece of work but she was amazing in her own way, and the amazing man that had put up with her being a stupid private eye for so long.

She loved them all.

A sharp jab of pain pulsed through her body and then Bettie just realised. The twins were coming out.

"Graham," Bettie said, through sharp pain. "Be a dear and get the midwife. It's showtime,"

***

15th September 2022
Canterbury, England

A few hours later, Bettie felt completely exhausted as she laid on the hospital bed with the thin blue sheets tightly wrapped around her lower half and she just held the two most amazing babies she had ever seen.

Sean, Harry and Phryne had all left shortly after the birth with Sean and Harry confirming they were definitely gay and never wanted to see a birth again. And Bettie had kicked Phryne out when she commented about Bettie's extreme screaming.

Bettie felt Graham's handsome face resting on her shoulder as they both just looked at the two cutest babies they had made together nine months ago.

The entire room smelt pleasantly of lemons, apples and oranges from an organic solution that the midwife had washed the room down with, and Bettie was just glad to have another smell in the room and it was so amazing to hear the light subtle breathing of her two twins.

At least Bettie's largest fear had been unfounded about the babies being identical, she had always known that they would have a boy and a girl, but she was still scared.

Bettie kissed both the cuties on their little warm heads and both of them smiled at the gesture. They still hadn't been cleaned yet because it was the rules that the babies had to have skin contact with their mothers for at least two hours before anything else was allowed to happen.

And Bettie loved that rule.

"We really have come a long way," Graham said.

Bettie just smiled. "Yep. But a stupid private eye and a idiot cop. We've had some great fights, great cases and great loves,"

Graham kissed her and Bettie loved the feeling of his lips on her.

And then they both went back to looking at their delightful twins in her arms. They really had come so far with each other, now their lives had truly changed forever and there was no going back now.

Bettie knew the next chapter of their lives wouldn't be easy, plain-sailing or completely joyous. There would be challenges. But in Bettie's experience that was exactly the same for all worthwhile things in life.

Bettie had never needed easy, she had only ever needed possible.

And she was really, really looking forward to being a mother and hoping beyond hope that she was going to be an amazing one with her sexy Graham by her side and her sensational family firmly behind her.

And that thought just delighted Bettie more than she ever wanted to admit.

AUTHOR OF THE ENGLISH BETTIE PRIVATE EYE SERIES

CONNOR WHITELEY

FINDING A ROYAL FRIEND

A BETTIE PRIVATE EYE MYSTERY SHORT STORY

FINDING A ROYAL FRIEND
12:00 pm
8th September 2022
Canterbury, England

Private Eye Bettie English had always liked the royal family in general, and when she had met the Queen a couple of times during her Private Eye work, Bettie had loved their kindness, charm and style even more, even though Bettie purposefully said she was never ever a royalist in the strictest of terms. But she did love them anyway.

Bettie sat at her dark oak desk in her bright white office playing some calming classical music (definitely not her first choice of music) as Bettie was in her large office above the cobblestone high street of Canterbury. Bettie had always loved her office's dark brown wooden walls, cream ceiling and her personal favourite was the mini-bar area tucked away in one corner.

Bettie had always loved working and living and breathing in Canterbury high street, because she really liked the wonderful sounds of students walking past, talking and shouting about how great their day had been.

All the little bakeries and cafes and restaurants leaked their sensational smells into the air, and even though Bettie had been a vegan since her pregnancy because animal products made her vomit. She still loved the sensational aromas of freshly baked bread, rich juicy pork and the sweetest creamiest cakes she had ever smelt.

Living in Canterbury was amazing.

The mini-bar really helped to make the office feel more luxurious, posh and expensive, all with the added bonus that it really helped to impress brand-new clients whenever they walked in. Bettie might have been a millionaire because of her private eye work, but she preferred to show her skill and wealth in a lot more subtle ways.

The mini-bar was one of them.

Granted the mini-bar was becoming a bit of a pain recently, especially with Bettie being so pregnant and she really, really looking forward to finally giving birth in the next few weeks, but she was such a workaholic that she didn't want to take "real" maternity leave from her Private Eye work so instead she was just working in her office on a bunch of background checks from various government sources and earning a very nice amount of money whilst she waited to give birth.

And Bettie knew that lots of brand-new private eyes hated background checks and believed all the myths about private eyes working grand cases, but that wasn't true in the slightest. The only reason why she had worked a lot in the past was because she had earned herself a reputation for being amazing at her job. And those high-stake cases always tended to find her anyway.

As Bettie was also the president of the British private Eye Federation, after she had been voted in as the new president after all the chaos and stupidity of the last one, David Osborne, she was slowly making changes, giving good people certain roles and making sure that the Federation could survive without her for a few months.

Something she was still a little unsure about.

Especially as because of Bettie banning all the far-left and far-right members of the organisation, she had lost millions of pounds worth of membership fees, sponsors and other political donations from dodgy foreign powers that Bettie had had absolutely no idea invested so much in the Federation for nefarious reasons.

It had only been in the past month that Bettie had realised how fanatically corrupt her beloved Federation and fellow private eyes had been. Something she was desperate to fix but it was her fixing that had meant the Federation was twenty million pounds out of pocket and that number was only growing.

Bettie's computer buzzed a little and Bettie didn't know in the slightest who would be wanting to video chat with her.

Bettie answered it.

She instantly smiled when she saw it was Agent Daniels of MI5, a great, amazing, wonderful man that Bettie and her boyfriend had had the great pleasure of working with a few months back. Bettie had to admit he looked great in his tight well-fitting black suit that framed his face amazingly and he just looked perfect.

That was instantly how Bettie knew something was wrong.

"Agent Daniels," Bettie said, "what do I owe this unexpected pleasure?"

Daniels pretended to smile but Bettie could see that something was paining him.

"What's wrong and I'll put the Federation on it?" Bettie asked.

Daniels shook his head. "In thirty minutes Buckingham Palace will put out a statement saying the Queen in under medication supervision to start preparing the nation for..."

Bettie hated seeing Daniels so choked up and concerned and she instantly knew what was going on.

The Queen was dying.

That realisation slammed into Bettie like a ton of bricks, she had never been a royalist but the Queen was amazing, kind and such a great woman that Bettie couldn't imagine her not being around anymore, but why was Daniels calling her?

"I'm sorry to hear that," Bettie said.

Daniels slowly nodded. "And the Queen has requested something but she knows she cannot ask MI5 or 6 or any government-run security service,"

Bettie leant forward, that was interesting to say the least. Bettie knew that if it was revealed that the Queen had asked the security services, that were funded by taxpayers, to do a personal errand then it risked inflaming and growing the UK's thankfully small republican movement.

Something Bettie really didn't want.

"Miss English," Daniels said, very formally. "The Queen has asked you to find an old friend of hers. She wants to see one of her oldest friends again before she dies,"

Bettie couldn't speak, even the realisation that the Queen was dying made a lump form in her throat.

"We know you're very pregnant and we wouldn't be asking this unless it was critical," Daniels said. "But in 1952 when the newly married Princess was living in Malta and her father had just died,"

Bettie got out a pen and paper from her top desk draw and started making notes.

"The Princess was mugged and attacked by some anti-monarchy English people on holiday in Malta," Daniels said. "The Princess was alone at the time so she didn't have any help but a little girl, aged 13, did intervene and effectively saved the princess from the English,"

Bettie nodded that was great news.

"When the Princess became Queen the incident was sealed and because of all the new responsibilities, political pressures and more, the Princess and the little girl lost touch. The Queen wants you to find her old friend again if you can," Daniels said.

Bettie just smiled because it was an impossible request and ask, she was extremely pregnant due to give birth any day now, but she so badly wanted to help the Queen so she was going to have to call in all the help she could get.

Then Bettie realised there had to be another reason why Daniels had called her just as her email pinged.

Bettie opened the email from Daniels and it contained all the information she needed to find the little girl, who was now called Sarah Attard, and she had moved to the UK in the late 90s and she was retired now and living somewhere in Rochester, England.

Now Bettie understood why Daniels had called her because Sarah was close enough and thankfully there was an address attached, but Bettie instantly recognised it as the address of a house that burnt down two weeks ago.

The only reason why Bettie knew about it was because her and her boyfriend Graham, a cop, had been in Rochester going out for dinner when the fire happened.

"I'll do my best," Bettie said. "What happens when I find her?"

Daniels smiled and it was great to see him so relieved. "Call me and I'll authorise a helicopter to pick you and Sarah up and we'll fly you to Balmoral to see the Queen,"

Bettie couldn't help my smile that was going to be amazing.

"But Bettie," Daniels said, "the Queen is dying and we really don't know how much longer she has. Time is critical here and it is not on our side,"

Another lump formed in Bettie's throat and she simply nodded ending the video chat.

Bettie took out her phone and made some calls. If she was going to get this done then she really needed help.

And with Graham working on anti-drug operations all week and her sister being next to useless in these sort of situations there was only one person who Bettie could call.

Bettie needed to talk to her nephew. Now.

***

12:40 pm

8th September 2022

Rochester, England

Bettie carefully got out of her nephew's little black car being ever so careful not to knock herself and her very large baby bump at all, Bettie had checked constantly on social media and news sites since the news broke about the Queen and the nation was truly devastated.

Thankfully no one had dared to imagine this was it for the Queen, Bettie felt so guilty and almost burdened by the knowledge but she just had to crack on and find Sarah Attard.

Sean had parked on a slightly sloped road on the edges of the historic city of Rochester with the remains of the flint roman wall close by, the noisy cobblestone high street with all of its Victorian buildings standing proudly, and the massive castle and cathedral being visible over the tops of houses in front of Bettie.

The road they were on wasn't the best that Bettie had ever seen with its massive potholes, little terrace houses with dirty windows and overgrown front gardens.

But Bettie was a lot more interested in the large burnt out remains of a house a little further up the road, that even now still made the air smell of charred wood, destruction and smouldering wreckage.

Of course because the fire had been two weeks ago, Bettie just knew that she was imagining the smell for the most part, but she still hated seeing burnt-down houses.

"Auntie," Sean said, wearing tight blue jeans, a loose grey t-shirt and his very tasteful and great-looking pink highlights in his longish blond hair were starting to grow out ever so slightly, which was a shame because they really did suit him.

Bettie gestured to the house up ahead and she went as quick as she could over to the burnt-out husk of the house, which wasn't easy considering how pregnant she was.

Bettie was really glad that was Sean was here though, him and his boyfriend Harry had been amazing help on other cases, and it was very useful that he could drive now, so she could use him as a family taxi service. And considering him and his boyfriend were living with Bettie and Graham whilst Harry recovered from a brain injury it was the least they could do.

And thankfully Sean was only too happy to help.

"What are you we looking for?" Sean asked.

Bettie wasn't sure exactly as she stared at the exploded-out windows, blackened bricks and Bettie just knew that the inside was completely destroyed. She couldn't even imagine the pain of knowing that all of a person's processions were destroyed in an instant.

"This is the only address Daniels had on Sarah so I'm hoping we'll manage to find some trace of her and where she went," Bettie said.

Sean nodded and as he went over to knock on the door of the house to Bettie's right, she was just horrified that a person's entire life could be destroyed so quickly and easily by something as simple as fire.

But Bettie had a job to do.

Bettie went over to Sarah's next neighbourhood to her left, which was a very attractive little house with dirty windows, and a messy garden but the front door was bright yellow with little flowers painted on by hand very well.

Bettie knocked on the front door and moments later a little old lady opened the door wearing a little dirty jumper, black trousers and glasses that made the woman definitely look her age.

Bettie almost wanted to gag at the woman's body odour it was so discussing and Bettie had never smelt anything of bad.

"Hi dear," the woman said.

"Hello," Bettie said showing the woman her Private Eye ID, something she had made all Private Eyes have to have under UK law to prove that they were licensed by the Federation.

"Are you looking for Sarah?" the woman asked.

Bettie slowly nodded. It was strange she would just know that.

"Relax dear," the woman said, "two other elderly men came round yesterday looking for her. You look kinder than them though and much more successful than those low lives,"

Bettie bit her lip she really didn't like the sound of that because now she was just worried about why other people were looking for Sarah.

The time seemed too strange.

"What did you tell them?" Bettie asked.

The woman shrugged. "Just that Sarah was a great neighbour to me and we played blackjack and watched quiz programmes together every Monday, Tuesday and Friday and it broke my heart when she had to move after the fire,"

Bettie smiled, Sarah really did sound like a great neighbour and friend.

"But where did she move to?" Bettie asked.

The woman looked down at the floor. "Um… she said she had a son in Dover that she was moving in with and I was meant to come down and see her next week. You know to see how she was getting on,"

"And don't come back you gay boy!" an elderly man shouted as Sean ran back to his car and a jar of something smashed on the ground behind him.

"Oh I couldn't recommend anyone see Terrance these days. Terrible racist, homophobia and sexist pig you know," the woman said.

Bettie just shook her head. "I cannot stress this enough but it's very important I get to Sarah before these men do. Can I please have that address?"

Bettie hated seeing the little old lady's face turn pale and she slowly nodded as she stood out her little black flip phone and showed Bettie the address.

It wasn't even in Dover but Sarah's son was in a large seaside town close by.

Bettie hugged the little old lady and thanked her for her time and stormed back to Sean's car.

Bettie didn't know what was going on but she just had to get to Whitstable now before the men hunting Sarah got to her.

Because Bettie just knew that only bad things would happen when the men found her.

And Bettie had to find Sarah and take her to Balmoral. She morally didn't have another choice.

Time was definitely running out now.

***

1:45 pm
8th September 2022
Whitstable, England

Bettie seriously hated the bad traffic and how long all of this was taking, the Queen was dying and Bettie would feel like such an utter failure if she didn't find Sarah in time. Things were getting really bad and Bettie was definitely starting to feel the pressure.

Thankfully Sarah's son lived in an apartment above the restaurant him and his wife owned along the seafront so Sean had parked the car as quickly as he could and Bettie and him were walking as quickly as they could along the seafront.

Bettie had always liked Whitstable seafront with its wide concrete sea wall that formed the pathway for tens upon tens of people to walk on, the very wide range of restaurants serving the freshest of seafood lining one side of the seafront and the stunningly crystal blue sea on the other side.

The air was crisp, salty and so refreshing that Bettie really loved it but they had to find Sarah's son.

"Where's the restaurant?" Sean asked.

"It should be up ahead," Bettie said.

After a few more moments of walking Bettie saw a very large black restaurant with tons of nautical theme decorations on the outside and it was packed. Bettie could smell the freshly fried fish and chips and other wonderful seafood delights from metres away.

Bettie almost wanted to be sick because seafood was another food group that her pregnant body hated to smell, touch or eat, but Bettie just had to manage.

Bettie rolled her eyes at the very short line and supposed it might serve their purpose better if they at least waited in line instead of being rude and forcing their way into the restaurant.

Bettie and Sean waited in line with three young families and an adult couple in front of them. Bettie was going to give the line five minutes to get to them before she forced her way towards the women seating everyone in the restaurant.

"How goes the Federation's money crisis?" Sean asked.

Bettie laughed. She really did love having Sean and Harry living with them because they were some of the best and smartest and most loving people she had ever known but they definitely had a habit of listening to "private" conversations between Bettie and her inner circle in the evenings.

One of the young families were seated.

"Awful," Bettie said. "I'm pouring tons of my millions into the Federation to keep it afloat and I suspect the Federation will be bankrupted by the end of the year because of the stupidity of David,"

Sean hugged her. "You're clever everything will be fine,"

Bettie really hoped he was right.

The other couples and young families got seated because they were part of a massive group and Bettie waved at the young woman who was seating everyone.

Bettie showed the woman her Private Eye ID. "I must speak to Sarah Attard please,"

The young woman gave Bettie a weak smile and waved Bettie to get closer.

"That's impossible Miss English," the woman said. "Last night we had a break-in and this morning when I arrived Mr and Ms Attard were gone and there was a lot of blood on the floor,"

Bettie felt Sean put his hands on her shoulder and rubbed it gently. None of this was good and this was the last thing that Bettie needed.

Sarah and her son were kidnapped and now they had no leads on where they were and each second the Queen was one second closer to death.

Not ideal but Bettie needed to be more demanding and proactive now for Sarah would definitely be joining the Queen in death she feared.

"Show me the apartment now," Bettie said firmly.

The young woman shyly nodded and led Bettie and Sean into the restaurant.

Bettie just hoped Sarah and her son were still alive if the men had taken them.

***

1:50 pm

8th September 2022

Whitstable, England

Bettie was completely shocked as she went into the gutted apartment belonging to Sarah's son with its smashed-up wooden dining table, ripped-up sofas along the back wall with a stunning sea view and even the smart TV had been knocked over but what really caught Bettie's attention were the massive drag marks in dark rich red blood coming towards the door.

"What did the police say?" Bettie asked as her and Sean and the young woman went into the apartment.

The young woman just stood by the door not daring to come into the apartment but Bettie and Sean were used to this sight and crime scenes so they hardly had a problem with it.

Sean went into one of the smaller rooms that shot off the much large living table with the sofa, TV and dining table. Bettie was fairly sure Sean was looking through the kitchen area.

Bettie went over to the smart TV.

"The police said there was nothing they could do," the young woman said. "They tried to find fingerprints and other evidence but they said everything had… washed or something,"

Bettie nodded but if the men were smart enough to wash things down that would get rid of their fingerprints then why not clean up the drag marks in blood.

"Auntie," Sean said from the kitchen. "If Sarah's son runs a seafood restaurant then why is there no fish in his fridge and plenty of EpiPens in draws?"

Bettie just looked at the young woman. That was a great question because surely a chef that loved seafood so much would be creating dishes and experimenting with seafood in his private apartment, and surely he wouldn't be working with shellfish or other seafood if he needed an EpiPen because of allergies.

"Unless the EpiPen belonged to Sarah," Bettie said as she went over to the young woman who was looking at the floor. "And what really happened this morning?"

Sean came out of the kitchen and folded his arms as he stood next to Bettie.

"We know this apartment is off," Bettie said. "Your boss is famous in Whitstable for his love of seafood so why would his shellfish-allergic mother come here? Or tell other people she was?"

Bettie really didn't like this young woman hiding things from her.

"It wasn't meant to go like this," the young woman said. "My boss had called his mum all concerned because some men were looking for her. Sarah had been out when the fire started and the police ruled it an accident but it wasn't,"

Bettie just nodded, that would actually make a lot of sense.

Sean stepped forward. "Then Sarah told your boss and, yourself, where she was really going but made you both promise to say and act like she was here,"

Bettie nodded. "So your boss got rid of his fish and shellfish and Sarah probably sent him a bunch of old EpiPens just so if the restaurant was being watched it would look like he was preparing for the arrival of his mother,"

The young woman nodded.

"But that doesn't explain where's the wife is and what happened to your boss," Bettie said.

The young woman leant across the doorframe and shrugged. "I don't know. I guess that men had come after him and took him and his wife,"

Bettie just looked at Sean. If there was any chance that they were going to get Sarah, her son and his wife back safe and alive then Bettie had to know where Sarah really was.

Sean nodded to Bettie as he hugged the young woman gently.

"Please," Bettie said. "Just tell us where Sarah is. We can help her and her family we just need to know where,"

Sean stepped away from the young woman and Bettie really hoped the young woman trusted them enough.

"She's in Canterbury. There's a small hotel on the outskirts that she went to," the young woman said.

Bettie and Sean rushed out the apartment.

"Thank you!" Bettie shouted as her and Sean raced to find Sarah before the men got to her first.

And probably killed her for some reason.

***

3:20 pm

8th September 2022

Canterbury, England

Bettie wasn't messing about in the slightest as her and Sean walked across the large car park towards a very small bright blue hotel that only had ten rooms with trees lining the car park as the wind lashed and slashed at them.

Bettie and Sean were about to go in through the large glass door when she noticed out of all the five cars parked at the hotel only one was dripping something onto the concrete below.

Bettie focused on the large black SUV that was dripping something and she went over to it. Sean knelt down on the ground and nodded at Bettie.

She just knew that it was blood and as much as she didn't like breaking into cars, if there was an injured person or dead body in the car then she had to know.

"I'll open the car," Sean said.

Bettie nodded and got out her lockpicks that weren't designed for cars but they were just as effective in her experience. And Sean started to pick the car.

Bettie looked around making sure no one was watching. She seriously doubted the security cameras above the glass doors of the hotel actually worked anyway.

A few moments later Sean had the car doors pop open and he unlocked the boot.

Bettie pushed open the boot and gasped as she saw a man and woman laying there with massive gashes to their head and each of them were tightly holding each other and their chests.

Each trying to apply pressure to the stab wounds.

Sean shook his head when he saw them and immediately called for an ambulance.

Bettie pressed each of her hands firmly on the stab wounds of Sarah's son and his wife and they hissed but Bettie was a lot more concerned about Sarah.

"Who did this?" Bettie asked.

Sarah's son fell unconscious and the wife started crying. She wasn't going to get answers from either of them.

"Sean," Bettie said firmly.

He came back over.

"Place your hands over their stab wounds and apply pressure like you did with Harry on the night of the attack," Bettie said.

It might have been harsh to remind him of the attack but Bettie didn't have time and Sean probably understood.

"And don't let go until the ambulance arrives," Bettie said. "And call Daniels,"

He nodded.

Sean took over from Bettie and she kissed him quickly on the cheek and went into the hotel through the large glass doors.

Bettie hated the chemically smell of the small bright white reception area with fake plants everywhere and no one was on duty and the dark blue carpets looked awful in this place.

"Help me!" a woman shouted.

Bettie hid behind a large fake palm tree near the entrance.

"Shut up bitch," a man said.

Bettie saw three large muscular men, clearly English, dragging Sarah who was a small elderly woman towards the door.

Bettie stepped out from her cover and stood firmly in front of the glass doors.

"I cannot let you leave," Bettie said.

The three men laughed at her. And Bettie really focused on their awful artic white beards, fragile frames and then it all made sense to

Bettie.

"You're the men who attacked the Queen in 1952," Bettie said.

Bettie was shocked but it made perfect sense. The men were clearly in their nineties but they would have been teenagers when they attacked the Queen in Malta and they had clearly looked after their bodies to be this capable after so long.

Just like the Queen and Sarah assembly had.

Each of the three men whipped out a knife and gestured they would kill Sarah if Bettie didn't leave.

"You're going to kill her anyway," Bettie said. "And why do all this? Why kill the woman that stopped you from killing the Queen seventy years ago?"

The three men laughed.

The man holding Sarah spat at Bettie. "You see what the Monarch's doing. Costing British taxpayers millions of pounds. The Monarchy must die and all those that support them must die too,"

Bettie really wanted to point out whilst 2022 or 2021 (she never had paid attention to the year) had been the first time the monarchy had cost the taxpayer over £100 million pounds, the Uk still had a government that had written over billions of pounds of fraud for no reason, gave million-pound contracts to their friends in exchange for faulty goods and used so much taxpayer money to line their own pockets.

Why was that right but the monarchy wasn't?

But political differences didn't seem like a good idea here.

"You're monsters!" Sarah shouted.

"Shut up!" the man holding her shouted. Slapping her across the face.

Bettie took a few steps forward. "You don't want to do this. You haven't killed anyone yet and you have only injured a couple of people,"

The three men laughed.

"Stupid woman," the man holding Sarah said. "We know what ya trying to do. It wouldn't work,"

The three men raised their knives.

Bettie rushed forward. The three men stared at Bettie.

The large glass doors smashed open.

Everyone looked at the broken glass.

Smoke grenades flew through the air.

The three men were confused.

Bettie shot forward.

Whacking the man holding Sarah in-between the legs.

He released Sarah.

Bettie grabbed her. Throwing her to one side.

Two men grabbed Bettie's arms pulling them in opposite directions.

The last raised the knife.

He was going to kill Bettie.

Bullets screamed through the air.

Heads exploded.

Blood painted Bettie's face.

As the three corpses fell to the ground Bettie had to get to Sarah, she rushed over to Sarah and threw the elderly lady over her shoulder. Bettie's twins kicked in excitement inside her.

Men and women in full body armour stormed into the reception area, their faces completely covered and Bettie just ignored them.

Bettie went outside the hotel and Sean took Sarah from her and gently threw her over his shoulder.

Bettie smiled as Agent Daniels in his tight black suit waved her and Sean over.

Daniels led them into a wide open field at the back of the hotel and a black helicopter activated to take them away.

"Who are you?" Sarah asked as her weak body struggled in Sean's grip as they all hurried towards the helicopter.

"Bettie English Private Eye, my nephew Sean and Agent Daniels MI5. The woman you saved in 52 wants to see you before she dies,"

Bettie was waiting for Sarah to start punching Sean's back or something but she just smiled.

"Fucking hell young man start running," Sarah said.

And as Bettie, Daniels and Sean with Sarah over his shoulder ran towards the helicopter Bettie just hoped beyond hope that the Queen would still be alive by the time they got to Balmoral in Scotland.

Bettie just couldn't fail.

***

6:32 pm

8th September 2022

Balmoral Estate, Scotland

Bettie had actually forgotten had slow compared to planes Helicopters were but she was rather amazed that the helicopter (because it was a military one) hadn't needed to refill at all during the journey.

Bettie had always absolutely loved the amazing highlands of Scotland, and whilst she really hoped Scotland gain its independence from the corruption of Westminster and London, she was so glad to be here in beautiful Scotland for this very special occasion.

Bettie was sitting against an icy cold window with Sarah and Sean next to her in a very uncomfortable seat as Daniels and the pilot continued to descend into the Balmoral estate, Bettie loved seeing the immensely wide open green fields of the estate and very tall pine and oak and other types of trees almost rise up to greet them.

Even though Bettie was in the helicopter she could still smell the delightful crisp refreshing piney air as the helicopter landed on the thick green grass with the Balmoral mansion just tens of metres away.

And it really did look like the most beautiful and perfect stately manor Bettie had ever seen, it looked right out of something from Downton Abbey.

But as the helicopter doors slid open and Bettie stepped onto the thick cold grass, she instantly knew that something was wrong and they were far too late, and judging by Sarah's smiling face it was only Bettie that had picked up on the change of tension in the air.

Bettie looked at Balmoral mansion and she frowned as a long life of ten servants, both men and women, in fine black suits and uniforms walked towards them in perfect step with each other, she just knew that she had been right.

Daniels took Sarah towards the servants and Sean just wrapped a thin youthful arm around Bettie, and she just rested her head on his shoulders.

"She's dead isn't she?" Sean asked.

Bettie felt a lump form in her throat and she just nodded.

The Queen of the UK and commonwealth was dead after an amazing 96 years of her life and even more amazing 70 years of constant love, service and dedication to her duty as Queen.

Even as Bettie stood there just watching Daniels and Sarah talk to the servants that were teary and looked just as upset as Bettie felt, she really wondered if she would still be doing her duty as a private eye at 96 years old.

Probably not, because as much as she loved being a private eye, the President of the Federation and newly expecting mother, things couldn't last forever, and at some point Bettie just knew she would have to choose what she really wanted in life.

But somehow the amazing Queen had managed to keep focused on duty, service and doing everything she could for this country. And Bettie damn well respected her for that.

Sarah's cries and screams of emotional pain ripped through the entire estate, and Bettie almost wanted to join her because she felt like such a failure but Bettie already knew that she had done a lot of good today.

As Bettie and Sean watched the most upset servant hug and try to reassure and grieve *with* Sarah about their own traumatic loss, Bettie just watched as the oldest of the servants slowly make her way over to Bettie holding a scroll of some sort.

Whilst the oldest servant made her way over, Bettie was rather amazed at how upset the Queen's workers were, because she had always heard stories of how much of a great sensational boss the Queen was, but to actually see how much her staff loved her.

That was something else entirely.

"Miss Bettie English, Private Eye and Madame President of the British Private Eye Federation," the woman said as poshly as Bettie ever could have imagined one of the Queen's servants to talk.

Bettie stopped leaning on Sean and stood up perfectly straight.

"Her Majesty wished me to give you this on your arrival," the woman said. "It was one of the last acts of business she ever did during her glorious life and before she made sure she told each of her family members how much she loved them,"

Bettie forced herself not to cry. It was amazing that the Queen had forced herself to do something for Bettie before she died, but Bettie just had a feeling that was the sort of amazing woman the late Queen was.

The woman passed Bettie the scroll and she opened it.

Bettie was amazed that it was a short letter to Bettie personally from the Queen informing Bettie that because she was just a good private eye, one so good that even the Queen had heard of her and her dedication to the UK. The Queen was officially requesting the new King to knight Bettie, and the Queen was gifting the Federation one million pounds to help them out.

Because apparently the Queen admired Bettie's courage and even though the Queen never ever wanted the royal family to have political power again, she would have liked to imagine she would have had the same amount of courage as Bettie in that situation with banning the far-left and right from the Federation.

Bettie felt her eyes turn wet as she handed the scroll to Sean, and she simply bowed to the servant and the servant smiled before heading back to her friends and Sarah and Daniels.

Bettie just leant against the icy coldness of the helicopter as the news of everything sunk in and she had to admit that even though she had technically failed to bring Sarah to the Queen before she sadly died, Bettie with the amazing help of Sean had still managed to do some incredible things today.

They had saved the lives of Sarah, her son and his wife from certain death, they had stopped three ninety-year-old men from spreading their hate and criminal views onto others that they were bound to have done after the killings, and most importantly Bettie had actually done exactly what the Queen had wanted.

Because Bettie, Sean and Sarah had all been here when it mattered most and they had protected the innocent.

And now the Queen was sadly dead, Bettie just knew that tonight was going to be a sad night, but that wasn't what the Queen would have wanted. She would have wanted a great night filled with stories, laughter and true friendship and as Daniels waved her and Sean over to them, Bettie just knew that was exactly what she was going to get.

And that was definitely going to be the greatest of endings to a very strange, dangerous and sad day, because how many people could honesty say they had been to the Queen's Balmoral estate as a guest.

Bettie couldn't think of a single person, and that just excited her way more than she ever wanted to admit.

AUTHOR OF THE ENGLISH BETTIE PRIVATE EYE SERIES

CONNOR WHITELEY

INVITATION TO SECRETS, LIES AND DECEIT

A BETTIE PRIVATE EYE HOLIDAY MYSTERY SHORT STORY

INVITATIONS TO SECRETS, LIES AND DECEIT
2nd December 2022

Canterbury, England

No one thinks about the walls.

Before Private Eye Bettie English had fallen in love, before she had become President of The British Private Eye Federation and before she had given birth to two amazing kids, Bettie actually got a lot of cases through strange invitations. Hell, she loved it and she had gotten some of her best and most exciting cases from invitations from mystery senders.

But as she sat at a massive oak round table with only four other people she was really starting to regret her joy of receiving weird invitations.

The dining room she sat in was rather nice and almost magical in a way with beautiful red, green and bright pink tinsel hanging all over the walls and ceiling and the tinsel shined like stars off the crystal chandelier (that was probably real), Bettie had seen some impressive families do great on their Christmas decorations but this family might have topped it.

There of course wasn't one or two or even three massive pine trees in the dining room, there was one in each corner. And Bettie was amazed that each Christmas tree was decorated in an identical way with rainbow coloured LED lights gently pulsing Christmas magic, golden tinsel hugging the tree loosely and little naked candles burning on the trees filling the air with the sweet scents of frankincense and myrrh.

Bettie wasn't exactly sure why the hell these four people wanted to burn naked candles on their trees (surely they knew that was a fiery death sentence) but Bettie didn't really want to argue.

Not when she had received a very panicked letter two hours ago wanting her to attend because someone was going to die tonight.

Bettie had originally planned to spend the night with her amazing, sexy boyfriend Graham as they went through all the great (and utterly rubbish) Christmas decorations that her 70-year-old mum had given her and then Bettie was going to read her two little angels a Christmas bedtime story before she put them to bed (but them sleeping when she wanted them to was a joke at this moment. Four-month-old babies didn't like sleeping).

But the invitation had changed those plans in a flash.

"Welcome everyone," the very tall woman, probably 32, at the head of the table said with a massive smile.

Bettie rather liked the woman's blue jeans, white shirt and shoeless feet, because it made her look normal and calm and like she was there to make sure everyone had a good time. It was just a shame that the other people at the table didn't look like that.

The other three people at the table were tall middle-aged men and wow did they look the part, and not the good or normal part, the three men were dressed in what Bettie could only describe as "grandad clothes" with their tan slacks, monocle and knitted red jumpers that looked so old they were about to fall apart.

Bettie was looking forward to seeing what these people were meeting about, and most importantly who was going to die. Something Bettie was hoping beyond hope that she could stop.

"We all know why we are here tonight," the tall woman said. "Three years ago, my father Lord Admiral Collins of the British Royal navy disappeared,"

"Happy Collins Day," the three men returned.

Bettie was shocked that she was actually attending Collins Day. She had read about it in the paper recently because his daughter,

Beatrice and presumably the tall woman was her, had been launching new campaigns in search of information about her father's disappearance.

Bettie had even had a crack at the case whilst she was on maternity leave during those extremely precious moments when her beautiful angels were finally sleeping.

The case was as strange as it got. Mr Collins had been on leave from the Navy for a month because Beatrice was getting married to the love of her life and Collins wanted to be there for the wedding and Christmas and New Year.

So he left the Naval Base at Portsmouth, England and drove to Canterbury two hours away, he kissed his wife hello and quickly popped to the shops to get some wine to celebrate his return (that was his wife's idea) and then he was never seen again.

There were no witnesses, no security footage that saw him on the second of December 2019 and his wife never heard from him again.

"Beatrice," Bettie said leaning forward, "why did your mother not get the wine?"

Everyone just looked at Bettie like she was a crazy woman.

"Who are you?" the oldest of the three men asked and Bettie noticed a minor scar under his chin like he had been punched there.

"This is Bettie English, the best private eye in the UK and somehow *she* received an invitation tonight," Beatrice said.

Bettie forced herself not to seem surprised at that comment. She was sure that if anyone had requested her presence tonight it would be Beatrice, but she certainly didn't invite Bettie with *that* tone.

"My question," Bettie said again, not really caring for the group's concern towards her.

"My mother was a woman in her late fifties who had just broken her leg after she fell down the stairs. She could barely let my father into the house let alone getting some wine," Beatrice said.

Bettie slowly nodded. That made sense.

"Nibbles Mrs Collins," a man said behind Bettie.

Bettie turned around and smiled when a very young man, maybe 19, walked in wearing a black waiter's uniform carrying a large silver tray of wine, freshly roasted nuts and smoked salmon.

Bettie loved all of those things but one part of herself she had never gotten back after her pregnancy was the ability to eat animal products. Bettie forced herself not to react to the amazing smell of the salmon despite her stomach churning.

Clearly these people didn't know about the possible death threat as the waiter placed the wine and nuts and salmon on the table and then bought out five silver plates and cutlery for them to enjoy the salmon on.

Bettie was starting to wonder if the person who actually invited her was really at the table.

"Are you not drinking Miss English?" the waiter said with concern edging his voice.

"No thank you," Bettie said. "I'm driving and I have two kids at home so I don't anymore,"

"Oh please Bettie," Beatrice said. "This wine is from the hills of Southern France, an area that my father loved. This is how we honour him on Collins Day,"

Bettie politely nodded and pretended to take a sip or two but she did not. The waiter just smiled at her and Bettie was almost a little concerned that everyone wanted her to drink. What if there was poison or something in the wine?

"What have you discovered about my father?" Beatrice asked the three men.

The youngest of the middle-aged man who Bettie was only realising now had a black eye smiled at Beatrice.

"We found one person who remembers selling your father a bottle of wine on the night in question," he said.

Bettie leant forward. "How? I didn't think the Police or Military police found anyone,"

The man with the scar under his chin sighed. "It's a great shame of our society that time loosen up tongues a lot better than a murder,"

Don't say that," Beatrice said. "My father is not dead,"

"My apologies Mrs Collins,"

That was a strange comment and now Bettie was seriously starting to wonder how the hell these people all knew each other. Bettie had believed they were friends or something but surely friends use first names and not formal surnames?

Beatrice started coughing a little and holding her stomach.

"Are you okay?" Bettie asked standing up.

Beatrice took a sip of the wine and smiled as she started picking at her salmon a little.

Bettie really wasn't liking this situation at all. She felt like a fish out of water but the mother angle was still annoying Bettie.

"Beatrice," Bettie said, "is this the same house that your mother lived in all those years ago?"

Beatrice coughed a little more and nodded before picking up a massive chunk of flaky salmon and eating it.

Bettie paced around the wooden table a little. "I assume your mother would have been in here with similar decorations when your father rang the doorbell,"

"Of course," Beatrice said grinning. "These are even the exact same decorations that were up on the night of the disappearance,"

Bettie almost felt sorry for Beatrice because she was clearly so obsessed with finding what happened to her father that Bettie was concerned she didn't have much of a life outside this hunt for the truth.

If Beatrice's mother had told the truth to the police then there was another problem, if she really had broken her leg and was on crutches then Bettie had to admit the mother was strong to walk herself all the way to the front door.

"I hadn't focused on it before," Bettie said, "but your dining room is at the back of the house and you cannot walk straight through the hallway to get from the front door to the dining room,"

Beatrice slammed her fork down on the table.

"You have to go through a number of other rooms with lots of twists and turns and this house probably has tons of hollow walls. If your mother really did that then why wasn't she more tired? And where was the waiter?"

The three men looked at Beatrice and nodded.

"You seem to be obsessed with keeping everything the same so there had to be a waiter, probably the same waiter, three years ago. Why didn't he answer the door? Or better yet, why didn't your father open the door with his front door keys?"

Beatrice downed her wine in a single gulp. "I don't know damn you. I don't know what happened to my father. I don't know what happened to my mother that night. I don't know anything,"

Bettie went over to her and folded her arms. "What do you mean you don't know what happened to your mother that night? Did she lie to the police?"

All three men stood up and went over to Beatrice. Their arms folded.

Beatrice held her stomach a little tighter. "My mother was out that night. She texted my father saying she would be home soon so he went to get the wine as a surprise,"

Bettie looked at the men. "She was having an affair, wasn't she?"

"No. No. No," Beatrice said. "That ain't true. My mummy was not having an affair,"

The last of the men that Bettie hadn't focused at all on yet just looked to the ground. And Bettie noticed his massive balding patch.

"How long did you sleep with her mother?" Bettie asked calmly.

Beatrice folded her arms and looked like she was about to cry.

"I didn't mean to sleep with her," he said not daring to look up. "I didn't mean to have sex with her. I didn't mean, well, any of it,"

Beatrice hissed a little.

"It was just my wife left me years ago, your mother was so nice and she was annoyed at the Navy for always taking her husband away from her. We were both lonely," he said.

"Damn you Jasper," Beatrice said.

Bettie went over to Jasper and gently raised his head with a single finger. "Did you kill Mr Collins?"

Jasper didn't even smile like that was a stupid thing to say, instead he simply shook his head as his eyes turned wet and Bettie knew, really knew that he was telling the truth.

Someone collapsed to the ground.

Bettie spun around.

The man with the black eye was gasping for air.

Bettie laid him perfectly straight, tried for a pulse and she didn't find one.

"Call an ambulance!" Bettie shouted.

Bettie immediately started CPR as hard and fast as she could.

Moments later the man gasped as air rushed into his lungs but he didn't open his eyes or move. But he was breathing and for now that would have to do.

Bettie picked him up and placed him gently back into his chair allowing him to lay unconscious, with his head tilted to one side so in case he vomited he wouldn't choke on it.

"I called an ambulance. They'll be here in the next hour," Beatrice said.

Bettie laughed because that really was a testament to how bad the ambulance service was getting in the UK.

"What's going on?" Jasper asked.

Bettie looked at the half-eaten plates of salmon plus her own intact plate and Bettie shook her head.

The food had to be poisoned but it also made no sense. Why poison that particular man? Why not poison Jasper or Beatrice or even herself?

Hell maybe they had poisoned Bettie.

"The waiter," Bettie said. "He smiled at me before he left and at the time I thought he was smiling at me because he knew I wasn't drinking. What if he was smiling because I was about to die?"

Beatrice shrugged. "Look at Tom's wine,"

Bettie presumed Tom was the black-eye man and Beatrice was

right, Tom hadn't touched his wine so the poison hadn't come from there.

Bettie waved her hands in the air. "So I received an invitation two hours ago saying someone was going to die and they needed my help to stop it,"

"Great job you did," Beatrice said.

"Did any of you send the invitation?" Bettie asked.

The three people just looked at each other like none of them would dare do such a thing.

Bettie had to agree with them. If any of them had sent the invitation they would have known not to drink or eat or touch anything just in case poison was being used.

"So we have three problems to solve," Bettie said. "I need to know who sent me the invitation, what happened to your father and who tried to kill Tom here,"

Both Jasper, the man with the scar under the chin and Beatrice laughed.

"I'm sorry," Bettie said to the man with the scar. "What's your name?"

The man laughed. "Believe it or not, I'm the uncle of the family. Jeremiah Collins, the bum of the family who has apparently never accomplished anything in my life,"

Beatrice hissed and Bettie thought she was actually going to spit at him, there was definitely no love lost between them.

"How did you get your scar?" Bettie asked.

Bettie loved watching all the colour drain from Jeremiah's face.

"Um," he said. "I was cleaning snow off my drive two years ago and the shovel hit me,"

"We didn't have snow two years ago," Bettie said.

"And you had that scar… three years ago but not before," Beatrice said.

"Fine," Jeremiah said trying to go for the hallway but the waiter appeared and blocked him. "I saw my brother that night he disappeared,"

"And you never said anything," Beatrice said trying to control her rage. Bettie took a few steps back just in case she lashed out.

"I was scared. I met my brother at the house that night and paid the waiter a thousand pounds the next day to say I wasn't,"

"And you still work here?" Bettie asked to the waiter.

The waiter smiled. "I love the family and I actually love the work,"

Bettie was surprised but the waiter seemed nice enough.

"I met my brother here after he found out about the affair because his wife had sent nudes to him instead of Jasper,"

Jasper looked as if he was about to die and really wanted the ground to swallow him up. Bettie loved hearing about people's secrets.

"I never wanted anything to happen but it simply turned into a massive argument. I said just divorce the woman but he didn't believe in divorce,"

"So you kept pressing daddy and he swung at you," Beatrice said as she rubbed her left arm.

"When did the argument happen? Before or after he went out to get the wine?" Bettie asked.

"After and we never drunk the wine. He was saving it for the wife,"

Bettie was glad these people were revealing their secrets to her because at least the night of the 2nd December 2019 was starting to make sense.

Mr Collins travelled home after deployment to find his home empty and his wife said she was on her way back so he goes out to get a bottle of wine, then Collins received a series of nude photos of his wife that wasn't meant for him and he suddenly realises she was having an affair.

Yet Bettie couldn't understand another question now, what had happened to the wine?

"I need to speak to your mother," Bettie said to Beatrice with a lot more force than she intended to.

Beatrice looked at the ground. "You can't. She's... fragile. She isn't right in the head. And she... isn't a fan of Collins Day,"

"My boyfriend is a cop. One call from me and he will come running and he will investigate all of this including the assault from Jeremiah, the affair and everything else," Bettie said.

Beatrice stood up perfectly straight so Bettie knew there was more secrets to uncover but she believed that everyone was allowed to have at least secrets to themselves. Hell she certainly did.

"I took her to a home yesterday," Beatrice said. "She has advanced dementia for the past year and a half. She kept thinking that the waiter was my father and, nothing has been going well for her,"

Well that was another dead end for the case.

Bettie just looked at poor unconscious Tom and really hoped that when the ambulance and paramedics got here she could have them run a little test for her.

She needed to know exactly what poison had tried to kill Tom.

Yet Bettie was still no closer to knowing who had wanted her here tonight, who had tried to kill Tom and most importantly what had happened to Mr Collins.

***

Bettie's boyfriend Graham had to be the sexiest man alive and she seriously loved Senior Scientist Zoey Quill because she had agreed to go late into the lab tonight to run a few tests for Bettie, Bettie was definitely going to have to buy Zoey and her husband and her children a very special present for Christmas.

A few hours later, Bettie was sitting at the wooden table again with Beatrice, Jasper and Jeremiah with the air still smelling of fresh salmon, freshly roasted pecans and strong bitter coffee that the waiter had just bought out when her phone buzzed with the test results.

There was no way in hell that Bettie could even pronounce or read the name of the toxin used against Tom but thankfully (and because Zoey was so amazing) she had included a layman's version of the toxin.

"A very rare nerve agent was placed into the salmon tonight,"

Bettie said. "And this particular nerve agent has to be programmed with the DNA of the victim before it activates,"

"So we're safe?" Jasper and Jeremiah asked at the same time.

Bettie nodded but was still a little surprised that Jeremiah was Beatrice's uncle yet she had been hissing, coughing and holding her stomach all night like she had been poisoned.

"What's wrong with your stomach?" Bettie asked knowing that she really needed to get answers now.

Beatrice looked past Bettie and weakly at the young waiter. Bettie didn't know whether to be concerned or not that it was fair to say the waiter had gotten Beatrice pregnant.

"That's why you stay as the waiter," Bettie said. That made a lot of sense but the nerve agent could only have come from one source that was possible for Bettie to understand.

The waiter went over, stood next to Beatrice and kissed her. And it was nice to see that they were in true love and not some fling that had ended in a pregnancy.

"Did your father ever bring back things from the Navy?" Bettie asked.

Beatrice held the waiter's hand so tight that her knuckles had turned white. "Yes, he bought back little things but he always kept them locked in a safe,"

Bettie just laughed because she finally realised what was going on, how someone had tried to kill Tom and what had happened to Mr Collins three years ago.

Someone, not Mr Collins, was living in the walls.

"Have you ever heard sounds in the walls?" Bettie asked. "Have you ever heard sounds like someone was walking about at night?"

Beatrice's eyes widened. "My mother... she said someone pushed her down the stairs when she broke her leg I never believed her. I lied about when she broke her leg but she did break it four months before my father disappeared,"

"And my brother constantly moaned about food going missing," Jeremiah said. "Nothing weird has happened for years though. No food or anything,"

Bettie just nodded. "This old house has a lot of hollow spaces in-between the walls and I think if we open up some of these walls then we'll find something very disturbing,"

"You think… my daddy's inside?" Beatrice said.

Bettie took out her phone and called Graham. She didn't have the heart to agree with Beatrice but they did need a team of crime scene techs here immediately.

There was a lot of answers to find. No matter how disturbing they might be.

***

The constant low sounds of crime scene techs in their white uniforms, police sirens and Beatrice and the two remaining men giving statements filled the air as Bettie stood there outside in the icy cold winter night with her beautiful sexy Graham standing next to her.

Thankfully he was wearing a massive thick coat that Bettie clung to in case it would warm her up, Bettie was just glad that their little angels were asleep with Bettie's nephew Sean and his boyfriend harry watching over them. At least they were warm and toasty tonight.

Despite all the police cars and white crime scene vans outside, Bettie was still pleased that Beatrice's house looked beautiful and Christmassy outside as it had earlier with plenty of gravity-defying light displays in the shapes of angels, reindeer and snowmen. It was like you were about to walk into a winter wonderland.

And not a house filled with lies, deceit and secrets.

Graham's phone buzzed, took it out and gasped before showing the photo to Bettie. Bettie was amazed that the crime scene techs had found an entire network of narrow spaces in-between the old walls with remains of food wrappings, matches and water bottles littered throughout.

Yet the photo was of the perfectly mummified body of Mr Collins who was wrapped up tightly in a tarp and stuffed at the end of one of the passages that the person living inside the walls had made for themselves.

Bettie felt so disgusted because it was flat out wrong for someone to live inside the walls instead of living in their own house. The things this person could have seen was a horrific invasion of privacy but at least it explained a lot.

It explained why Beatrice's mother had said a man pushed her down the stairs, it explained why Mr Collins' brother didn't know what had happened to his brother after he left and what had happened to the wine, and it finally explained what happened to Mr Collins the night of the 2nd December 2019.

"What do you think happened that night?" Graham asked as he finished texting the crime scene techs because apparently the scene was far too busy, fragile and chaotic to risk Graham contaminating it.

"I think the man or woman came out the walls looking for food that night. He found Mr Collins angry and frustrated about his wife's affair and Mr Collins caught him or her. There was a fight and Mr Collins died," Bettie said.

"Then the killer took him into the walls to avoid anyone finding the body. But just imagine living with your own murder victim for so long?" Graham asked.

Bettie just laughed. "Babe, you realise what we do for a living. And you think a man living in the walls is the weirdest?"

"Fair point," Graham said, kissing her on the head.

"But where is the man or woman now?" Bettie asked. "And we know what happened to Mr Collins but what happened to Tom and who invited me?"

"Detective!" a uniformed officer standing by the police tape shouted to Graham and then the officer gestured to a man engulfed in the shadow of the bright streetlamps.

Graham waved him through and Bettie instantly knew who this man was. He was the man living in the walls.

Bettie just stared at the very, almost dangerously thin man walk towards them, he was clean-shaved, in good health and looked rather handsome for a man in his late fifties.

The man was wearing black jogging bottoms, a very nice red t-shirt and a thick puffer jacket that suited him perfectly.

"Why kill him?" Bettie asked. Graham didn't seem to be following.

"I never meant to do that Miss English," the man said. "I was made homeless after my divorce and I had nothing but I was once a bricklayer and my father worked on this house,"

"So you knew about the gaps in the wall," Bettie said.

"Of course and my father was a cowboy builder. He didn't put in any insulation or anything so it was hardly a health hazard,"

"It's still illegal," Graham said.

Bettie waved him silent and gestured the man to continue.

"I knew the family always celebrated their silly little Collins Day tonight so I wanted... I wanted someone to finally discover the truth, because, he keeps talking to me,"

Bettie hugged the man for some reason she didn't understand but she could tell that he wasn't a bad person, he was just a man that had been forced by a situation to react.

Granted Bettie never would have decided to live in the walls of a house if she was homeless, but she could understand if someone was desperate enough.

"I never meant to kill Mr Collins but he caught me and I hate living with that corpse anyway. Please arrest me. At least you guys have heating, meals and free water. You have any idea how annoying it is having to wake up in the middle of the night just to get a day's supply of water,"

Bettie smiled and shook her head as Graham cuffed the man and arrested him for murder.

"Why did you try to kill Tom? You must have seen where Mr Collins kept the illegal things we bought back from the Navy and programmed the nerve agent," Bettie said.

The man's smile deepened. "I never wanted to kill Tom. I was aiming for Beatrice. I didn't know you needed to programme the nerve agent so that only means one thing, doesn't it Miss English?"

Bettie waved Graham so he took the man over to the nearest police car and Bettie was just shocked at yet another secret this family held. Mr Collins had programmed the nerve agent to kill Tom before he died, Bettie wasn't even sure she wanted to know why Mr Collins wanted to kill him (maybe he believed it was Tom who was having the affair with the wife) but Bettie knew one thing for sure.

She was really glad that the man, whoever he was, had invited her tonight so she could uncover the secrets, lies and deceptions that had been eating this family away for so long. And now, hopefully, just hopefully Beatrice could find some peace and move on from Collins Day.

And as Bettie went home to kiss her two little angels goodnight, she really hoped that was true. Because she had seen first-hand the sheer cost of people not being able to move on from the past.

It never ended well and it never led to a happy Christmas.

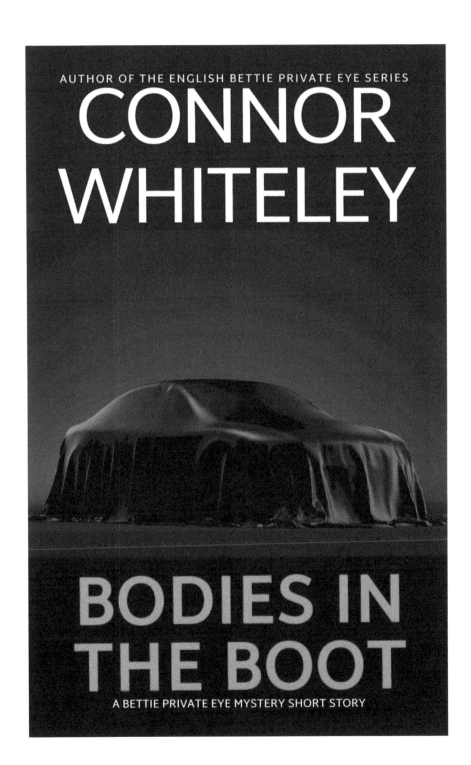

AUTHOR OF THE ENGLISH BETTIE PRIVATE EYE SERIES

CONNOR WHITELEY

BODIES IN THE BOOT

A BETTIE PRIVATE EYE MYSTERY SHORT STORY

BODIES IN THE BOOT
5th October 2023
Medway, Kent, England

"How many bodies could you fit in there Auntie?"

Private eye Bettie English just laughed and grinned as she leant against the icy cold metal pillar at the car dealership she was visiting with her nephew Sean. She had to admit that the car dealership was rather nice considering this was Medway of all places, with its wide forecourt that wrapped around the main metal building perfectly.

There was a great range of cars on display, and Bettie couldn't have cared less about their names and models, because she was useless at cars. But there were plenty of red, black and blue cars in all different shapes and sizes in neat little rows on the forecourt.

Bettie sort of recognised some of the brands like Fiat, Citroen and Ford, but she had to smile to herself because she was useless at their models. They all just looked the same to her, a metal box on top of four wheels.

Bettie waved at a young man in the dealership's tight black uniform as he led a young couple followed by a first-time buyer round the forecourt. She had no idea why a first-time buyer was looking at cars at this end of the court. They were stupidly overpriced and Bettie was only up here because she had wanted to play a game with Sean.

The game was simple and Bettie couldn't deny it was great fun. Whenever her and Sean opened a car boot, they had to guess how many bodies they could fit inside.

Bettie had no idea how she was going to tell her Detective boyfriend, Graham Adams, later on but she knew she would and they would laugh about it.

Bettie went over to Sean and he definitely had great taste. He was looking at a small black car that would be hard to notice, it would fit in small gaps easily enough and it was probably quicker than it looked. Bettie wasn't sure if the price tag of £6,000 was right and she could afford that from a single hour of work but she wasn't buying it for Sean.

The entire point why Bettie had come with Sean to the dealership was to help him find a good car (not that she knew what she was looking for) and she wanted to teach him that even though she was a millionaire and him and his boyfriend lived with them. It never hurt to learn money lessons, which was why Sean had to buy this car with his own money.

"I'm thinking two bodies," Sean said grinning and running a hand through his longish blond hair with tastefully done pink highlights.

Bettie smiled and shook her head. He wasn't wrong, the black car did have a big boot but it wasn't big enough for two adult bodies inside. Maybe an adult and a dwarf but not two adults.

"Miss English?"

Bettie turned around and forced herself to smile as the head of the dealership came over with a massive frown on her face. The woman looked rather good in a dirty white blouse with tons of creases in it, her black trousers had holes in and her high heels looked like they were about to break at any moment.

"Are you the President of the British Private Eye Federation?" the woman asked.

Bettie nodded. She loved being the President of the Federation who oversaw all private investigators in the UK that allowed her to help innocent people, improve lives and she had the power equal to some small countries thanks to the Federation's blackmail files.

Something she intended never ever to use.

"Yes I am," Bettie said. "Can I help you at all?"

The head of the dealership came closer and Bettie looked at her name tag, Cindy. Bettie wanted to cough as the sheer awful hints of fish, chips and fried food filled her senses. It was awful.

"I found a body of sorts in the boot of my car attached to a note that says I'm going to die in ten minutes,"

Bettie looked at Sean. As much as she wanted to keep looking for a new car, this was definitely going to have to wait. Cindy was in danger and Bettie couldn't let anything bad happen. And it would be good for business to (Cindy might even give them a free car out of it).

"I need to see your car," Bettie said.

"Of course," Cindy said. "Oh thank you, thank you Miss English,"

Bettie just grinned at Sean because she had a feeling that this case was going to be wonderfully weird, chaotic and very odd indeed.
***

A few moments later, Bettie frowned as Cindy opened the booth of her large silver Fiat in the back car park of the dealership. There was a high, thick green fence that ran along the sides of the car park, and you could only come through it by the forecourt and a small blue door that led into the main building.

Both required a passcode.

Bettie liked how Sean looked like he was playing on his phone, but he was probably already "hacking" into the dealership's security cameras. She loved having a postgraduate with her specialising in Advanced Technological Engineering, or a drone and computing degree as she liked to describe it.

"Here you go," Cindy said. "I hate this, I just hate this,"

Bettie gently rubbed Cindy's shoulder as she went closer to the boot. There was a large manakin inside without a face, features or any clothes on. But there was a handwritten note that had been taped to the face of the manakin.

Bettie wanted to focus on the note but she leant into the booth of the car for a moment. She carefully looked around the rusty trim of the boot, and checked for any fabric, fibres or anything else that might tell her who did this.

There was nothing.

The sound of customers laughing, making offers and bargaining made Bettie smile. She really hoped everyone here was getting a good deal for their cars and everything was working.

She had heard way too many horror stories of dealerships selling bad cars to too many innocent people. She really wanted everyone to get good cars here, it was the least the people of Medway deserved. Most people in this district could barely afford heating and food, let alone a new car.

Bettie put on her gloves that she always carried with her, and she read the note out to Sean.

"In ten minutes, I'm going to kill you, bury you and make you pay for what you're doing here," Bettie said.

Sean smiled. "Well, that would explain what I've found in your security logs and your computer systems?"

Bettie folded her arms and just looked at Cindy. She knew something wasn't right here.

"You," Sean said, "have been coming to the forecourt at 2 am at night every Monday for the past four months. You log in and you've been changed financial records to increase the interest people are paying after they've already signed the contracts,"

Cindy leant against her car. "You have no right to hack into my systems. That's a crime,"

"I could call my detective boyfriend and see what he has to say about this," Bettie said.

Sean took a step closer to Cindy. "Even worse, you keep digital records of all the faults in your cars, but the paperwork you give to buyers say they are perfectly in order,"

Bettie really hated Cindy. How the hell could she betray, hurt and con so many innocent people that only wanted a cheaper car instead of going to a franchise of a major brand. It was disgusting.

"My death threat though," Cindy said.

Bettie nodded. "We'll investigate that but I promise you there will be a price to pay for your criminal activities,"

Cindy shook her head. "Just find out who wants to kill me,"

Bettie was about to say something but Cindy just walked off, so Bettie focused on the note and noticed it had been written on the dealership's own branded paper.

"You know someone here wants revenge," Bettie said. "Cross-reference all the employees and their families with any purchases in the last, two years,"

"Okay," Sean said.

Bettie went over to the thick green security fence that separated the forecourt from the secured parking area. The small silver pad was perfectly clean with no marks, fingerprints or signs it had been interfered with.

Bettie was sure it was an employee of the dealership and that only confirmed her theory even more. If an outsider had done this then there would be signs of someone trying to break in.

"No signs of anyone coming or going on the security footage, but I think it was looped round so it wasn't really recording. It isn't even picking us up now," Sean said.

Bettie really liked having Sean with her. He was always a brilliant crime-solving partner. She felt lucky to have him in her life, unlike his mother.

"Anything on the purchases?"

"Still cross-referencing,"

Bettie nodded and she headed over to the blue door on the other side of the secure parking area and went inside the main building. She needed to talk to someone and she needed to get to the bottom of this threat before a woman died.

Cindy might not have been innocent but she never ever deserved to die.

***

"You could fit tons of bodies in that car," Sean said grinning.

Bettie laughed as she stood in the middle of the beautiful showroom in the main building, and she was shocked at how great it looked. The grey tile flooring was shiny, sterile and Bettie was slightly pleased to see she had lost most of her baby weight (at last) in her reflection.

There were eight posh, expensive BMWs, Land Rovers and a lot more expensive cars she didn't recognise, lined up against the floor-to-ceiling windows facing the forecourt, and the small offices looked impressive behind the glass wall behind her.

Bettie had no idea how the hell people were meant to afford the BMWs, Land Rovers and other cars, but this dealership clearly had ambition.

And Bettie couldn't deny Sean wasn't wrong about the boot of the Land Rover. A killer could probably fit tons of bodies inside, something she hoped would never ever be tested.

"Can I help you?" a middle-aged man asked.

Bettie was glad her plan had finally worked. Being President of the Federation had always meant she had needed to look imposing, scary and powerful time to time, and apparently she had the *look* down perfectly these days. So she could activate it whenever she wanted.

And con artists, like this dealership, always liked money and power.

"We're looking for a car for my nephew and I'm wondering what would you recommend," Bettie said. "Can we talk in your office?"

Bettie noticed the middle-aged man's name tag said Carl, and he was a step down from Cindy. Maybe he wanted to kill her to take over.

"No, I'm afraid some trainees are in my office at the moment," Carl said gesturing behind him where there were five trainees watching someone on a computer.

Bettie hadn't realised there might be trainees here, and there was a chance that someone might have gotten a job as a trainee to target the dealership. They wouldn't pop up on the main employees list because they were "only" a trainee.

"Um," Sean said clearly making the same connection, "how many trainees do you have at the moment? I have a friend that might want a job,"

Carl's face lit up. "Oh that is wonderful. We always need more trainees and we have a lot of great benefits, but I'm afraid we're fully booked at the moment with trainees. We only have eight spaces you see,"

Bettie cocked her head. That didn't make any sense, because there were only five trainees behind the computer and she couldn't see any more in the showroom.

Bettie went over to the massive floor-to-ceiling windows and noticed only one trainee outside showing people round the cars.

"Where are the other two trainees?" Bettie asked.

Carl shrugged. "I don't know. They are all meant to be here,"

Bettie checked her watch and bit her lower lip. It was probably already past the ten-minute mark, so they might already be too late.

"I need you to find them now," Bettie said.

"Who the hell do you think you are bossing me about?" Carl asked.

"I am Private Eye Bettie English, President of the British Private Eye Federation and unless you want your boss to die you will help me,"

Carl stumbled back a little like Bettie had actually hit him or something. Bettie just glared at him and Carl hurried off.

"Should we look ourselves?" Sean asked.

Bettie shook her head. Something wasn't right here. Clearly the dealership was ripping people off, changing interest payments after contracts were signed and selling bad cars as good ones. That made sense, and as much as Bettie didn't want to admit it that was normal in the dealership game.

But why the manakin?

Bettie couldn't understand why use the manakin in the car boot to scare Cindy or warn her. It made no sense because if the trainee or whoever really was going to kill Cindy then why not just kill her?

Unless Cindy was never meant to die and she had set up this plan in the first place.

"Where's Cindy's office? Did you see it on the security footage?"

Sean led Bettie across the showroom and into a large corner with more desks, chairs and cabinets than Bettie had ever seen before. The entire office smelt of coffee, chips and fried fish, which made Bettie really want to vomit. It was so overwhelming.

Bettie went over to the perfectly arranged desk and found a notepad that Cindy had been writing on. Then she compared the writing on the notepad to the note on the manakin.

It was a match.

"Why do this?" Bettie asked. "Why would Cindy want us to investigate and why would she threaten herself?"

Carl came into the office. "I've found the two trainees, they were making out in the toilets. Typical young men and women,"

Bettie was glad that loose thread was dealt with, so Cindy was clearly up to something but she had no idea what.

"Carl," Bettie said, "why would Cindy threaten herself?"

"Bloody bastard," Carl said. "She's going to abandon ship and leave me for the cops. I knew it was wrong, it was bloody stupid but I needed the money,"

Bettie leant across the desk. "If you want any chance of not going to prison then you need to tell me everything,"

"Auntie," Sean said taking out his phone, "cross-referencing came back and every single current and former employee was forced to buy a car and they are still paying it off,"

Bettie couldn't believe that. That was outrageous and extremely illegal, and that was just messed up.

"Talk," Bettie said.

"Fine, me and Cindy started this dealership after university because we wanted some fun, we wanted a business and we used to steal cars for a living. It wasn't hard to fake reports and MOTs,"

Bettie rolled her eyes. She really didn't like these people.

"Then we realised running a business is a little hard so we got more and more employees. But when we had to cut their wages, they threatened to leave so Cindy offered them a *discount* on a car,"

"And," Bettie said, "that's when you nailed them because they brought the car on finance and then you changed the interest rates so much you trapped them. What was the deal Carl? If they keep working and shut their mouths, you do it interest-free?"

Carl nodded and looked to the ground.

"What changed?" Sean asked.

"One of the trainees who brought a car off us was outraged, she spoke up and went to the cops. We increased her interest rates to crippling amounts so she didn't retract her statement from the cops,"

Bettie clicked her fingers. There was something on the local news (the only thing that seemed to make her baby boy sleep at the moment) about this. A 19-year-old woman had died in a drunk car crash last week, she had been drinking and upset over crippling interest repayments.

"You killed that woman," Bettie said. "You might not have crashed the car but she wouldn't have been drinking if you hadn't done that,"

Carl shrugged. "Business is business,"

Bettie just looked at Sean. She hated these people and she was going to make them pay, and Bettie was going to do everything in her power to give the victims of this con their money back.

Bettie went round the desk and got very close to Carl's ear.

"So the cops are coming here and Cindy has probably run. I have the power and influence to get you a reduced prison sentence but you have to come clean about your operation,"

"I can't," Carl said. "Cindy will ruin me,"

Bettie laughed. "Then you have clearly never met the Federation. You are conning tons of innocent people and you caused a young woman to die. If you don't do the right thing then I will use the

Federation's resources to bury you alive,"

Bettie forced herself not to frown as she stood up. She hated being like this but she hated people like Carl and Cindy even more. It was just unforgivable to take advantage of so many innocent, good people that only wanted a damn car to get to work.

"She does have the power to do it," Sean said. "Especially with the evidence I've found,"

Carl stood up and paced round the office for a few moments. Bettie really hoped he was going to make the right choice.

"Fine," Carl said. "I'll testify to everything that happened here and I'll even tell you where Cindy probably is. Just don't... send me to jail,"

Bettie laughed because Cindy was finally going to get justice and she actually had an idea about what to do with dear old Carl.

***

A few hours later, Bettie leant against an awfully cold metal pillar in the forecourt of the dealership, and she just smiled at all the flashing red and blue lights of the four police cars that blocked the road entrance inside. There weren't any cars left on the forecourt and Bettie was surprised to see so many weeds had cracked the concrete under the cars.

Apparently all of them had been stolen from one place or another, and her sexy, wonderful boyfriend Graham had confirmed the dealership had been running this scam for about two decades. Cindy wasn't even as young as she looked.

Bettie watched as one of the police cars drove away with Carl and some of the other employees in the back. She didn't feel sorry for Graham or the other detectives that were going to have to sort this mess out. Thankfully, she would send off all the evidence they had collected in a moment, so hopefully that would allow the detectives to get home to their families sooner.

A small group of young men and women in hoodies and black jogging bottoms were gathered just at the road entrance. Bettie didn't like how sad, hopeless and disappointed they looked because they had all probably brought cars here at one point or another. And they had probably figured it out that they were conned.

So a ton of their money was wasted at a time when no one could really afford it.

Bettie waved as Graham, in his sexy white shirt and trousers, and Sean came over after opening the main building's door for a bunch of uniform officers to carry out boxes of paperwork.

The cold night air smelt of strong bitter coffee, fried fish and chips and Bettie was so looking forward to going home to her two sweet twins. Then she was going to go for a shower, she really didn't want to smell of fish and chips anymore, the damn smell had probably soaked into her clothes.

"My officers picked up Cindy a few minutes ago trying to flee to Dover," Graham said. "She's silent but there are records and laptops in her boot. We'll nail her for this fraud,"

"Thank you," Bettie said blowing the man she loved a kiss. "What's going to happen to Carl and the others?"

Graham shrugged. "That's up for the Crown Prosecution Service to decide. Carl was a big player but testifying will help him, and the others were only victims in truth so we only need a statement,"

"Good," Sean said playing with some brand-new car keys in his hands.

"You didn't," Graham said playfully hitting Bettie's arm.

"Well, it isn't my fault they left the car keys unattended and their computers open," Bettie said. "As a private eye, I only care about solving crimes, helping people and benefiting my business,"

"I so did not hear that," Graham said before giving Bettie a kiss on the cheek and going over to some uniformed officers.

Sean folded his arms and grinned. "What are you going to do about the victims?"

Bettie smiled. "Oh you know, what's the point of being a millionaire if you can't help people? All the victims will suddenly and mysteriously be sent £10,000 tomorrow afternoon with a small note,"

"Mysteriously, sure," Sean said hugging Bettie. "I love you

Auntie,"

"I love you too Sean,"

Bettie followed Sean over to the other side of the secure parking area, and there was only one car left a massive black Land Rover and Bettie was seriously impressed. That would be a great car for a high-speed chase.

"Open the boot," Sean said climbing into the front seat.

Bettie popped up the boot and gasped as ten manakins popped out from under a big blue blanket.

Bettie just laughed and laughed and she really did love her nephew, and at least the age-old question was answered. How many bodies could you fit in there, and Bettie had to admit she loved being a private eye, an auntie and a girlfriend to a detective a lot more than she ever wanted to admit.

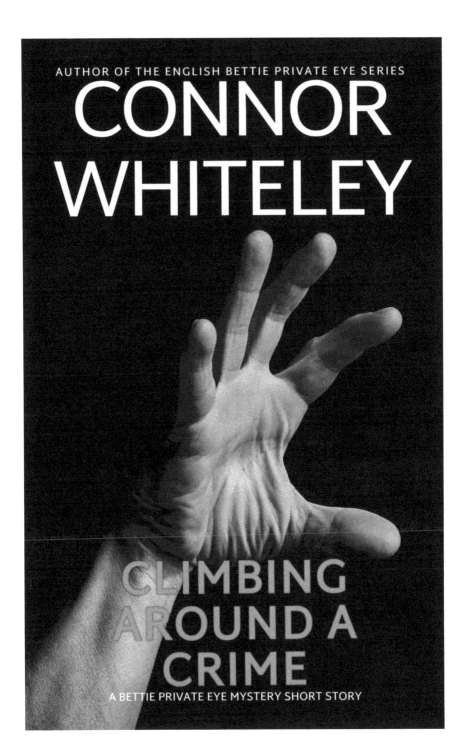

AUTHOR OF THE ENGLISH BETTIE PRIVATE EYE SERIES

CONNOR WHITELEY

CLIMBING AROUND A CRIME

A BETTIE PRIVATE EYE MYSTERY SHORT STORY

CLIMBING AROUND A CRIME

Of all the ways private eye Bettie English had wanted to spend her Friday evening when her best friend and personal assistant Fran had suggested they have some "fun", Bettie certainly hadn't expected to be doing bouldering of all things.

Bettie was a good ten metres up in the air and barely clinging to the purple handholds that pretended to look like rocks. There were only a few millimetres of the handhold for her to actually hold onto and even she had to admit, she might have pushed herself a little too far this time.

She had already been climbing for over an hour in the massive bouldering centre. A large grey warehouse-like building with fake wooden rock-like walls covered in orange, grey and purple handholds with each of them being a different difficulty.

Bettie had wanted to try the red, blue and white handholds but she wasn't crazy enough to try them. They were way too hard and her arms, legs and bum ached.

It had been ages since she had done "this" type of exercise that required such a firm grip that she couldn't train herself by chasing bad guys, defending herself from criminals and doing her normal cardio.

Bettie hissed a little as her fingers grew more and more tired and she could see the next purple handhold a little further up from her. She could reach it, she knew she could and she was determined to do it.

Bettie wasn't exactly a fan of the gentle hip-pop music playing in the background but a lot of other people clearly liked it as they laughed, talked and planned their next climb with each other.

She looked over to her left and there was a short little kid, maybe twelve, just shooting up a red handhold route without a sweat. When her two beautiful twins were old enough, she was so bringing them here.

Bettie hissed as she realised bouldering required weird hand strength that she seriously didn't have, but she loved it anyway. It was so much fun climbing up the handholds, stretching herself and proving that she was a strong independent woman that could do anything she put her mind to.

Except she could feel her fingers were about to give out on her.

She fell.

Bettie landed straight down on the soft, spongy grey floor below and she laughed to herself. She had always liked falling and this had been a great idea of Fran's to come here after work.

"Are you okay?" Fran asked.

Bettie got up and laughed at she looked as her best friend, smiling and wearing her black gym top and activewear jogging bottoms. Apparently, Fran did this a lot but Bettie was rather impressed she was doing a lot better than her friend on her first time.

"I'm going to start myself off again on a grey route," Fran said going over to the climbing wall.

Bettie nodded. She couldn't blame Fran at all for wanting to take the easiest route, her fingers and arms were killing her but that was all part of the fun.

Someone screamed.

Bettie spun and gasped as she saw a young woman fall twelve metres through the air with two handholds flying off the wall.

The woman landed with a thud and Bettie rushed over.

She knocked people out the way as she rushed over the other side of the centre. She even leapt over a small child.

A group of other people were already surrounding the young

woman and Bettie just pushed past them.

"Who are you?" someone asked in Adidas sportswear.

"Bettie English, private eye," she said kneeling down next to the young woman.

Bettie was surprised at the sheer sponginess of the floor as she knelt down next to the young woman who was hissing in pain, holding her ankle and her black, tight sportswear was hugging her slim body.

Bettie wasn't exactly a fan of how all the men and women at the centre crowded around her like they were trying to suffocate her, but they were asking questions and trying to help.

The worst of it was the awful hints of sweat, sweat and more sweat that filled the centre. Bettie didn't mind it too much but she was looking forward to getting some fresh air later on, but right now she just needed to help this young woman.

"What happened?" Bettie asked as calmly and reassuringly as she could.

The young woman held onto Bettie's hand. "I was climbing like I've done a thousand times and the handholds just gave way. They spin rarely but never fall off,"

"Excuse me. Excuse me," a man said as he pushed himself through the crowd.

Bettie rubbed the woman's hand gently before she stood up and let the man in his first-aid uniform take over.

She went out of the crowd and enjoyed the slightly less intensely sweaty air, and then she went over to Fran who was taking photos of the handholds.

Bettie knelt down next to them and Fran followed. She had liked it how resourceful, clever and focused Fran was. Fran had probably already sent the photos to the Federation for some kind of analysis that Bettie didn't want to focus on right now.

"Here," Bettie said pointing to the handholds. "The attachments to the walls have been cut,"

Bettie hated seeing the perfectly smooth almost saw-like

markings on the handholds. And Bettie wouldn't have been surprised if someone had tried to kill or hurt the young woman on purpose.

"How long have you been coming here?" Bettie asked Fran.

"Maybe four months," Fran said looking over at the young woman. "Bethany was here before I started and she's a competitive one. She represents Kent at national competitions. She's really nice too,"

Bettie nodded. She had heard of national contests for all sorts of weird and wonderful sports but bouldering just seemed a little too niche.

"How many of the people here are competitive?" Bettie asked standing up.

"Most of them actually. There's a set of trials coming up and everyone has to requalify or get in for the first time,"

"Show me the person who might do this," Bettie said not knowing if Fran was observant enough to guess who might be responsible.

A few moments later, the crowd surrounding Bethany broke apart and the man in the first aid uniform carefully walked next to her as she went across the centre to the reception area. Bettie was glad she seemed okay and nothing was broken, so hopefully she had "only" sprained her ankle.

But for the sake of Bethany and the others at the centre, Bettie wasn't leaving until she found out who could have done this.

"Lukas," Fran said.

Bettie smiled as a very fit man in his early thirties came over topless showing off his massive biceps and six-pack, and long brown hair. He winked at Bettie and she just frowned.

"It's a shame about Beth, right?" Lukas asked. "I told her, she gonna be more careful,"

Bettie smiled. "You almost sound like you wanted this to happen,"

Lukas pointed a warning finger at Bettie. "No. Beth is the only one that climbs that route tonight, she practises all tonight doing the exact same route because it's one of the hardest here. All of us have to train on lesser routes,"

Bettie tried to remember how long Beth had been here before or after them. Beth had turned up about the same time as them so she had been doing the route for about an hour before it broke.

That didn't make any sense.

"Do you know how to damage these handholds enough?" Bettie asked.

"No, no one does except Mike, the manager. I come here to train, socialise and become good enough to compete. That is it and I do not waste my time on pretenders like Beth. Now if you excuse me, I have training to do,"

Bettie folded her arms as Lukas went away and the idiot turned round to flex a little for her. It wasn't a bad sight but she hated guys like that.

"He isn't wrong Bet," Fran said gesturing they should go to the reception area.

Bettie followed Fran as the two of them went across the spongy floor with the hints of sweat, manly musk and chalk filling the air.

"I know," Bettie said. "I have little idea how someone could change and damage the handholds so easily. Considering this has been open all day and I presume other people have used the route,"

"I'll get the camera footage,"

"Thank you," Bettie said.

Bettie stepped out the way of a small child as he leapt off one of the walls and almost took her out.

"I'm so sorry," his mother said.

"It's fine. Your son's great at climbing," Bettie said.

She went over to the reception area which was nothing more than a large front desk, a row of black metal tables and some horrible black chairs that Bettie seriously didn't want to sit in. They just looked plain uncomfortable.

Bettie waved at Beth as she was sitting on one of the horrible chairs with an ice pack on her ankle, and she was playing on her phone.

"Some people call you a pretender," Bettie said.

"Ha," Bethany said. "Lukas and the other guys just can't accept that I qualified for nationals every year since I was 18. I'm good at bouldering, I work hard and I make sure other people benefit from my work,"

Bettie leant on the back of a chair. "How do other people benefit?"

"This centre. A few years ago, it needed to up its membership cost to keep its doors open, and every April it wants to increase its costs. I donate a few tens of thousands to keep prices down,"

Bettie was amazed. That was brilliant of Bethany and she had no idea there was that much money in bouldering competitions that she could afford to donate like that.

"I live off my day job and my competition money pays for very nice holidays with my boyfriend," Bethany said. "And this place was where I fell in love with bouldering, so why shouldn't others have the same chance?"

Bettie nodded. That was a great point but maybe that was what had annoyed someone enough to attack her tonight. She had learnt over the years with her own extreme acts of charity (the benefits of being a millionaire) that it always annoyed certain organisations and people more than they ever wanted to admit.

"Thank you for your time," Bettie said going back over to Fran.

"At least six other people have used that same route today. No accidents, no problems, no time to damage the handholds," Fran said closing her phone.

Bettie shook her head. It was worth a shot but that would have been too easy.

"I presume you got the Federation to run background checks on Bethany," Bettie said.

"I am offended you needed to ask Bet,"

Bettie laughed as she waved over a large man with the nametag "Mike."

"Everything checks out with Bethany," Fran said. "No problems, no money issues and she is basically keeping this place afloat,"

"Find out everything you can about rival businesses and people that want to see this place shut,"

Bettie nodded her thanks to Fran as she went over to Bethany and sat down. Fran's face twisted into a mixture of pain and just being uncomfortable as she sat down.

"Miss English," Mike said, "it is a pleasure to have you here tonight. I presume you're working to find out what happened to Bethany?"

"I am," Bettie said gesturing to the other people bouldering. "Do you think any of them could have done it?"

"God no," Mike said. "It isn't possible because these are all good people and everyone knows that Beth is keeping this place open. It's public knowledge and we all owe Beth a great debt,"

"Does anyone not like you being open?"

Mike rolled his eyes. "My wife. No, I'm joking. Maybe Lukas because his father wanted to redevelop this site and expand the centre so we do other sports as well,"

Bettie looked at Lukas at the very top of the bouldering wall after completing the blue and white route, which was meant to be the hardest one. He was skilled, he didn't like Bethany but she just wasn't sure he could damage the handholds.

"Help!" Fran shouted.

Bettie spun around.

Bethany was coughing and gasping and winded.

She collapsed to the ground.

Bettie rushed over.

She slammed an open hand on Beth's back.

Something flew out of Beth's mouth and she gasped in as much air as she possibly could.

Bettie knelt on the ground and inspected the small chunk of chalk that had shot out of Bethany's mouth. It was small and neatly cut, this wasn't something someone had quickly broken off. Someone had planned this carefully and purposefully.

Then Bettie noticed Beth had a small plate of energy balls in front of her. And she realised someone really wanted Bethany well and truly gone from this competition.

She went over to Beth's plate and broke up some of the remaining energy balls and shook her head. All of them contained chunks of chalk designed to choke Beth.

Bettie looked at Mike. "Who the hell made these?"

He shrugged. "I don't know. I normally make them from scratch just for Beth. Not tonight though, not after the fall,"

"Fran, did you see anyone?"

"No sorry. I was deep diving on my phone,"

Bettie so badly wanted to roll her eyes, but Fran was just doing her job and Bettie couldn't moan at her for that. And she supposed it was slightly her fault too, she had just never expected someone to try and kill her again so soon.

"No," Bethany said. "You did make these for me,"

Bettie folded her arms, because something wasn't adding up here.

"I was talking to Miss English, I couldn't have given them to you," Mike said. "And you keep this place afloat, why would I want to kill you?"

Bettie clicked her fingers and smiled. This was all starting to make sense because Mike had probably owned this centre for more years than she wanted to think about, he had trained and had great athletes train here like Beth. She would have been surprised if there was anything he didn't know about bouldering.

Including the handholds.

And Bettie was willing to bet if she had a Federation-approved lab test the handholds there would be some kind of substance, maybe glue, on the handholds that would have lasted until tonight. So only Beth could would have been affected.

"What did you study at university?" Bettie asked Mike.

"Chemistry,"

Bettie laughed. "Chemistry students would know about chemicals, substances and bonding strengths. How long did the handholds have to last until Beth came?"

Mike took a few steps back.

"And actually," Bettie said, "it didn't matter if you got one of the other staff members to give her the energy balls. You had already made them and why would your own staff assume you wanted to kill her?"

Mike took a few more steps back. Bettie and Fran followed him onto the spongy floor.

"Here it is," Fran said. "Two years ago your wife filed for divorce and retracted it at the same time as a massive gym company made you an offer to sell the centre,"

Bettie placed her hands on her hips. "But you couldn't sell and save face with Bethany giving you money. As you said, this centre is great because you've trained hard-working people. You couldn't shut down easily just because of a buyout,"

Bettie smiled as everyone had stopped bouldering now and everyone was starting to gather around Mike to stop him from escaping. But there was a large patch of bouldering wall exposed with a purple route.

Bettie seriously hoped he didn't climb up there to escape (not that there was anywhere to go).

"So what?" Fran asked. "Why try to kill Beth now?"

Bettie just shook her head at Mike. "The gym group has remade their offer haven't they? Your wife wants you home more and you want to get rid of this place and you want to save face. You can't have everything,"

"Traitor," Lukas said. "How dare you want to sell this place. The heart of our community. We trusted you,"

Bettie bit her lower lip as she realised just how seriously people took bouldering and now she truly focused on their postures, their manners and when all the men and women looked up, she noticed the truth.

Most of these were university students, bankers and office workers. Most of them had high-stress, intense jobs so this was their escape and this was their chance to relax and have fun with friends.

If this place went, then so many amazing benefits would be lost for them too.

"I wasn't trying to kill her," Mike said. "I only wanted to stop her competing so the money would dry up,"

Bettie went towards Mike and Mike just ran for the bouldering wall.

Bettie followed him.

Mike shot up the purple route.

Bettie didn't think. She only reacted. She climbed up the wall as fast as she could.

Mike was already at the top.

Bettie hissed as she climbed up. Her fingers and legs ached. Her forearms flooded with pain.

Her fingers felt like they were going to let go. She kept on climbing.

Everyone was cheering Bettie on and she just grinned as she climbed harder and harder.

She moved one hand at a time behind Mike and then she grabbed Mike's ankle and she leapt off the wall.

Mike screamed and Bettie laughed as the two of them fell to the ground and then Bettie climbed on top of Mike and pinned his arms behind his back.

"Fran," Bettie said, "please call Graham. I have a little gift for him,"

And as Fran went away to call Detective Graham Adams, Bettie just grinned at the chance to see her wonderful, sexy boyfriend again.

At least she had a hell of a story for him.

***

About two hours later, Bettie held sweet, cute baby Harrison in an adorable black puffer jacket outside of the centre surrounded by the bright red and blue flashing lights of three police cars. Bettie was rather impressed the police cars could fit inside the little car park that could barely fit ten cars inside, but they managed it.

The night was icy cold and Bettie was really enjoying the aromas of damp, strong bitter coffee and chocolate coming from the energy ball Fran was devouring next to her. It was so much better than the awful hints of sweat that had filled the bouldering centre.

Bettie loved how Graham was holding Elizabeth as she slept in his arms whilst he spoke to some uniformed cops about bagging and tagging the evidence and interviewing everyone. She had already passed her evidence over to him and he had mockingly hit her on the arm.

Apparently, Graham couldn't trust her to go anywhere without getting involved in a crime in one way or another. And Bettie couldn't really disagree but she loved her job, she loved helping people and she loved putting bad people away even more.

"Thank you," Graham said to the uniformed officers before coming over to Bettie and Fran. "Bethany's going to make a full recovery before the tryouts,"

"Good," Bettie said as she bounced Harrison a little.

"Mummy," Harrison said pointing to the energy ball in Fran's hand.

"No, sweetheart you can't have nuts until you're older,"

Harrison just buried his face in her neck and Bettie kissed him lightly on the head. She really did love her kids.

"What's going to happen to this place now?" Graham asked. "The owner's been arrested, Beth probably won't want to keep funding it and I don't like how the gym company's going to buy it,"

Bettie just grinned and hugged little Harrison even tighter. She had absolutely no intention of allowing the gym company to buy the bouldering centre, shut it down and convert it into something new.

The local community needed the bouldering centre to destress, have fun and socialise after a hard day's work, or just to have fun.

"Fran," Bettie said grinning.

Fran took out her phone and showed Graham something.

"The British Private Eye Federation," Graham said clearly reading from something, "strongly believes in supporting businesses critical to the local community,"

Bettie nodded, because it was why she did what she did. She solved crime, helped people and improved lives.

"You're buying the centre and who's running it?" Graham asked.

"Once the paperwork goes through privately so the gym group will never have a chance to outbid us," Bettie said. "Someone from the Federation will manage it until Bethany has retired from competitions. Then she has agreed to run it on our behalf,"

"I love you," Graham said kissing Bettie on the lips.

Bettie seriously loved the feeling of his soft, beautiful lips against her.

And as Bettie and Fran took the twins home and left Graham to do what he did best as a cop, Bettie felt amazing because she had done a lot of good today. She had saved a life, stopped a man from graduating to murder and she had saved a business critical to the local community.

If that wasn't something to celebrate then Bettie seriously didn't want to know what was, and it was only possible because she had been climbing around a crime.

AUTHOR OF THE ENGLISH BETTIE PRIVATE EYE SERIES

CONNOR WHITELEY

DAY TO REMEMBER

A BETTIE PRIVATE EYE MYSTERY SHORT STORY

DAY TO REMEMBER

20th November 2023

London, England

She was about to have the most chilling phone call of her life.

"Just have a coffee already,"

As much as Private Eye Bettie English really liked her personal assistant Fran because she was kind, helpful and an amazing assistant that basically oversaw the day-to-day running of the British Private Eye Federation, so Bettie could focus on helping people and solving cases, Bettie just had to admit Fran was being a nightmare today.

Bettie had never really liked coming into her massive, executive office at the Federation's headquarters in London. Sure, she loved the massive floor-to-ceiling windows that allowed her to see all over London, and its immensely impressive skyline. She had always liked to watch the little white boats on the Thames, watch people coming and going in from the Houses of Parliament and see the happy tourists walking about below.

But the office just wasn't her home, or even where she liked to work.

Bettie wanted to be out on the streets, in the community and talking to the amazing people that her and her fellow private investigators helped every day. She seriously loved being President of the Federation but not when she had to give speeches.

"Do you want a coffee?" Fran asked.

Bettie just looked at Fran across her massive black glass desk with her three computer screens to one side, her laptop open with her emails and a small plate of Danish pastries.

Bettie would have preferred if Fran had gotten the pastries from a small local business instead of a major international corporation, but Fran had been in a rush apparently.

But Bettie couldn't deny the pastries smelt great with hints of vanilla, sugar and sweet strawberries filling the office. She could almost taste those wonderful strawberries on her tongue, but she wasn't going to give in to temptation just yet. She had a speech to write.

And she was really hoping something was going to pop up in the meantime to stop her.

"No, thank you," Bettie said. "I don't want a coffee. I want to get this speech done,"

"Why are you even doing a speech on Pro-Transgender Healthcare? We all support trans people but we're private investigators, not politicians or doctors?" Fran asked.

Bettie smiled as she heard the muttering and shouting of people walking outside her office.

That was actually the question Bettie had been wondering herself. She had only been talking to her wonderful nephew, Sean, and his boyfriend last month about the awful state of transgender rights and healthcare in the UK. She completely agreed it needed to improve and these great people needed to be supported.

But she couldn't remember the exact moment where she had signed up to give a major keynote at a medical convention later on tonight.

Thankfully, she had six hours left.

Bettie just knew that wouldn't be enough time to write something worthy on the topic, considering how many lives and livelihoods it could affect.

She was the President of the Federation, her words had power. She could influence people positively or damn entire communities. That was a hell of a burden.

Bettie's phone rang.

Fran went to grab it from the desk but Bettie grabbed it first and answered.

"Miss English, is that you?" a man's voice said on the phone.

"Yes, who is this?" Bettie asked.

"I'm sorry for the call but you don't know me. I got your name and number from Percy Munchin, he said if I was ever in trouble you would help me,"

As soon as the caller said Percy's name, Bettie just grinned. She hadn't heard from Percy for years but he was a great man, a brilliant speaker and one of the kindest men Bettie had ever had the privilege of meeting. Granted she had thought he was a serial killer for a few days but after that business was sorted out, he was delightful.

"Yes, I can help you. I think," Bettie said gesturing Fran to run a trace on the call.

"Percy also said you would trace the call and try to work out who I was. I'll save you the trouble. My name is Penelope Gray and me and my friends need your help because someone is threatening to kill us all tonight,"

Bettie gasped and nodded at Fran.

The voice, the chosen name of Penelope and the fact it was the 20th November made Bettie realise instantly that these death threats had to be connected to what today was for the trans community. Transgender Day of Remembrance was today, a chance for everyone in the world to remember, honour and want to support all the trans people that had been murdered in the last year for the simple reason of wanting to be themselves.

Bettie had stopped checking the numbers a few years back because the number of murders only increased year on year.

It was disgusting but Bettie had a chance to save lives and she fully intended to take it no matter how heartbreaking the situation might be.

"I'll be there immediately," Bettie said hanging up as Fran finished the trace.

***

20th November 2023

Canterbury, England

One thing Bettie did love about being President of the Federation was the UK Government allowed it to have its own array of vehicles with blue flashing lights, it meant she never had to wait in traffic. She loved that little detail.

As the massive black SUV she was in the back of started to drive into Canterbury, Bettie smiled as she was home. She liked seeing the thick oak, pine and silver birch trees lining the exit off the motorway. And in the distance, the impressive flint city wall that dated back to Roman times stood proudly.

Bettie couldn't wait to go home later on and see her boyfriend Graham, two beautiful kids and Sean. No doubt he would love her even more for helping out innocent trans people on today of all days.

As much as Bettie wanted to focus on her speech, something she had barely started writing on the way here, she just wanted to save the lives of these innocent people. She wouldn't allow another person to die, especially on a day that was meant to be about remembering the murdered.

Not adding to that evil tally.

She settled back in the soft, wonderfully warm car seat as Fran passed over an iPad with photos. Bettie was surprised by the slight coldness of the iPad but she took it.

Bettie couldn't believe how disgusting the images were. They were all photos of the outside of a local church with red paint, animal blood and anti-trans comments painted on the cream-bricked walls of the church.

Bettie felt her stomach tighten as she read the warnings, the death threats and all the disgusting stuff the attackers were saying. She just couldn't believe that people in the 21st century could be so foul to other people just because politicians and bigots said this was okay.

It was disgusting.

"We'll be there in a minute Madame President," John said from the front of the SUV.

Bettie just nodded. She had always liked John as her new head of security. She didn't think she needed John for a slight second, but she wanted to keep beautiful Graham happy after a massive assassination attempt (more like attempt*s*) were made on her a few months ago.

"What did the police say?" Bettie asked passing the iPad back to Fran.

"Nothing. Simple case of vandalising and this is not the job of the police where there are more important cases to investigate," Fran said.

Bettie laughed. "Let me guess, the police aren't interested in actionable death threats made against trans people,"

"Of course not," Fran said.

Bettie shook her head as the SUV pulled to a stop and John opened the door for Bettie.

She got out and shivered a little and pulled her thick black trench coat around tighter. She wasn't exactly a fan of the small square car park they were in, but she supposed John would have liked it with its thick tree cover, high brick walls covered in death threats and no one else was about.

Even though Bettie really didn't like the cracked roof tiles and the plastic pipes hanging off the roofs of the surrounding, almost abandoned former council houses.

Of the few windows Bettie could see behind the tall walls, they all looked cracked, cold and ugly. Bettie had a bad feeling about this.

Something just felt off.

The rich aroma of curries, spices and crispy bacon filled the air and Bettie was so tempted to find whatever restaurant that was coming from. Then she laughed as Fran brought over a small box of Danish pastries and ate one.

"I'm not leaving these behind," Fran said.

"Fair enough," Bettie said smiling before turning to a very tall woman coming towards them.

Bettie had to admit Penelope was an impressive woman with her long brown hair, slim body and tight black peacoat that highlighted her feminine body really well.

"I like your coat, it's great," Bettie said trying to be as supportive and affirming as she could.

Penelope nodded her thanks and gestured to the death threats painted on the walls.

Bettie shook her head but these were different from the ones in the photos. There were brush marks, angles and even small pieces of fabric mixed into the paint here. The words were written too quickly and harshly to be readable but Bettie understood the general message.

This person wanted every single trans person to die in the world.

"I didn't send photos of these because, I don't know. We don't know who did these ones," Penelope said clearly trying to practise her voice training.

"Who did the photos you send us?" Bettie asked.

"Just some local kids. The children of the Priests of another church,"

"Why?" Fran asked coming closer. "And why would a trans group meet in a church? I thought the Church hated trans people,"

Penelope nodded. "On principle yes, but there are some churches that accept us and other queer people. This is a good one,"

Bettie looked at the massive church a few metres away from the car park, she wanted to force a smile. She couldn't. She just couldn't forgive churches and religion for what it had done to the queer community and her beautiful nephew.

Bettie went over to the rough writing Penelope was focusing on. She took a pair of blue crime-scene gloves that Fran gave her as she also came over.

"I have no idea who did this," Penelope said, "but I just don't want my friends to die,"

Bettie nodded as she knelt down and inspected the markings on the walls. The paint wasn't exactly dry and it was sticky and thick. It might not have been paint at all.

"Why do these idiots think you'll be easy pickings tonight?" Bettie asked after reading a line of hate.

Penelope frowned. "We have a Trans Day of Remembrance Service tonight in the Church. We'll be reading out over 390 names,"

"Jesus," Bettie said.

That was way too many dead people and Bettie hated it how her stomach twisted at the idea of the speech tonight.

Bettie shook the thought away and focused back on the hate writing in front of her. The ground was awfully cold and rough but Bettie ran a finger over the writing and a red sticky substance came off the wall.

"Fran," Bettie said, "is this fake blood from productions and film sets?"

"Definitely," Fran said. "My daughter uses this a lot in her productions. It's really cheap stuff but it's effective for budget movies,"

Bettie was really pleased Fran's daughter was finally getting the chance to produce her own indie films, and Fran was travelling to Venice next year to hopefully see her daughter get an award. Bettie couldn't have been more pleased for Fran.

"Why use false blood from film sets?" Penelope asked.

Bettie stood up and looked over at the walls of the church. Even from a small distance, Bettie could see the markings, writing and death threats were all different.

These definitely weren't done by the same person.

"Stop there!" John shouted.

Bettie froze and saw that John was pointing his small sidearm (something Bettie forgot he had) at a young man walking into the car park.

He was focused on Penelope, dressed in all-black and Bettie just knew he was here to hurt Penelope.

Something she wasn't going to allow.

"I said stop. I'm licensed to shoot," John said.

The SUV's horn went off.

Bettie looked around. There were more young men in all-black entering the car park.

Most were climbing over the walls.

"Stop!" Bettie shouted with as much authority as she could. "You will *not* harm her!"

The young men all stopped and Bettie couldn't tell them apart in their all-black clothing.

"He ain't a woman," the young man said that John was aiming at.

"He's an unholy slut. He ain't in the bible," another young man said.

Bettie also wanted to point out the bible said a person could be stoned for wearing two different types of fabric but this probably wasn't the time for bible lessons.

"She is a woman," Bettie said. "It is ridiculous that you have nothing better to do than attack people and threaten them,"

Bettie gestured to the vandalism on the wall behind her.

"We ain't do that bitch," another young man said.

Bettie was about to protest but she believed him. These were young men, clearly religious, and Penelope had said sons of priests had attacked the church.

Someone else was behind these focused death threats.

The young men charged.

John fired.

The bullet screamed through the air.

Hitting the man's leg.

He went down.

The other young men charged.

Bettie grabbed Penelope. Throwing her towards John.

John gripped her. Throwing Penelope into the SUV.

Bettie charged forward.

Rushing towards the young men.

They stopped.

Bettie didn't.

She punched them.

Giving them a left-hook. Then right-hook. Then jabs to the stomach.

Two young men fell to the floor.

Bettie ducked.

A fist shot past her from behind.

Bettie spun around.

Punching another man in the balls.

He slammed to the ground.

Bettie stood up and just grinned as there were no more attackers around and Fran and Penelope were getting back out of the SUV.

"Madame President how am I meant to protect you if you don't get to cover?" John asked grinning.

Bettie shrugged as she went over to the young man that John had shot. She was more than glad not a lot of blood had come out of the wound and it seemed to be just a flesh wound.

Of course the young man was rolling about, acting like a big baby but Bettie placed her right boot on his chest and looked down at him.

His eyes opened and Bettie just smiled.

"I never like hurting people," Bettie said. "I hate it but this was self-defence,"

"I'll call an ambulance," Fran said, "and the police."

Bettie had no idea what the point of calling the police was. If her boyfriend Graham was still a cop then he could deal with this but some corrupt officials had made that option impossible.

"Why are you defending a bitch?" the young man asked.

Bettie took her boot off his chest and helped the young man up. She threw one of his arms round her shoulders and Bettie grabbed him by the waist.

"Look at her," Bettie said. "Actually look at Penelope, she isn't a monster, she isn't crazy. She's just a woman wanting to live a normal life,"

"He ain't a woman!"

Bettie took her arm off his waist and the young man struggled to stand so he fell back down to the ground and Bettie shivered a little as an icy cold breeze blew in the car park.

"Who did this?" Bettie asked. "You have to know something about this. You cannot be the only transphobe in Canterbury,"

The young man grinned.

Bettie went over to him and searched his pockets. He tried to protest but it wasn't hard to find his locked phone.

"Fran, I need the unlocker please?" Bettie asked.

A moment later Fran came off and passed Bettie a small USB stick-like device that Bettie held over the phone screen and a moment later she was in.

"That ain't legal," the young man said who turned out to be Charlie.

"I'm a private eye. I don't need to follow the law at times,"

Bettie wanted to add on how she would never follow the law if it meant saving lives but she didn't want to get Charlie fired up again.

Bettie went through his contacts and apps, and she found a strange social networking app called *TwoG*. Bettie rolled her eyes as soon as she clicked on it and the motto *there are only two genders* popped up on the screen.

A second later, Bettie was scrolling through thousands upon thousands of anti-trans messages. There were pictures of dead bodies, mutilated corpses and extremely transphobic memes.

Bettie shivered and closed the app. That was outrageous and sickening and just disgusting. Some of the pictures of dead trans people barely seemed to be 18.

She just looked at Charlie and she took a deep breath of the rich curry-scented air. It barely calmed her down enough not to kick him in the nuts.

It was the least he deserved.

Fran took Charlie's phone, gasped and then looked like she was doing some techy stuff to do it with more advance gadgets the Federation had access to.

The loud beep of sirens filled the air as two ambulances and two police cars came into the car park. Bettie just rolled her eyes. This wasn't what she needed.

Two police constables came out with handcuffs and started to walk towards Bettie, but Bettie just showed them her Federation ID, the constables sighed and went off to the real criminals that were still rolling and screaming about on the floor.

She was more than glad the police were too scared to arrest Federation members at times.

"Bet," Fran said coming over as paramedics dealt with Charlie, "look at this contact,"

Bettie sadly looked at the app again and noticed how Charlie was constantly talking to another user called *Gender2*. Bettie didn't want to read them as she felt her breakfast and lunch start to crawl up her throat again.

"Find him," Bettie said.

"Find *her* you mean," Fran said. "The user might have used a VPN so I couldn't find their IP address, but photos on their profile gave me information about their phone. I eventually got a serial number and I know who owns it,"

"Who?" Bettie asked wanting back over to the SUV.

"Layla Taylor a local lecturer of religion at Kent University," Fran said.

Bettie slammed the door shut as the SUV roared away.

She was going to deal with Layla once and for all. No one got away with attempted murder, not if she could help it.

***

20th November 2023

Hales Place, Canterbury, England

Bettie just grinned to herself as she walked down a very long main road just on the outskirts of Canterbury. The area used to be a massive council estate but mainly students used the small cheap houses as places to live.

Bettie rather liked the little white small houses that lined the wide road. A few blue, black and red cars drove past making a small cold breeze blow past her, only adding to the already bitter temperature surrounding her.

Bettie pulled her coat tight as she smiled at Layla Talyor who was currently getting out of her little black Fiat outside a small house. She had to admit Layla wasn't an awful-looking woman, she was skinny, attractive and her wavy black hair was probably attractive to a lot of men.

Including young male students.

"Layla Taylor," Bettie said.

"Um yes," she said looking at Bettie.

"Or should I call you *Gender2?*" Bettie asked. "It's hard to keep track of names, isn't it?"

Layla frowned. "I do not have time for this,"

Bettie took two large steps forward and closed the gap between her and Layla. Bettie wasn't allowing Layla to get away.

"You incited a young man called Charlie to try and kill an innocent woman today," Bettie said.

"I don't know what you're talking about,"

Bettie just grinned. She liked difficult suspects because it meant she got to play with them, and hopefully that would give Fran more time to work with Sean and his boyfriend Harry on the computer stuff to find what she needed.

"Penelope was an innocent person. Why attack her and her group?" Bettie asked. "Because the bible told you to do it?"

Layla glared at Bettie. "How dare you. How dare you use the Bible in *that tone?*"

Bettie took a few steps away from her as she noticed the awful aroma of sweat and urine filling the space between them.

"I have my people investigating all your online activity as we speak. You might be able to explain away the extreme transphobia but what about your relationships with students?"

Bettie loved it how pale Layla went.

"You should technically be at work you know. It isn't 5 pm yet and why would you be going to a student's house?" Bettie asked.

Layla came over to her and Bettie felt a cold knife press against her stomach.

"Leave me alone,"

Bettie shook her head. She couldn't do that. There were innocent people and lives at stake. She wasn't going to back down.

"Then die bitch,"

A shot screamed through the air and Bettie just gasped as warm blood splattered over her face and her entire body went icy cold.

She slowly looked to her right and nodded her thanks as John stood a good twenty metres further up the road.

***

20th November 2023

London, England

Bettie still shook a little as she sat in the wonderfully warm, soft SUV as it slowly drove through the busy, packed and noisy streets of London later that night. The gentle humming of the SUV running, the loud honking of car horns and people shouting outside made Bettie smile a little.

This really was a typical night of traffic in London. John had asked about using the blue flashing lights but Bettie had shaken her head. She actually wanted the time to think.

She was already late for the medical conference but they were still allowing her to present whenever she got there. Bettie just didn't know if she could say anything worthy after today's events, the attempted murder and the death threat of Layla.

Bettie looked at Fran as she typed away on her laptop, probably finishing up their official statements for the Federation and the police. Then Bettie looked down at the small wooden box of amazing, delicious-looking Danish pastries that looked so good in between them. The rich aromas of strawberries filled the SUV.

Bettie reached down and picked one up, enjoying the touch of the buttery pastries as it coated her fingers in butter and rich icing. She was looking forward to having one of them after all.

"You feeling okay now?" Fran asked putting her laptop away.

Bettie shrugged. She had seen people die before in different situations but never exactly in front of her. She had seen her personal assistant die before in front of her but that situation had been different.

That was an assassination attempt not a killing done by her own security detail. Layla's death had to happen but Bettie never wanted it to happen though.

"I've sent the Federation's tech unit information about the app," Fran said. "They'll pass on everything to the police in time and we'll make sure the police deal with the hate website,"

"Thank you," Bettie said bringing the pastry closer to her lips. "I don't know what I'm going to say tonight,"

The car jerked a little as it hit a pothole.

Fran laughed. "Just do what you always do. Talk from the heart, and enjoy it. It's why the members love you talking and it's why I love listening to you,"

Bettie grinned and just nodded to herself because that was exactly right and that was exactly what she was going to do tonight. She might have been President of the Federation but that didn't mean she had to write official speeches.

She was a woman of the people and she was a woman of action. Bettie's place wasn't in some office, it was on the streets solving crimes, helping people and improving lives. She had never needed to write a speech.

"Use the blue lights now please,"

"Of course Madame President,"

Bettie just grinned as the SUV started its blue lights and they slowly started making progress through the traffic, because she had a speech to deliver to some medical and political folks.

Because it was Transgender Day of Remembrance. It might have been a day about honouring the murdered and dead trans people, amazing people whose lives had been cut too short. But there was a purpose as well.

It was making sure none of those people died in vain. So Bettie was going to go on that stage and she was going to convince people to help, support and improve transgender healthcare because everyone was entitled to healthcare, even trans people.

Because at the end of the day trans people were just people wanting to live a better life, which was what everyone wanted, so why should trans lives be harder or lesser than anyone else's?

They shouldn't.

And Bettie was so glad she had finally realised that simple point and that certainly helped to make today a day to remember. A day where she had solved a crime, saved lives and made sure a horrible transphobe could never hurt people ever again.

If that wasn't a day to remember then Bettie really wasn't sure what was.

AUTHOR OF THE ENGLISH BETTIE PRIVATE EYE SERIES

CONNOR WHITELEY

THE MYSTERY IN THE STUDENT HOUSE

A BETTIE PRIVATE EYE MYSTERY SHORT STORY

THE MYSTERY IN THE STUDENT HOUSE

10th January 2024

Canterbury, England

"My love for you is only matched by my contempt for you now auntie,"

Private Eye Bettie English playfully hit her favourite nephew in the entire world Sean, as they went into the awfully small white porch of the house they were secretly investigating. Bettie had to admit there was clearly a reason why these houses in this part of Canterbury were so cheap.

They were disgusting.

Bettie really didn't like the massive single panel of glass that covered three "walls" of the tiny porch, allowing out all the heat and allowing in the icy coldness of outside inside. It was so pointless. Even the red tile flooring was ugly, but Bettie supposed she couldn't complain.

It wasn't like she was actually here to help her nephew check out a house. He had already graduated with his Masters, but the house owners didn't need to know that.

"Please take off your shoes," a woman said from inside the house.

Bettie rolled her eyes as the loud hammering of the rain pounded the thin tin roof above them, so much so Bettie could barely hear herself think. Let alone the woman.

All she wanted was a moment to warm up her hands, that were

still aching and freezing from standing outside for ten minutes in the pouring rain waiting for the woman to show up. Bettie hated when people were late.

Bettie did as she was told and realised maybe it wasn't the best idea to wear boots today that went halfway up her shins. She knelt down on the icy cold floor and started untying her shoes.

Why this woman didn't have blue crime-scene shoe covers was beyond her. That would have made it so much easier for her to do this.

Bettie smiled at Sean as he just slipped off his shoes and leant against the doorframe just waiting for her. He ran a hand through his longish blond hair with tasteful pink highlights and he smiled at her.

She knew he was just as excited about the idea of trying to find DNA evidence as she was, because Sean was a brilliant private eye in his own right. It was just a shame he preferred the tech world to the private eye world.

Something she seriously wanted to change.

"This way," the woman said from inside the house.

Bettie put her shoes to one side and went into the tiny hallway. The overwhelming aroma of garlic, sweat and burnt toast hit her nose and Bettie coughed.

Even when she had been at university, her and her friends had never allowed the house to smell *this* bad. This was something else entirely, she just wanted to find something with DNA on and get the hell out of here.

She had been hired a few hours ago by a young university student, Rachel Pierce, from one of the more arty universities in Canterbury that reported she had been assaulted and *interfered* with coming home last night. She had gone through all the appropriate channels and reported her attacker to the police, but Rachel couldn't prove it.

So Bettie had tracked down Adam Green to this house, he was out enjoying his lectures whilst Rachel was with Bettie's boyfriend Graham trying to calm down and feel safe enough to return home.

Bettie flat out hated seeing Rachel like that, so she was going to do everything she could to put Adam away. He needed to pay and Bettie had to find DNA to match to what Rachel had given the police last night.

Bettie supposed the hallway itself wasn't that bad with the tiny staircase to her left, a weird L-shaped bend that led to the living room judging by the floorplans (Bettie was still so grateful to her personal assistant Fran for them), and the dark blue fluffy carpet was rather pleasant.

Maybe the porch was the only bad part of the house.

The pounding of the rain behind her got even louder and Bettie pretended to smile as the realtor woman stepped into view and Bettie looked at her properly for the first time. She was rather young and pretty, which surprised Bettie because she sounded rough and a little tired on the phone. Instead the woman was tall, fit and stood in front of her like she was a bundle of energy.

Bettie knew the woman clearly didn't have kids, because Bettie had two twins and she was never going to look like that again. But she loved her twins more than anything in the entire world.

"What room are interested in seeing first? This is a wonderful home with so many amazing features, you and your friends are going to love it," the woman said to Sean. "My name's Caroline,"

Then Caroline looked at Bettie like it was a little weird she was here.

"I'm just here because his friends have lectures and they don't trust him to look at a house alone," Bettie said grinning.

Sean playfully poked his tongue out at her.

"Let's see the living room first," Sean said.

Bettie supposed that was a good place to start, she had to find something with DNA on. She really didn't want an attacker and potential assaulter to go free.

She had to get justice for the victim.

The awful aroma of burnt toast was even worse, if such a thing was possible, as Bettie followed Caroline into the large rectangular living room with dark white walls, two very ugly orange sofas and a smart TV hanging off (not on) the wall.

"We will obviously replace the TV before you move in," Caroline said clearly not knowing about the damage before today. "What are your thoughts?"

Bettie subtly nodded to Sean to signal she wanted to do some investigating and she wanted Caroline gone for a little while. So Sean started talking about the living room and how bad the damage was to the smart TV.

Then Sean subtly walked towards the floor-to-ceiling French doors at the end of the living room, so Caroline had to have her back to Bettie.

Bettie seriously did love her nephew, he was just brilliant.

The constant pounding of the rain hitting the French door covered Bettie's footsteps as she really focused on the living room. Including the two small wooden tables next to the sofas and there was a small black waste bin next to them in a corner.

Bettie went over to it. She knelt down and managed to just about hide behind one of the ugly sofas and she just grinned at the waste bin because it was clearly fake.

The bin was simply filled with perfectly clean, not-used tissues that were barely roughed up enough to even remotely pass as used. Bettie just listened to Caroline cheerfully talk about the property and then she realised that there was an edge of panic in her voice.

Caroline was concerned about something and then Bettie didn't doubt the smart TV hanging off the walls wasn't concerning her. And she hadn't heard a single sound in the entire house, when her tenancy in her student house back in the late 00s was close to ending, Bettie had always made sure to be home when the new tenants came round. Mostly just because she was nosy and wanted to check out if any of them were hot, but also to make sure they didn't mess up anything.

Her friends had sadly experienced some problems back in the day, so she was determined to avoid a similar fate.

There was no one else in the house though and Bettie just

couldn't understand why.

"Sean," Bettie said standing up and folding her arms, "no one lives here and Adam certainly isn't here,"

Caroline frowned. "What? What do you mean? Who the hell are you people?"

Sean laughed and gestured towards Bettie. "So not my department,"

Bettie took out her Private Eye ID card that also showed that she was the President of the British Private Eye Federation, a powerful organisation with more power than the governments of small countries.

Caroline took a few steps back. "I need to contact my boss. This isn't what I wanted. I don't want to deal with you people,"

Bettie took a few steps forward. "Caroline, I'm investigating a serious assault against a young woman last night and I need to find Adam, one of the tenants here,"

"Where is he?" Sean asked.

Bettie loved it how menacing and intimidating Sean was trying to look but it seriously wasn't working.

"I don't know," Caroline said taking out her phone. "He was meant to be here to let me in, that's why I was late. I had to drive back to the office to get the spare keys,"

Bettie went over to the Smart TV. It had clearly been pulled off the wall but it was at an angle with a slightly cracked screen, suggesting someone had been pushed into it and fell backwards.

"What about the other tenants?" Bettie asked. "My assistant said there were four people living here,"

Caroline shook slightly and Bettie went over and placed a gentle hand on her shoulder.

"I don't know," Caroline said. "This… this is all a bit much. Can I just call me boss?"

Bettie just looked at Sean. He subtly smiled at her and Bettie liked that smile, because they both knew this case was just about to get started and that excited her a lot more than she wanted to admit even to herself.

"Don't bother," Bettie said, "I'll get my assistant to find your tenants and hopefully your employer can get their rent,"

"Thank you," Caroline said.

Bettie shook her head as she put her boots back on because she couldn't believe that Caroline sounded like she was only interested in rent and not the lives of the tenants that could be in danger because if Bettie had learnt anything over her career. It was never to underestimate how dark situations could get.

Little did Bettie realise just how true that idea was.

***

Bettie nodded her thanks to Fran as she passed Bettie a large mug of piping hot ground coffee as soon as she came into the living room of her house. Bettie loved how the rich, intense aromas of real coffee filled the large living room, instead of the instant rubbish she had been buying lately to save money. Not because she needed to save but it meant she could donate to charities even more.

"Mummy," Elizabeth said as she charged at Bettie.

Bettie flat out loved her little 16-month-old bundle of joy. Elizabeth was the most beautiful, precious and most amazing kid she had ever met and Bettie really did love both her kids equally. She was also rather impressed Graham had dressed Elizabeth properly today instead of letting her run around in PJs like he normally did.

Not that she could blame him because both the twins were so cute in their PJs.

Bettie picked up her beautiful daughter and hugged her tight after putting the coffee mug on the large walnut coffee table in the middle of the living room. At least she didn't have to go out in that awful rain that was still hammering outside.

Then Bettie nodded at the three massive white boards Fran had thankfully put up whilst Bettie had driven over here. The white boards were pushed against the far wall of the room so she couldn't see the TV but that didn't matter. She was here to solve a crime, not watch TV.

The whiteboard to the left was covered in notes about Rachel and the attack last night using everything they had gotten from the police report, Rachel herself and any other evidence they could find.

Bettie had to admit she would have liked a lot more detail on that particular board, but this was a tough one. They only knew Rachel was attacked in an alley by Adam and then she had managed to run to the police station before breaking down, crying and succumbing to shock.

Thankfully she had managed to give her statement first. Bettie was really impressed with how brave, amazing and courageous Rachel had been. She doubted she could hold off shock and crying that much.

"I can't actually find that much on the other tenants," Fran said sitting down on one of Bettie's two massive sofas.

Bettie smiled as Sean and his wonderful boyfriend Harry came down the stairs holding hands before sitting on another sofa.

Having her wonderful family here made Bettie a lot more excited than she had any right to feel because now she knew, truly knew they were going to find Adam and the other tenants. Together her and her family and friends were unstoppable.

"I could only find references and odd social media posts about the other tenants. Joshua, Nathan and Ethan all lived in that house yesterday," Fran said. "But today, no one has seen them,"

"Doorbell footage?" Bettie asked bouncing Elizabeth a little in her arms.

"Nothing," Harry said.

Bettie rolled her eyes. If there was doorbell footage of the tenants then Harry would have found it, so Bettie had no reason to doubt it. It was just annoying as hell these tenants looked like they had simply disappeared.

"Auntie, why would the tenants leave?"

Bettie smiled. "What connections are there between Rachel and Adam and the other tenants? I know they all go to the same university and Rachel and Adam had seen each other at clubs and bars before,"

"That's it," Fran said shrugging. "My initial and secondary searches all reveal there are no other connections. No classes, no social groups and nothing else that links Rachel to Adam or anyone else,"

"How did she know his name?" Harry asked.

Bettie smiled as everyone went deadly silent and she just let the question hang in the air between them all. That was a brilliant question and she wished she had thought of it herself because it was stupidly true.

Fran was an amazing computer person and personal assistant, and Bettie believed her when Fran said the searches came up blank. Bettie had little doubt Harry had done a computer deep dive on Adam, Rachel and the tenants because he was sensational with computers.

All the searches had come up blank, so why did Rachel know Adam's name? And why was she able to identify him as her attacker?

Bettie gestured Sean to come with her and then Bettie gave Elizabeth a little kiss on the cheek before giving her to Harry.

Then Bettie and Sean went upstairs into Sean's and Harry's bedroom where the subtle aromas of lavender, lilacs and roses filled the large bedroom from a little romantic gesture from Harry to Sean yesterday.

Bettie smiled at how clean, tidy and filled with great personal items like holiday photos and romantic gifts covered all the walls and cabinets. It was why she had wanted Rachel to be in here today, because it was such a happy room filled with love, protection and devotion between lovers.

It was a safe place.

"Hi," Graham said in his tight sexy jeans and tight black hoody (Bettie was so taking that off later on), where Rachel was playing with Harrison.

Bettie had to admit it was great seeing Rachel smiling, laughing and with a little more colour back in her face. Bettie had hated seeing

Rachel this morning with cuts, bruises and extreme fear on her face.

She didn't even want to question Rachel now but she was going to have to, the case might depend on it.

"Harrison," Bettie said as joyfully as she could, "can you show Sean where the ice lollies are please? He's forgotten again,"

Cute little Harrison sat up immediately and started wiggling towards the end of Sean's bed before jumping off with so much energy Bettie was almost scared.

"Sean's so silly isn't he mummy?" Harrison asked.

"Yes he is sweetie,"

Bettie laughed as Harrison just gently took Sean's hand in his and he led Sean back down up.

"Mummy!" Harrison shouted, "can I have one if I do this!"

"Yes sweetie and make sure your sister gets one,"

"Okay. Thank you mummy,"

Bettie laughed and Graham just shook his head at her. Then Bettie frowned a little as she went over to Rachel and sat on the opposite end of the bed to her.

"Rachel I need to ask you a simple question, is that okay?" Bettie asked.

Rachel looked at the floor. "I've already told Graham everything I know,"

"I know but it's important," Bettie said knowing Graham had been trained to talk to assault victims so if she had said anything major then he would have told her by now.

"Please," Graham said. "Bettie is an amazing woman and she will help you, but remember like I said, you need to trust us,"

Rachel nodded so Bettie weakly smiled at Rachel. "How do you know Adam? We can't find any record or evidence of you knowing each other? He never spoke to you at the bar, you don't share classes, social groups or anything,"

Rachel looked up at Bettie. "You calling me a liar,"

"No," Bettie said shaking her head. "I'm just curious and a defence barrister will be a lot harsher than me when this goes to trial,"

Rachel laid down on the bed and buried her face in the pillows.

Bettie wanted to move closer and gently hold Rachel's hand but she didn't dare, and she couldn't help but feel that something was off.

"I met him once," Rachel said. "It was first year, so two years ago, there was a rave near the River Medway. No phones, no tech and no cameras,"

Bettie nodded. She had heard about the rave because the police had broken it up and it was on a small sea fort island in the river Medway near Upnor and Hoo Marina.

It had been a massive rave and no one could exactly figure out how over 100 young people had gotten on the island in the first place, but after the drugs were found, high-price lawyers for the rich kids had brought down their power on the police and whatnot, no one had ever thought about it again.

"I was swinging from one of the rope swings and Adam started chatting to me. He was nice, sweet and we exchanged names and whatnot," Rachel said. "Then he tried to kiss me and I said no. He wasn't happy,"

Bettie nodded at Graham.

"Then I saw him last night for the first time since the rave. He was happy to see me and I tried to get away from him but… it didn't work out, did it?"

Bettie got off the bed and paced around a little. At least that was the connection and why Rachel was able to identify the attacker, but there were still more questions. Thankfully, she only needed to ask Rachel one more.

"Joshua, Nathan and Ethan, they live with Adam," Bettie said. "I need to know would any of them fight Adam to protect you,"

Rachel sat up on the bed and smiled. "Ethan would, bless him, he was so cute. Adam hated him for being a transman but no one else cares. He was so cute, so sweet and so… perfect,"

Bettie smiled. It was great to know how much she cared about Ethan, and that explained a lot about what had happened last night.

"Final question," Bettie said, "I'm guessing you and Ethan met at the rave and you haven't spoken since,"

"I wanted to get his phone number that night but Adam was so focused on me, I just couldn't. I didn't even realise he was trying to control me that night," Rachel said then she threw her head back and accidently hit the headboard.

Bettie nodded because things were finally starting to make perfect sense. She didn't doubt for a moment that after the attack Adam had gone home to his housemates, bragged about the attack then Ethan would have been outraged.

Then Bettie completely understood if Ethan was angry enough to start a fight and him or Adam or maybe one of the others had been pushed into the smart TV, causing the damage.

It was only what happened next Bettie didn't understand yet.

Why stage the property to look like it was being lived in when it clearly wasn't? Why not just run instead of preparing the scene like the waste bin? It made no sense.

Bettie took out her phone and called the Federation, she was going to need a helicopter.

She had to get to the sea fort immediately. She didn't know how but she just knew Adam and the others would be there.

And Bettie was going to get the truth out of Adam no matter what.

***

Bettie flat out loved the power, resources and all the good vehicles the Federation had access to as she waved the massive black helicopter away after it had carefully dropped her off next to Fort Darrett in the River Medway via rope winch.

The soft wild grass was soft and rather warm for a change under Bettie's feet and she was so glad the damn rain had stopped about two hours ago, so her boots weren't getting wet. The very last thing she wanted was to be stuck on an island when it was wet and cold and just draining.

The Fort itself was rather impressive with it being a massive ring of concrete and bricks going up one storey with a flat roof. Yet because the Fort had been designed for 11 guns, there were 11 flat sides to the ring with wide openings to shoot through.

Even though the Fort never saw any action.

Bettie was glad it was in such good condition considering it had finished being built in 1872 as part of plans for the defences of Chatham Dockyard where England had kept most of its naval power in the 1800s.

Bettie just couldn't help but smile at the old Fort because she wanted to know what the Fort could have been if the original ideas for two tiers had been completed. The cost of the project had caused it to be finished in 1872 and it was impressive enough, but Bettie would have liked to know what it could have been.

The rich aromas of sea salt, smoke and cooked meat filled the air as Bettie went over to the small hole in a massive rusty sheet of metal that had been placed over each gun opening.

Bettie could hear muttered voices and she really hoped that Graham, Sean and Fran could convince Kent Police to bring officers here as soon as possible.

She was about to climb inside when she noticed the wide moat around the Fort that dropped down into thick, sloppy mud below with steep sides on either side. The only way to get to the Fort was by climbing over a thick wooden beam and even that was only accessible after coming through a narrow opening through a thick bush of thorns that ran around the edge of the entire moat.

If Bettie got into trouble here then she was completely alone.

Bettie climbed inside and was surprised at the sheer grey stone curved walls of the Fort that went round in a ring. There was so much *stuff* on the ground like dust, sand and dirt that it was like nature was determined more than ever to reclaim the island.

Then she saw them.

In the middle of the Fort there was another moat that Bettie knew from her childhood dropped down tens upon tens of metres to flooded storage rooms. But after the drop-down, there was a large brick platform covered in bushes and trees and the people she was searching for were there.

Bettie recognised Adam immediately with his black crewcut, black eye and almost too-thin body. Then there were two other young men she couldn't really tell apart with brown hair and matching black clothes, they had to be Joshua and Nathan.

But it was Ethan that Bettie was more concerned about.

The young man with longish blond hair was holding his left arm like he had been stabbed and his once-blue hoody was now a lot darker, and Bettie just hated Adam more than ever.

Bettie went over to the edge of the moat and she was right next to a narrow brick walkway that led onto the central platform where the others were.

"Who the hell are you?" Adam asked clearly annoyed.

"She's Bettie English," Ethan said a little starstruck. "You know, the woman in the papers and the woman on the news. You're in shit now Adam,"

Bettie laughed because hopefully Ethan was right.

"You attacked Rachel last night, you committed criminal damage in your house and I'm sure this is private property. How did you even get here?"

Everyone looked at Bettie like she was the dumbest woman alive.

"There's a guy in Hoo Marina," Adam said, "you pay him and he brings you after dark,"

Bettie nodded and kicked some of the dust under her feet. At least that explained how all the students got here for the rave two years ago and how the four of them had gotten here after the attack.

"What happened at the house?" Bettie asked wanting to buy the police as much time as possible.

Adam pulled out a knife that was still dripping blood.

"It don't matter," Adam said. "None of this matters. Just leave us alone and go away,"

"I can't do that Adam and you know it. You attacked an

innocent woman,"

Bettie went onto the brick walkway and hated how a massive brick splashed into the water below. She wasn't sure how long this walkway would hold but she wasn't going to show Adam she was scared.

Adam grabbed Ethan's injured arm and pressed the knife against his throat.

"This is all your fault you bitch. Why don't you just admit you like Rachel? But we both know she won't like a pussy girl like you. You aren't even a real man,"

Bettie just glared at Adam. That was enough and she was going to make Adam pay for everything now.

Bettie took another step forward and two massive bricks splashed into the water below.

She went to get onto the platform but Joshua and Nathan picked up two broken bricks each and gestured they were going to throw them at Bettie.

Bettie seriously wasn't sure if she could dodge all four bricks without falling into the stagnant water below. She hated to imagine what disease or infection she would pick up from that water.

Adam jabbed the knife a little harder against Ethan's throat and Bettie hated seeing how defeated Ethan looked.

"She likes you a lot Ethan," Bettie said. "She doesn't care that you're a transman and you are a man to her, and me for what it's worth. People like Adam don't matter,"

Ethan looked into Bettie's eyes. "Really?"

"Her face lit up when she spoke about you," Bettie said.

Police sirens echoed around the Fort from the distance.

Ethan stomped on Adam's feet.

Adam let go. He was about to swing.

Bettie charged forward.

The walkway collapsed.

Bettie screamed.

She fell.

She gripped onto the edge of the central platform as the bricks splashed down below.

Bettie kicked against the wall but she couldn't get a grip.

Thunder roared overhead and rain started slashing down. The edge of the platform was getting wetter and wetter.

Bettie didn't know how much longer she could hold onto it.

"Leave her," Adam shouted.

Bettie tried to pull herself up as much as she could but she couldn't.

Her hands burnt. Her muscles ached. Pain flooded her arms.

She was about to let go.

Bettie shouted for help. No one came. She was alone. She was going to fall.

She fell.

Two hands gripped her arm.

Bettie slammed into the brick wall as someone pulled her up.

As soon as she felt the solid central platform under her she leapt up and hugged Ethan.

Then she broke the hug and listened for the police sirens. They were coming from the south side of the island and no other direction.

"The man gave us a crappy little speedboat on the north side of the island," Ethan said. "Is that important?"

Bettie nodded and she ran and jumped over the moat she had just almost died from. She rushed over to the nearest gun opening and climbed outside.

Ethan followed her.

Bettie started running towards the thick wooden beam. "Of course it's important. Even a crappy speedboat with a two-stroke engine would let them get to the mainland,"

Bettie went running and she went quickly and carefully as she got over the wooden beam that moaned and groaned as she went over it.

Bettie hissed in pain as the sharp thorns caught her as she raced through the narrow opening. The awfully soft ground was almost trying to slow her down but Bettie wasn't stopping for anything or anyone.

As soon as she got through the thorn bushes she saw Adam, Nathan and Joshua on the other side of a large area of cord grass. They were climbing into a small black speedboat that barely looked seaworthy.

They were going to die if they went out in that. Bettie couldn't allow that to happen.

Bettie ran as fast as she could.

The thick aroma of sea salt was almost choking but she kept running.

Icy cold breeze slammed against her but Bettie just kept running. Ethan ran behind her but Bettie was faster.

Bettie could barely hear the police sirens of the police boats as Adam pushed the boat into the water. Just as Joshua and Nathan were about to climb in Adam pushed them out.

Joshua and Nathan slipped on the mud and accidentally pushed the boat out into the raging River Medway.

The rain lashed down even harder and Adam activated the engine. The speedboat roared to life.

Bettie ran as fast as she could. But Adam just started to speed away.

A massive gust of icy wind made Bettie jump and created massive waves in the river. One slammed into the speedboat.

Flipping it over.

Bettie didn't think. She only acted. She charged into the River Medway and swam towards Adam.

She wasn't letting him drown.

He had to answer for his crimes.

***

A few hours later when the awful rain had finally stopped, Bettie wrapped a wonderfully thick white blanket round herself as she sat on her sofa facing the TV in her living room. When she had gotten home from the hospital where she had been treated for hyperthermia, given god knows how many statements to the police and been slightly told off by Graham for swimming into icy cold water during a storm, she had felt like the house was a little empty.

The three massive whiteboards were gone, Fran had gone home for the night and even Sean and Harry had gone out with some friends tonight. They had tried to paint it as a crazy night on the town, but Bettie knew it was code for just talking, laughing and enjoying themselves at a local pub.

Bettie had put the twins to bed earlier and she was just enjoying the silence of the house after a wonderfully hectic day. So Bettie allowed the softness of the sofa to claim her weight and she was so looking forward to what was going to happen next.

Especially with the delicious rich aromas of basil, garlic and cheese coming from the kitchen where Graham was finishing up one of his "famous" meals for her. Sometimes that meant great food from recipes from mainland Europe or sometimes it meant disgusting creations of his own, but Bettie loved him no matter what.

She was just hoping beyond hope it would be the first option.

After she had swam into the River Medway, getting colder and colder with each passing second, she had managed to grab Adam despite his shock and dragged him back to the island Fort Darnett was on. Then she had handed them all over to Graham and the police and they had gone to hospital to be checked out.

Bettie was glad she had only needed to be warmed up with more tea (not coffee sadly) than she wanted to admit. She so wasn't drinking English tea after that hospital trip, it was disgusting.

At least Adam had confessed (and DNA confirmed) to seeing Rachel at the party last night then he had followed her on her way home and when she had taken a shortcut down an alley, he had attacked her. Bettie had almost vomited during his graphic account of the attack.

She never wanted him to see the light of day ever again.

Then Adam had gone home after kicking Rachel in the stomach to see his housemates. He had bragged about it because it made him feel powerful and manly so Ethan had flipped out at him for attacking an innocent woman. Especially a woman that had been so kind to him.

They had fought and Ethan had been pushed into the smart TV making it hang off the wall. So Joshua and Nathan being Adam's good little pets had sided with Adam and made Ethan help with the staging of the house.

The idea behind that had been to give them a day to decide what to do with Ethan and where they were going to run away to. They knew Rachel was going to talk so their time was limited.

Bettie was still surprised they had gone to the Fort but considering that was where all of this had started two years ago, it sort of made sense and Bettie probably would have done the same if she was them.

Once at the Fort Adam had started a small fire to keep them warm and Ethan had tried to get Adam to turn himself in. Adam had slashed Ethan's arm to make him shut up.

Then Bettie arrived and judging by the sheer look of anger on Adam's face at the hospital when Ethan had walked past his bed, she didn't doubt Ethan would have been dead if she hadn't arrived.

Bettie was more than glad she had. Especially because Rachel had gone to the hospital to see Ethan and they had spoken, kissed and they had agreed to go on a date.

Bettie couldn't stop smiling as the man she loved came into the living room without any food and a massive guilty grin on his face. He might have been a rubbish chef but she loved him more than anything else in the entire world.

"Let me guess," Bettie said, "takeaway and sex tonight?"

"You read my mind,"

Bettie threw the blanket at Graham as they laughed and kissed and made out like two horny teenagers. And after the hecticness of today, Bettie was more than looking forward to all the fun she was going to have tonight and all the nights after that.

GET YOUR FREE SHORT STORY NOW! And get signed up to Connor Whiteley's newsletter to hear about new gripping books, offers and exciting projects. (You'll never be sent spam)

https://www.subscribepage.io/wintersignup

About the author:

Connor Whiteley is the author of over 60 books in the sci-fi fantasy, nonfiction psychology and books for writer's genre and he is a Human Branding Speaker and Consultant.

He is a passionate warhammer 40,000 reader, psychology student and author.

Who narrates his own audiobooks and he hosts The Psychology World Podcast.

All whilst studying Psychology at the University of Kent, England.

Also, he was a former Explorer Scout where he gave a speech to the Maltese President in August 2018 and he attended Prince Charles' 70th Birthday Party at Buckingham Palace in May 2018.

Plus, he is a self-confessed coffee lover!

Other books by Connor Whiteley:

Bettie English Private Eye Series

A Very Private Woman

The Russian Case

A Very Urgent Matter

A Case Most Personal

Trains, Scots and Private Eyes

The Federation Protects

Cops, Robbers and Private Eyes

Just Ask Bettie English

An Inheritance To Die For

The Death of Graham Adams

Bearing Witness

The Twelve

The Wrong Body

The Assassination Of Bettie English

Wining And Dying

Eight Hours

Uniformed Cabal

A Case Most Christmas

Gay Romance Novellas

Breaking, Nursing, Repairing A Broken Heart

Jacob And Daniel

Fallen For A Lie

Spying And Weddings

Clean Break

Awakening Love

Meeting A Country Man

Loving Prime Minister

Snowed In Love

Never Been Kissed

Love Betrays You

Lord of War Origin Trilogy:
Not Scared Of The Dark
Madness
Burn Them All

Way Of The Odyssey
Odyssey of Rebirth
Convergence of Odysseys

The Fireheart Fantasy Series
Heart of Fire
Heart of Lies
Heart of Prophecy
Heart of Bones
Heart of Fate

City of Assassins (Urban Fantasy)
City of Death
City of Martyrs
City of Pleasure
City of Power

Agents of The Emperor
Return of The Ancient Ones
Vigilance
Angels of Fire
Kingmaker
The Eight
The Lost Generation
Hunt

Emperor's Council
Speaker of Treachery
Birth Of The Empire
Terraforma
Spaceguard

The Rising Augusta Fantasy Adventure Series
Rise To Power
Rising Walls
Rising Force
Rising Realm

Lord Of War Trilogy (Agents of The Emperor)
Not Scared Of The Dark
Madness
Burn It All Down

Miscellaneous:
RETURN
FREEDOM
SALVATION
Reflection of Mount Flame
The Masked One
The Great Deer
English Independence

OTHER SHORT STORIES BY CONNOR WHITELEY

Mystery Short Story Collections

Criminally Good Stories Volume 1: 20 Detective Mystery Short Stories

Criminally Good Stories Volume 2: 20 Private Investigator Short Stories

Criminally Good Stories Volume 3: 20 Crime Fiction Short Stories

Criminally Good Stories Volume 4: 20 Science Fiction and Fantasy Mystery Short Stories

Criminally Good Stories Volume 5: 20 Romantic Suspense Short Stories

Connor Whiteley Starter Collections:

Agents of The Emperor Starter Collection

Bettie English Starter Collection

Matilda Plum Starter Collection

Gay Romance Starter Collection

Way Of The Odyssey Starter Collection

Kendra Detective Fiction Starter Collection

Mystery Short Stories:

Protecting The Woman She Hated

Finding A Royal Friend

Our Woman In Paris

Corrupt Driving

A Prime Assassination

Jubilee Thief

Jubilee, Terror, Celebrations

Negative Jubilation

Ghostly Jubilation

Killing For Womenkind

A Snowy Death
Miracle Of Death
A Spy In Rome
The 12:30 To St Pancreas
A Country In Trouble
A Smokey Way To Go
A Spicy Way To GO
A Marketing Way To Go
A Missing Way To Go
A Showering Way To Go
Poison In The Candy Cane
Kendra Detective Mystery Collection Volume 1
Kendra Detective Mystery Collection Volume 2
Mystery Short Story Collection Volume 1
Mystery Short Story Collection Volume 2
Criminal Performance
Candy Detectives
Key To Birth In The Past

Science Fiction Short Stories:
Their Brave New World
Gummy Bear Detective
The Candy Detective
What Candies Fear
The Blurred Image
Shattered Legions
The First Rememberer
Life of A Rememberer
System of Wonder
Lifesaver
Remarkable Way She Died
The Interrogation of Annabella Stormic

Blade of The Emperor
Arbiter's Truth
Computation of Battle
Old One's Wrath
Puppets and Masters
Ship of Plague
Interrogation
Edge of Failure

Fantasy Short Stories:
City of Snow
City of Light
City of Vengeance
Dragons, Goats and Kingdom
Smog The Pathetic Dragon
Don't Go In The Shed
The Tomato Saver
The Remarkable Way She Died
Dragon Coins
Dragon Tea
Dragon Rider

All books in 'An Introductory Series':
Clinical Psychology and Transgender Clients
Clinical Psychology
Careers In Psychology
Psychology of Suicide
Dementia Psychology
Clinical Psychology Reflections Volume 4
Forensic Psychology of Terrorism And Hostage-Taking
Forensic Psychology of False Allegations
Year In Psychology
CBT For Anxiety
CBT For Depression
Applied Psychology
BIOLOGICAL PSYCHOLOGY 3RD EDITION
COGNITIVE PSYCHOLOGY THIRD EDITION
SOCIAL PSYCHOLOGY- 3RD EDITION
ABNORMAL PSYCHOLOGY 3RD EDITION
PSYCHOLOGY OF RELATIONSHIPS- 3RD EDITION
DEVELOPMENTAL PSYCHOLOGY 3RD EDITION
HEALTH PSYCHOLOGY
RESEARCH IN PSYCHOLOGY
A GUIDE TO MENTAL HEALTH AND TREATMENT
AROUND THE WORLD- A GLOBAL LOOK AT
DEPRESSION
FORENSIC PSYCHOLOGY
THE FORENSIC PSYCHOLOGY OF THEFT,
BURGLARY AND OTHER CRIMES AGAINST
PROPERTY
CRIMINAL PROFILING: A FORENSIC PSYCHOLOGY
GUIDE TO FBI PROFILING AND GEOGRAPHICAL
AND STATISTICAL PROFILING.
CLINICAL PSYCHOLOGY